The Wond...
SYDNEY ...

Berkley Books by Sydney J. Van Scyoc

BLUESONG
CLOUDCRY
DARKCHILD
DROWNTIDE
STARSILK
SUNWAIFS

DROWNTIDE

SYDNEY J. VAN SCYOC

BERKLEY BOOKS, NEW YORK

DROWNTIDE

A Berkley Book, published by arrangement with
the author

PRINTING HISTORY
Berkley edition / May 1987

ISBN: 0-425-09775-7

ONE

KEIRIS WOKE AT dawn and lay for a moment with eyes closed and breath held, listening—hearing nothing but the distant rush of the sea. The palace and the smaller, clustered structures of Hyosis stood high on a curving spine of land, the sea washing the rocky shore below. Night and day the sound of the breakers penetrated every part of the palace. In the seaward chambers the ocean crashed restlessly. In other, more landward wings of the low, spreading structure, the water spoke in a bare whisper, except when Systris and Vukirid combined forces to whip the tidewaters to frenzy.

But it was not the sea Keiris listened for now. It was the other sounds that customarily came with morning: the slap of feet in the corridor, the brush of heavy mops on walls and floors, the voices of cooks and cleaners. He did not hear those today. Nor did he hear his mother's sounding horn from the seaward plaza or the smaller steering horns of the fishing vessels in the cove. He heard none of the sounds he usually heard at dawn—except the sea.

He drew a ragged breath, dread settling in his stomach again. *Nandyris* . . .

He had only to think of his half sister and his throat closed with fear. Reluctantly Keiris sat. Beyond his window the sky was clear, stained with color. Dawn polished the pink stone of his walls and made his bare stone floor glow with rosy color. Surely Nandyris could not be lost on a day when everything was so much as it should be. Surely she could not be lost on a day when his flagged floor was swept and polished, when his cushions were piled carefully in the corner, when—he rose and went to the window to assure himself—the cleaners had already swabbed the landward plaza.

Surely she could not be lost. The worst storms of winter were past now. Although land and water had begun to warm, the wrecker-fish normally were sluggish this early in the spring; the blood-lilies had not yet sent their treacherous streamers across the ocean's surface; it was early for lizard hatchings. And Nandyris had been steering, and she received the voice of the dais more clearly, more distinctly, than the part–Adenyo who steered the other vessels of the fleet that harbored at Hyosis.

But if Nandyris' vessel had come to shore during the night, he should have heard the horns. And he had heard nothing, not in the early hours of night when he lay waiting for his mother to call him to her chambers to tell him what had happened, not in the later hours when he slept fitfully, realizing the summons would not come.

Keiris pressed his stomach with one hand, trying to ease the pain that fear brought. The distant wash of the sea was insistent. He could not screen it out. When he thought of how deep the water ran, when he thought of the many things that lived there and all the ways in which they were strange . . .

Quickly he left his bed and pulled on the clothes he had laid out the night before. The trousers he had chosen were sea-blue, the color Nandyris liked best. The shirt was bleached white, like the shirts the sea crews wore. The boots were made from the hide of a hatchling sea-lizard. Nandyris had helped take the lizard herself, from the prow of the vessel she crewed with. She had given him the boots to wear for winter festival, and it had seemed to him last night that if he prepared carefully enough for the morning, that if he thought of every detail, daylight could only bring the sound of Nandyris' laughter in the corridor. It could only bring her to the morning table to eat with him. It could only bring her back from the sea.

Apparently it had not. Keiris stared around the chamber bleakly. Then he rolled his bed and tied it and emptied a beaker of water into the container of vines he grew. When he finished, the corridor beyond his room was as silent as it had been before. Reluctantly he left his chamber.

He did not meet Nandyris in the corridor or in the morning room when he reached it, although her place was carefully laid at the table. In fact, he met no one, although this was the hour when the palace staff was normally busiest. Keiris looked briefly out the broad window at the stony slopes where fruit trees grew. The last blossoms had already been torn away by the wind. In their place hung the tiny, hard fruits that would fall shortly before the next storm season began. Turning back, Keiris stood for minutes, staring down at the table, at the two brightly tasseled cushions that waited beside it.

Their meal was carefully arranged in a series of thin-shelled bowls: reef-apples; weed bread; chips of smoked yillie-fish; and the tiny, salty-sweet brill-nuts that Nandyris liked so well. Normally Kristis, who kept their kitchen, counted out the nuts frugally. But today she had filled an entire bowl with the precious delicacies. That told Keiris he was not the only one trying to bring Nandyris back. Kristis was trying, too, with offerings at the table.

He gazed down at the table a moment longer, his stomach cramping sharply. Then he glanced up at the scuff of feet.

Kristis stood with her hands knotted in the pockets of her work apron, her stocky shoulders hunched. She hardly seemed to belong to this room, with its finely polished surfaces and brightly tasseled silk cushions. She was like a knot of sea-wood left by the tide, heavy, gray, gnarled. And today her heavy Nethlor face was ravaged, her eyes inflamed. She shrugged, nodding at the carefully set table. "I thought you might take something before you go to the docks."

"The others are at the docks?" He should have guessed. Where else would the people assemble on the morning after two fishing vessels had failed to return—one of them bearing the successor to the dais?

"They're waiting there for the first horn. If you'll sit, if you'll stop a moment to eat—"

"No. No, I can't." The pain in his stomach warned him against that. If he ate now, he would only be sick. He glanced at her with quick concern. "Are you coming? Do you want me to walk with you?" The path to the docks was steep, and Kristis' balance was no longer sure.

She shook her head and wiped angrily at her reddened eyes. "It'll make no difference where I hear the horn from. Here, the bottling room, the smokehouse. You go and I'll leave everything here for you. And, young Keiris . . ." She touched his arm with a staying hand and spoke with rough emotion. "If the sea has her, young Keir, you still have us. You still have all of us. We're a family to you too."

"Yes," he said gratefully, squeezing her hands before he slipped away. If Nandyris was lost, he still had the people of the palace staff, a family without the kinship of blood.

He had three older half sisters, too—Lylis, Pendirys, and Pinador—but he had never been close to them, not as he was to Nandyris. They had been women when he was born; they had gone to live at the academy at Sekid when he was still a child. Only he and Nandyris had grown up together. Only he and Nandyris had run together on the shore, picking up whatever treasures the sea offered.

They had run in the corridors of the palace, too, just as noisily. They had splashed in the rain collectors on the roof. They had ventured into storage rooms and rifled trunks packed away decades ago. Sometimes they had even slipped from the storm-safes when the winds lashed, and huddled together at the corner of the landward plaza to watch lightning crackle from the black-bellied sky. Other times Nandyris had lashed ropes to stunted trees and dropped herself over sheer cliff sides when the tides were high, swinging her feet just above the black rocks and seething waters. Keiris had waited with painfully-held breath, certain she would slip, but she never had.

They had talked, too, endlessly, of the time when they would be called to the plaza to test at the horns. When the test was passed, they had told each other, they would sail with the fishing crews to learn the sea. And when they had done that, they would be ready to take their mother's place when she came to her cessation.

Keiris frowned, hurrying down the corridor. Nandyris had quit sharing those tales with him years ago. And once she had been called to the dais, she had told him very little of her experience with the horns. Still, the tales had been real once. For a while, as a child, he had believed he would be one of the rare males to blow the sounding horn and tune himself to the thoughts of the great sea mams who lived in the depths beyond the headland. He had believed he would blow the steering horn, too, and relay what he had learned from the mams to the crews of the fishing vessels at sea.

He had even forgotten, in the blaze of Nandyris' enthusiasm, how he felt when he stood on the cliff side with her and looked over the thrashing water. He had forgotten that he feared the sea: its depth, its power, the strange creatures and things that lived in it.

His fists tightened briefly. As a child he had believed he would use the horns. He did not believe it now. With his last birthday he was two years past the age when his mother should have called him to test on the horns. Apparently his lack of the necessary gifts was so clear, she saw no need to summon him, to test him. Certainly she had never done so.

But if the sea didn't give Nandyris back, she would have to test him—no matter who his father had been, no matter how little his background promised—because he was the only one of her children still untested.

Keiris frowned. He had seen his half sisters' genealogies. The match that had produced them had been carefully planned to produce an intermingling of the best Adenyo blood. Yet Lylis and Pinador had failed at the horns. They could not even use the steering horn; the tones they drew were clear enough, but their thoughts did not carry to vessels at sea. Nor, when they sailed with the fishing vessels, could they intercept the information their mother broadcast to them, the information she gleaned from the sea mams: impending weather disturbances, wrecker activity, the movement of schools of fish.

Pendirys had done better. She had learned to use the steering horns, but she heard no more clearly than the part–Adenyo steering-hands who already worked aboard the vessels. And no matter how carefully their mother had instructed her, no matter at what length, she had never learned to touch the thoughts of the sea mams.

Nor had any of his mother's nieces or cousins shown the gift when summoned from the academy at Sekid. Only Nandyris had it. And if Nandyris was lost, Keiris was the only one left untried.

His stomach knotted. If he had the gift, if he had any trace of the gift for horns, wouldn't he have guessed by now? Wouldn't he have felt it? Instead he felt only an uneasy fear of the sea—and a balancing dread of being dismissed from the palace to join his mother's kin at the academy at Sekid if he did not learn to use the horns. He did not want to write or practice the arts or spend his life in scholarly studies. The palace was his home. Kristis, Tracador, Tardis, Norrid—they were his people, even if they were not kin. If he could learn to be at ease with the water, if he could learn to hear just well enough to become a steering-hand . . .

Yet each time he thought of doing those things, of letting

the sea touch him so closely, of admitting its voices into his very mind, he felt sick and frightened.

Torn, he ran through the corridors, his boots resounding on the polished floors, and emerged on the landward plaza. He paused for only a moment, glancing toward the deserted workstations and trade stalls beyond the plaza, then took the path that led beneath the tattered fruit trees to the cove.

The day was jeweled now with dawn. Sky and sea were brilliant with the early blaze of the sun. The palace was the most brilliant of all, a low structure of pink slabs set upon a cliff of dark rock. Keiris glanced up as he made his way down the steep path to the docks and saw sunlight dash from the tall columns that guarded the seaward plaza. His mother stood upon the dais at the edge of the plaza, the sounding horn on its stand before her.

The seaward plaza was not visible from the rest of the palace. No structure had windows that overlooked it, and no person was permitted to walk upon its polished flaggings without Amelyor's invitation. Nor could the plaza be glimpsed from the rockbound slopes that stretched beyond the palace environs. When Amelyor took the dais, no person could see her unless he looked up from the shore below or from a fishing vessel at sea. Then he saw only a silhouette, a distant figure.

Keiris frowned. *A distant figure* . . . His mother had always been that to him. She had little time to pass as Nethlor women did. When the vessels went to fish or to harvest the seabeds, Amelyor must stand at the dais. Even when the vessels were docked, she stood there, gathering information about weather and ocean activity. During the storm months she remained at her station for all of each day and through much of the night. Who else could hear what the sea mams had to tell? Neth, the land they lived upon, was little more than an elongated spine of rock thrust up from the sea. Its fruits were sparse; its orchards and farms yielded little. The people of Neth must look to the sea for survival. Only the women who blew the sounding horns could talk with the sea mams. The palaces that housed these women were scattered along the twisting coastline. At Hyosis, only Amelyor could use the sounding horn.

Keiris had grown up in his mother's palace feeling closer to half a dozen other people than to her: Kristis and Tracador, who worked in the kitchen; Norrid, who had told him stories

of the Nethlor and taught him knots; Sorrys, who had come
from Sekid to teach him to read and write; Unid and
Anegidor, who had let him carry their cleaning buckets and
wring their mops when he was small, who treated him like a
son of their own now. He felt as close to Amelyor this
morning, looking up from below, as he had ever felt.

She had not even called him to her chambers the previous
night to tell him why Nandyris' vessel had not returned. And
he had twice told Maffis, her aide, that he wanted to see her.

So this morning he knew only what everyone else knew:
that yesterday seven vessels had gone out at dawn; that
Amelyor had taken soundings from the sea mams until late afternoon, then abruptly put down the sounding horn and with-
drawn from the dais; that an hour later five vessels had returned,
their crews disembarking silently, refusing to talk to anyone.
He didn't know whether Nandyris' vessel had met some
hazard the sea mams had not sensed quickly enough; whether
Amelyor had relayed a warning that had not been intercepted;
whether, in fact, Nandyris' vessel was lost or just delayed.

Today everyone from the palace, everyone from the nearby
Nethlor villages, everyone from the fishery had gathered near
the docks. Hundreds of people had come. The crews, heavily
muscled men and women in sea-stained whites, stood silently
among them, gazing up at the plaza where Amelyor stood,
arms at her side. Men, women, children—their faces were
gray, frowning. They spoke but only in whispers. Keiris licked
bloodless lips and joined them, standing a little apart.

The sea did not appear angry today. Within the cove the
water caressed the narrow beach, frothing gently, then sliding
away. Tardis, captain of vessels, stood to one side, his long-
jawed face betraying nothing. The steering-hands were grouped
around him, eyes downcast. Whatever Adenyo blood they
owned was many generations diluted. It hardly showed in
their features, in their coloring. Their knack for steering was,
Keiris knew, a pale gift compared to Nandyris'.

Yet they could project and hear better than many who were
whole-blooded Adenyo. A puzzle. A continuing puzzle not to
be solved.

Keiris glanced around. The people gathered near the docks
showed their Nethlor blood clearly. They were as alike one
another as they were different from him: stocky and heavily
muscled, pale-haired, their eyes reflecting the colors of sea
and sky. Their features were rugged, half finished. He was

like Nandyris, tall and slender, dark. Even his face was like hers, so much alike that they might have shared a father as well as a mother.

But they had not, and perhaps that was why Amelyor had never called him to try the horns, because his father had come from a family less gifted than Nandyris' father.

Keiris shrugged. He knew nothing of his father. Not his name, not the palace he had come from, not what had become of him. Nandyris' father had died eighteen years ago, but people still spoke of him. His own father had gone instead, deserted the palace one night and never returned. And no one would speak to Keiris of him. No one ever had. Once Keiris had searched the library for his genealogy, but it had been removed—if it ever had been shelved there at all.

Where had he gone? Why? What was the use of asking himself those things when there were no answers? Keiris forced himself to relax knotted muscles.

Then they tightened again as he realized that the people around him had come to full attention. They gazed upward, breath indrawn. He peered up.

Far above, his mother took the sounding horn from its rack and placed it to her lips. She stood with back arched. Her hair was laced into a single, long streamer, and the wind molded her gold-threaded gown against her body. Keiris saw her draw a long breath, and the first melancholy wail of the horn shivered in the air.

The sound touched him as it seldom had before, making him shudder with sudden cold. For a moment he felt the lash of the sea. For a moment he tasted salt on his lips, as if he were at the helm of a vessel at sea. He knew the sea mammals his mother called did not hear the cry of the horn, not as he did. They heard something else instead, some silent call Amelyor sent out with the sound, and they answered in kind.

Perhaps they were answering now. Perhaps their response was already in the air. Briefly, frowning, Keiris tried to imagine what form such a message might take. *An alien voice, as deep as the clefts of the ocean bottom . . .* He shuddered again, the chill intensifying.

But surely his mother did not fear hearing that voice, as he did.

As he did without entirely understanding why.

The horn wailed again, and someone standing near him sobbed. Keiris squeezed his eyes shut as answering tears rose

in his eyes. If only he could work some magic and bring
Nandyris back himself. If only he could close his eyes, call
up a fully fleshed memory of her, and carefully, carefully
reach out his hand to it. . . .

It was not hard to create an image of her, long-limbed,
dark-eyed, her white teeth flashing against her sunburned
skin. Her hair was as dark as his. She wore it in a long coil
bound with white cord. Her features were like those of the
earliest carvings of Adenyo women, the nose high and proud,
the brow broad, the lips wide and smiling. She was dressed in
white, and she wore a shell horn at her neck—not a steering
horn but a smaller horn that sounded only a tiny note.

It was not hard to create an image of Nandyris. It was not
hard to make it walk toward him, holding one hand to touch
his as the sounding horn called again. It was not hard to
imagine, for those moments, that he had summoned her. That
he had reached out, that he had called, just as his mother
reached out to vessels at sea. . . .

But when he heard the people standing nearest him gasp,
the image shivered and dissolved. Opening his eyes, Keiris
turned numbly and looked where everyone else looked.

A dark shape slid under the water near the docks.

"Sea mams. Gray-beaks."

Startled, confused, Keiris couldn't even tell who spoke.
The words seemed to come from everyone, an awed whisper.
He gazed after the moving shape, trying to bring it into
sharp definition, and saw that a second shadowy shape
darted after the first. Dark fins cut the water. Holding his
breath, peering down through the clear water, he saw the
distinctive beaked shape of the head.

Afterward he didn't remember what made him respond as
he did. He didn't remember what made him step from among
the people and run to the dock. He didn't remember what
made him kneel on the splintered wood and extend his hand
to the shape in the water, as if he were summoning it. He had
not seen a gray-beak so close before. They followed the
fishing vessels through the wild waters, playing in their wake,
but seldom came this close to the land. He only knew them
from a few distant glimpses when he walked the sea cliffs
with Nandyris, from the talk of the fishing crews, and from
stories told in the storm-safes.

Now he knelt, his hand extended, and felt a shiver of awe
as one dark shape raced through the water directly toward

him. A lunging body, the brush of surprisingly silken skin—
Keiris gasped and drew back as the first of the two creatures
raised itself from the water and touched his hand—and then
lunged into the air. It happened so quickly, Keiris had no
more than the impression of a long, dark shape arching
briefly through the air, pausing only to waggle its sharp-
beaked head. The second mam followed, twisting its body in
midair and slapping its tail against the water as it dived back
under the surface.

Keiris jumped to his feet, shaking himself, brushing the
water out of his eyes. Nandyris had told him gray-beaks were
playful. But to come to the docks on this particular day to
play, when they had not come in all the years of his life . . .
A distracted glance toward the plaza told him his mother had
returned the sounding horn to its rack and stood with her arms
at her sides, gazing down. He could not read her expression.
Too much distance separated them. Her posture told him
nothing, either.

The two dark shapes circled now in the water, as if they
had come for some purpose that hadn't yet been met. Warily
Keiris sank back to his knees. But before he could extend his
hand gingerly, both creatures propelled themselves from the
water again. They lunged into the air, sleek and powerful,
flying over the docks, over Keiris' startled head. For a moment a single depthless eye met his, paralyzing him. Then,
splashing into the water again, they quickly swam away,
abandoning the cove.

And there at Keiris' feet on the splintered wood lay an
object. A small shell horn, its bell carved in a scalloped
pattern, a cord of intricately tied knots strung through a hole
drilled at the thickest part of the shell.

Keiris' pulse began to race. The pain in his stomach—
forgotten since he had descended the path—was sharp again,
cramping. He knew the horn immediately. He remembered
the day one of the weed-rakers had brought it to Nandyris.
That had been two years ago, at this same season. A few days
later he had sat with Nandyris on the rocks above the sea and
watched her carve careful scallops into the bell of the horn.
He had knotted the cord for her; thanks to Norrid's patient
teaching, he was good with knots. Nandyris had worn the
horn every day since.

She had worn it yesterday.

And today the gray-beaks had dropped it at his feet. Numbly

Keiris wound the cord in his fingers and cradled the small horn in one hand. Around him the people had grown still.

Everywhere he looked, eyes met his. Faces ringed him, stricken and grieving. The horn told them what they had come to learn. Nandyris, laughing Nandyris—Nandyris, who one day would have stood on the seaward plaza and blown the sounding horn, was gone. The sea had taken her and it would not give her back. Not today, not tomorrow, not at all.

In most eyes he saw grief or fear. In a very few he saw disbelief. Keiris clutched the horn, trembling now, and wished he could disbelieve, too, if only for a few moments longer. But he could not. Finally, slowly, he raised his head and looked toward the plaza where his mother stood. Then he took the shell horn and began the steep climb back to the palace.

TWO

THE SEA HAD taken Nandyris, and he did not know how or why. And so Keiris' first thought, as he climbed the path, was to go directly to Maffis, his mother's aide, and ask again to see Amelyor. But when he reached the palace, he found Kristis waiting on the landward plaza, her hands still knotted in her work apron. She saw the shell in his hand and tears scored her crumpling face. Before he could do anything else, he had to hold her. He had to permit her to hold him.

Then there were the others: palace workers, fishing crews, canners and smokers, farmers, herders, orchard keepers. They had followed him from the docks, and when his mother did not come to accept their condolences, Keiris accepted in her place. He accepted their speculative glances, too, and tried not to show how they frightened him. If they thought he might take Nandyris' place, if they thought that . . .

Keiris moved among the people with as much composure as he could summon, until Maffis appeared from the crowd, his broad, roughly formed face heavy with grief. "Young Keir."

"My mother—" Keiris' stomach tightened. *Not now. Not today. His mother wouldn't test him today.*

"She will see you now. You are to bring with you . . . what the gray-beaks brought." Maffis' pale eyes flicked to the shell horn.

Keiris nodded, but his chest felt weighted with stone as he followed Maffis through the arched entryway into the palace.

Their boots slapped against carefully swabbed palace floors. Light from high apertures brightened the long corridors and made the richly grained pink stone gleam. The public chambers were deserted, worktables and meeting tables bare, cushions carefully stacked and waiting in the corners. Everything was orderly. Everything was well kept. Keiris cupped Nandyris' horn in one hand, trying to make himself as calm as the empty palace.

The sound of the sea grew louder as they passed into the more seaward wings of the palace. At last Maffis pushed back the broad doors to Amelyor's suite. Keiris entered and halted, drawing a shaky breath.

The chamber was spacious and tall. Carvings stood in every niche. The low table at the center of the floor stood upon a mat of combed white fur. Bright cushions were carefully arranged around it.

Amelyor stood at the sunrise window, tall in her gold-threaded gown. Her dark hair was coiled around her head now, held with a shell clip. She had placed herself against the disk of the sun, but the sky behind her had lost the vivid colors of dawn. Her face was impassive, her eyes opaque, unreadable.

"I have brought young Keir," Maffis announced.

"Thank you. Leave us please, Maffis."

The aide inclined his head and withdrew.

They were alone. The sound of the sea was rushing and loud. Keiris' blood rushed almost as loudly as he waited for Amelyor to speak. Except for the tautness at the corners of her mouth and the slight pallor of her face, she seemed untouched. Her eyes were not reddened; her face was not ravaged. She appeared as always: poised, remote, contained.

"This is what the gray-beaks brought," he said finally, when she did not speak, when she only studied him silently. "Nandyris' horn. If you want it—"

She shook her head. "No, keep it." She stepped forward, her bare toes touching the white of the fur mat. "We have not talked much, have we, Keir? We have never talked much at all."

"No," he agreed, although this seemed a strange time to discuss that, when there was so much else to consider. "If you will tell me what happened to Nandyris, why her boat was lost— "

"Haven't you guessed?"

The bluntness of the demand made him pale. No one had said anything, but Amelyor had entered the middle years of her life and Keiris knew what people feared. And if those fears were true, surely the word was hers to say first. He licked his lips. "I would like to hear from you what happened."

Amelyor lifted her shoulders in a shrug. The uncalculated gesture emphasized the careless grace of her long limbs. "It's a simple matter. During this past year the sea-voices have become fainter for me. I hear them less clearly. They seem dimmed, muffled, as if they come to me from a long distance. And my friends in the sea tell me that my voice comes more faintly, less distinctly to them too. My gift for the horns is waning.

"That is only to be expected at my age. The cessation eventually comes to us all, and I'm not young. You know, don't you, that Kristis and I were playmates as children?"

"She's told me that," Keiris said slowly. Kristis had told him, and he had studied his mother covertly, trying—unsuccessfully—to find some sign of her age. He no more found it today than he had before.

She shrugged again, another careless lifting of her shoulders. "I've known that one day I would no longer be able to talk with my friends in the sea. If conditions had been right, I should have stepped down from the dais at the first sign of cessation. The interim period, until the final loss, is a period of intermittent failures—of the voice, of the hearing. But Nandyris was young. She had not finished her years on the water. She needed more experience to round out her perceptions. She was not ready for the dais.

"I waited—what was my choice?—and this is the result. Yesterday Nandyris took her vessel and its companion beyond the weed beds into the wild waters. They were pursuing a school of gillie. I had no reason to believe there was danger in the area. It's early for lizard hatchings. Early for wrecker activity.

"But soon after midday, both my oldest friend, the great gray, and the smaller mams I speak with warned me there were signs of bottom disturbance—and then the voices ceased. All the voices ceased: Nandyris' voice, the voices of the other steering-hands, the voices of the smaller mams, even the gray's voice. I could hear nothing. My voice to the vessels failed at the same time." She turned, pacing across the polished stone floor. "I stayed with the horns for a time, trying to find my voice again, trying to find my hearing. At last I withdrew. It was useless. So I secluded myself. I rested,

as much as was possible. When the sun set and Nandyris'
vessel had not returned with the others, Maffis brought me a
sedative tea and I drank it. I wanted to walk the plaza, I
wanted to sound the horns, I wanted to call your sister's
name. But I had no voice for the sea. And so I took my bed
and slept.

"I slept, hoping to see Nandyris' vessel at the docks when
I awoke. I awoke, hoping to hear her voice outside my door.
Of course, I did not. When the sun rose and I went to the
plaza, my voice had returned. I called to the oldest of my old
friends and she told me a tale, a simple tale.

"The disturbance my friends reported, the disturbance I
was not able to warn Nandyris of, was an early hatching of
Bights lizards, two nests of them laid closely together."

Keiris drew a sharp breath. The Bights, red-eyed, vicious,
each adult as long as three fishing vessels together, buried
their eggs in deep beds of sand or mud, scores of them nested
together. The eggs lay there for years, the embryonic lizards
slowly forming as the eggs sank deeper and deeper into the
ocean's soft floor. Then one day the hatchlings broke their
shells, wriggled up through layers of mud, and boiled upward
in a voracious mass.

"They went for the gillie first. If I had been able to call a
warning, the vessels might have escaped. But there was no
warning. The water boiled with lizards and gillie. Sea mams
came to the area. Gray-beaks. Yellow-fins. White-tails. Even
a large white. They tried to defend the vessels. They tried to
drive the lizards back to the bottom. If there had been only
one nest of hatchlings, perhaps it could have been done. But
there were two nests. They hatched simultaneously, the vessels
capsized, and no one was saved. The mams lost numbers
too."

Keiris put one hand to his mouth, his stomach cramping
tight. It was not hard to imagine the struggle, the confusion,
the thrashing of the water. It was not hard to imagine Nandyris
tumbling helplessly into the sea. It was not hard— But he
stopped himself there, biting hard at his lower lip.

Amelyor turned sharply, studying him. Her voice was flat,
as expressionless as her face. "So your sister died. Do you
blame me for it?"

"No," Keiris breathed, startled. How could she think that?
Her voice had never failed before. How could she have
anticipated what had happened?

This time Amelyor's shrug was more than a careless lifting of limbs. It was a gesture of pain. "Nor can I blame myself, reasonably. But I do. How can I forget? I was the one who failed her."

"No, she would never want that," Keiris said. Nandyris would want no pain lingering after her, certainly not that kind of pain. Impulsively he said, "If you want to test me . . ."

She seemed momentarily surprised by his offer. She studied him, her dark gaze narrowed, her brows drawn in a frown of concentration, as if she were trying to see his very thoughts. "Why do you speak of that now?"

He drew a deep breath, steadying himself. "Because I'm the only one you haven't tried. I'm the only one you haven't called."

Her frown deepened momentarily. Then she pressed her temples, as if there were pain there. Her voice was low. "I have called you, Keiris, many times. I have called and you never came."

He stared at her, not understanding her words or the emotion he heard behind them. "No," he said. "There was never a message from you. Maffis—"

"I didn't send Maffis with the summons. I called you as I called Nandyris. As I called your other sisters. I called you with the horns. But you didn't come. Did you never hear my voice? Even faintly?"

Keiris paled. She had called him with the same voice she directed to the sea mammals? To the steering-hands? And she had expected him to hear and respond? "I heard nothing," he admitted. "But I—I've wanted to come. Many times. I've wanted to come and ask when you would test me. I'm beyond the age when my sisters tested."

"You're beyond the age when your sisters heard my summons. Yes, even Lylis. Even Pinador. They tested poorly when they came, but they heard me call." When she saw his baffled disbelief, she went on quickly. "Let me tell you something, Keiris. Each of us has a voice—a silent voice. You have a voice. I have a voice. Every person with Adenyo blood has a voice, and so do most of the mammals of the sea. I don't know why it should be this way, when the Nethlor seem to have none. At least those Nethlor who have no Adenyo blood have none. But most who have voices—Adenyo and mams alike—are not able to project in such a way that others can hear them clearly. And most do not clearly hear the voices of the others around them. When I call through the horns, most of our kin hear only the horn. They hear the barest echo of my voice, if they hear it at all.

"Beyond these, few of us—among humans they are almost always pure Adenyo; among mams they come from the larger breeds—can hear and project clearly with little more than cursory training. Others can be taught, although their gifts are generally less useful. Some can never learn."

"I can never learn," Keiris said, letting the bitter words come—words he had never spoken aloud until now. "Is that what you're telling me? I'll never use the horns because I didn't hear you. I don't have the gift and I can't be taught. But if I had been a daughter instead of a son—"

"If you had been a daughter, the chances would be greater that you could use the horns. Those most gifted are usually full–Adenyo and female. You are neither of those things."

"I—" At first he let her words slip past without fully apprehending them. Then he glanced back at her, frowning, still not fully comprehending, and met eyes narrowed and measuring. A slow flush spread across his cheeks, as if his body comprehended her words before his mind made sense of them. "I am Adenyo," he said. "I am full–Adenyo."

Her eyes continued to measure him, narrowly. "If your father was not full–Adenyo, then you are not, Keiris."

What was she saying? Did he understand her? His face had grown very hot. At the same time his hands had become icy. His father had not been full–Adenyo? He could not believe it. Why would his mother have taken a part–Adenyo for her mate? Sometimes, of course, there were love matches between Adenyo and Nethlor. There had been from the days when the Nethlor had first found the Adenyo adrift on their rafts, fleeing the fire-cones that had washed their islands with flame. But no one who had a dais to fill could afford to dilute the blood of her children that way.

Yet his mother was telling him that she had. "Why?" Why would she have done that? And why had she never told him? Why had no one told him?

Amelyor sighed, glancing regretfully at the sun. "Why? Because I didn't guess what he was until the night he left me. The night you were born. Oh, I saw that he was more heavily built than most Adenyo. I saw that from the first day he came walking up the path from the sea. I thought it was simply because he worked himself hard. He loved the sea, and when he went with the crews, he didn't just blow the steering horn. He did all the things the others did.

"There were other differences, too, small ones. And I knew there were things he kept from me. I knew that long before I took him for a mate. When I questioned him about his family, about his palace, for instance, he answered me reluctantly, as if each word cost him a price. He won a place steering almost as soon as he came here, and even when we spoke to each other through the horns, I was always aware of some reserve. His voice was clear. It carried well. When he spoke, it was more song than speech. It was a song that sang inside me. Or perhaps it only seemed that way because of my feeling for him—and because I had so seldom spoken that way with another human. Even so, he never let me go as deeply into his thoughts as I wanted to go. He kept certain barriers between us.

"I'm not sure he was entirely pleased when I asked him to be my mate. But there was something undeniable between us, something I had not experienced before. I think he had not experienced it, either. He agreed to say the words with me.

"We didn't speak of having a child together. Nandyris was young, but I knew she would test well. I wasn't concerned for the dais.

"I was pleased, anyway, when I conceived. But when I told your father we were to have a child, he became distant. He was obviously troubled, but he wouldn't tell me by what. The barrier he kept between us grew more difficult to penetrate.

"I thought that would change when I delivered. He was good with children. And so, on the night you were born, he waited in the nursery and I had Maffis carry you to him immediately. Maffis left him there in the nursery with you. An hour later, when I had had time to recover from the delivery, I sent Maffis to bring him to me. Maffis returned and told me he was gone.

"I didn't understand. How could I? I went to his chamber myself. I was the one who found the dyes on his bureau—the dyes he had used to darken his hair and skin, to deceive me into thinking he was full–Adenyo when in fact he was of mixed heritage. And what proportion of Adenyo to Nethlor, I've never been able to learn.

"I didn't fully believe it even then, when I saw the empty room, the dyes on his bureau: that he had lied to me, that he had gone—without even telling me his intent. I thought there must be some explanation. I thought that if I could find him, I would hear it.

"But when I sent messengers to the palace at Rynoldys, where he told me he had come from, I learned he had not come from there at all. He had not come from any of the other palaces I queried, either. Nor had he come from the academy at Sekid or from Kastar or Lonorid. Even the name he gave me was false. There was a man of that name, but it wasn't him."

Keiris stared at the pale mask of her face. "You don't know who he was. You don't know where he came from. You don't know where he went." His voice was a hoarse whisper. No wonder no one had ever told him any of those things. No one knew.

"I don't know." She drew a long breath, standing before the disk of the sun again. "He stepped into my life, he stayed with me for a few years, and he stepped out again. And now I have a test for you, Keiris. A test different from any other. I want you to find him."

"Find him? My father?"

"Yes. I want you to take a message to him. When he left here, he took something that I have claim upon. I must have it back. And if in exchange he wants to keep what is his— then that is between you. That is between you and your father."

He shook his head, confused. "He took something from you?"

"He took my youngest daughter. Your twin." Seeing his incomprehension, she went on quickly. "There were two of you, Keir, born together. And by all the conventions your father was entitled to take you if he chose to leave. If parents part, the father may take the son, but the daughter remains with the mother. Instead of observing that convention, your father smuggled your sister away. He stole her the first time he was left alone with her, when Maffis took you both to him in the nursery. And now I must have her back."

"But no one said anything to me." Keiris stared at her, lost, dull with shock. He had not been born alone. But Maffis, the palace staff—if he had had a twin, they must have known. And they had said nothing. "No one told me."

"Very few members of the staff knew. I told them—I told everyone—that I didn't want to hear your father's name again.

Nor did I want your twin spoken of, if I could not quietly gain her back. And I could not. I searched, but I never discovered where your father went with her.

"Perhaps I didn't search as thoroughly or as openly as I should have." She shrugged, dissatisfied with her own effort. "But I was not then concerned for the dais. I had Nandyris. And your twin was fragile. There were . . . anomalies. From the limited examination Gesis and Fendon made of her, they were uncertain she could survive. It seemed likely I was searching for a dead child and a mate who would never come back to me even if I did find him. And I was reluctant to have it known what had happened. That I had been deceived. And deserted."

But now Nandyris was dead, and his mother must test her final daughter, if she was still living. Keiris' mind worked quickly. "She's only part–Adenyo. Like me."

"She is part–Adenyo, yes. If she is still living, she may not test well at all. But it is possible she has become stronger, and it is possible she can take the dais."

And on that slim hope she wanted him to go searching. But where? How? Slowly he let his breath seep away. "I don't know how to find her. I don't know where to look." He couldn't even guess how to begin.

"And I can give you very little help, except to tell you that your father was a steering-hand, a good one, and he loved the sea. He loved it more than anyone I've known."

So he had that one clue, if nothing else. There were few enough men who used the steering horns. People would remember him for that if they had met him. Keiris frowned as a new thought struck him. "What if he took her for the same reason that you want her back?"

"Because there is an empty dais somewhere? Because somewhere someone was approaching her cessation without a successor?" Amelyor's eyes narrowed and became hard. "Our ancestors forged our conventions for good reason, Keiris: to prevent disorder and hostility. One of the first conventions is that a mother always has first claim upon her daughter. Remind your father of that when you find him. Tell him that if he will not send my daughter willingly, then . . ." She turned to the window and stared out, her mouth drawing down in a hard line. "Then I will use what voice I have left to bring the great mams to my cause. And the ocean touches every shore. Tell him that, too: the ocean touches every shore. It touches our shore, and it touches the shore where he lives now.''

Keiris caught a sharp breath, recognizing the threat. ''Would you do that?'' Would she set the sea mammals against his father's people? ''Can you?''

She turned back, and for the first time he saw age in her eyes—the age of the ocean depths, opaque and cold. ''I can do many things while my voice stays with me. You see me upon the land. I stand in the sea, too, and there I have many bodies. I talk with the grays and the whites and the more gifted of the smaller breeds. With their help there are many things I can do. Tell your father that I will do them. I will do them rather than see our people suffer.''

Keiris expelled a slow breath, knowing as well as she what would happen if Hyosis was left with no one to blow the horns. The vessels would fall victim to wreckers, lizards, blood-lilies, and a dozen other hazards—and the people would go hungry. The people who had cared for him. The people who were his family. The Nethlor, whom he knew now were blood kin, however distant. He stared down at the floor, knowing he must do what she wanted. He must go and make the search, even if it was futile. ''I—I don't know how to find my father,'' he said uncertainly.

Amelyor studied him long and carefully. ''Listen for him,'' she said finally. ''And call to him.''

''What do you mean?''

''Your voice and your ability to hear are undeveloped now. But it may be that these abilities develop later and more slowly in males, if they are to develop at all. So I have heard over the years. It may even be that males expect so little of themselves that they don't take the necessary steps to develop what latent gifts they have. Take Nandyris' horn with you. Travel near the shore and try to speak, try to hear wherever there are docks and fishing vessels.

''The horns are only devices, you know. We don't blow them because they amplify our voices or enhance our hearing. We blow them to bring ourselves to a state of concentration. I can't tell you what steps we take to learn, what methods we use. Those are different for each of us. The important thing is simply to reach out—to continue to reach out until you can touch what you reach for. You can call and listen as well with Nandyris' horn as with any other—if you can learn to do those things at all. If you can discover how to teach yourself.''

If. If he could somehow teach himself to do those things—
and he felt no intimation that he could; he couldn't even guess
how to begin—perhaps he could find a sister he had never
seen and bring her to the palace. Keiris raised trembling
fingertips to his temples. "I don't think I can do these
things," he said in a half whisper.

Amelyor addressed him with a lingering glance before
speaking. "Nor do I think I can do the things I must do each
day, Keir." She turned away, frowning at the sky beyond her
window. "I've told you your father loves the sea. So did
Nandyris. I do not. It is a cold place to me, full of dangers,
which I must study. It is a large place, so large that I'm afraid
of losing myself in it. Yet I awake each morning and plunge
into the water. I stand at the dais when blood-lilies are
blooming, when wreckers are pummeling my friends the
mams, when storms come. I stand there while lightning bites
the land around me. I send my voice to the depths of the
ocean and I feel the weight of the water. I feel it crushing me.
I touch the minds of creatures so strange, their thoughts make
me fear for my own mind—even though these same creatures
are my oldest friends. Sometimes I'm afraid the sea will take
my humanity, that it will turn me into something else—some
creature from the island tales. You've heard those tales,
haven't you? Those old tales?"

"I have." Sorrys had told them to him: stories from the
oldest library scrolls of the rermadken, sea creatures said to
live in the waters beyond the Adens—creatures who appeared
human until one glimpsed their faces. There had been tales of
the tide folk, too, humans who lived as sea creatures, coming
to land only to give birth to their young or to seek shelter
from storms.

"Still, I go to the dais each morning. I leave other people
to feed my children and teach them. Today I watched my
daughter's death through the eyes of a creature larger than any
fishing vessel in our fleet. And now I'm asking my son to go
find a man whose name I don't know.

"I do all these things because there is no one else to do
them, Keiris. The Nethlor found us adrift on rafts when the
Isles of Aden were destroyed. They took us in. They fed us
and sheltered us and let us live upon their land, even though
they existed at the very edge of survival themselves. We had
nothing to offer them but our gift with the horns. They took

us in, not even knowing we could offer that. That's kindness, Keir—to offer life and expect nothing in return.

"That was long ago. They gave us much in the beginning, and they continue to give us much. We don't have their strength, their patience, or their numbers. They make us a gift of those things every day.

"What can you offer them in repayment? What can you do for them?"

What could he do for the people he loved? Keiris stared down at the floor, knowing he must do whatever he could—however little that might be. Finally he sighed. There was one final point that must be clarified. "My father—do you hate him still? Even after all this time?" It must be so. How else could she feel?

For a moment he thought the quick contraction of her pupils signaled anger. Slowly she released her hair from the shell clip and let it fall across her shoulders. It hung to her waist, a sheet of black silk. "Is that what I've led you to think?" She spoke softly, speculatively. "I've had two mates. The circumstances of my taking them were completely different. Nandyris' father was chosen for me, and the process was correctly observed in every detail, according to convention. Delegates went from my mother's family to the palace at Hensidor, carrying the genealogies. There were three men there to be considered; Kandris was the one selected as most suited to me. Contracts were drawn, and we met and said the necessary words and did the necessary things. He gave me four daughters, and he represented me at meetings and councils and on festival days, while I held the dais. He was a good man, and when he was gone, I was sorry.

"Your father came to me from nowhere, with dye in his hair. When I questioned him, he gave me a false name and told me false stories of his origins. He drew a genealogy for me once, at my insistence, but none of the things he put into it were true. I knew him too well to ask him to do the expected things. I never asked him to represent me at meetings or festivals—because he only wanted to work at the docks or be at sea. And I only wanted him to be there, at the steering horn.

"Because when he was at the steering horn, his voice touched me, and my voice touched him. There were barriers. There were reservations, but I had more from him than from any other person I've ever known. We shared thoughts, we shared feelings. We shared dreams that were like long songs we sang together. I stood alone at the dais, as it was my duty to do—but I wasn't alone at all.''

"And you didn't guess—you didn't guess what he would do?"

"I never guessed," she said. "I think even now that if you had been the only one born, he would have stayed with me. At least"—her brow furrowed—"at least until there was a second child."

"Until there was a daughter."

"Yes. Surely that was what he came for, a daughter. To fill a dais somewhere. Or for some private reason of his own. Perhaps only because he loved the sea and wanted a daughter who could talk to the mams." And there was no hatred in her voice. There was only regret.

"You cared for him."

"I cared. I still forget myself sometimes and listen for his voice. I still think of things to tell him." She turned and gazed into the sun for a moment, then turned back. Her hair spread in a fan across her shoulders. Her voice was very low. "I have given you two messages for him. That I want back what is mine and that the ocean touches every shore. Tell him, too, that there is a way he can keep his daughter. He can return here with her."

Keiris studied her and saw a tenderness he had never seen in her before. He felt his shoulders tense. The price of failure, he realized with sinking heart, had just grown steeper. Much steeper. "I'll tell him," he said. "When must I go?"

"After you have dropped the effigy for Nandyris."

His head snapped up sharply. "I'm to drop the effigy?"

"You were closer to her than anyone. The gray-beaks brought her shell horn to you. She would want the effigy from your hand."

"If you had been on the dock when the gray-beaks came—"

"But I was not. I was at the dais. Here . . ." She strode across the chamber to her bureau. Opening a lower drawer, she brought out a small shell box. From it she took a strand of amber beads. With a sharp motion of her wrist she broke the cord that held the beads and spilled them to the top of the bureau. She selected one and held it to the light. "This is the clearest, the best. Use it as the heart."

He accepted the bead numbly, feeling its weight in his hand. "I'll have to have cloth woven," he said. "Then I'll

have to stitch the effigy. That will take me two or three days.
And I'll have to gather the gifts from the people." The
Adenyo followed the old custom of dropping a single effigy to
those lost at sea. The Nethlor offered other gifts instead.
Some of them would take days to carve or fashion.

"I will tell Tardis he has five days to prepare a vessel."

Keiris nodded, pressing his temples. Tardis would want to
scrape and sand and paint and seal, so that the vessel that
went carrying gifts for Nandyris and the lost crews would be
like a gift itself. But at least Keiris would be busy while the
boats and the gifts were being prepared. He would have no
time to think—except of Nandyris and this one final thing he
must do for her.

His mother had turned back to the window. She gazed out,
her expression growing remote. "Come back to me before
you leave. There are likenesses of your father in storage. I
will have the vault keepers find them for you."

She was dismissing him. "Yes. I'll come," he said, and
turned quickly, suddenly eager for the privacy of his own
chambers where he could think clearly of what she had told
him, of what she had asked of him.

But when he reached the corridor, his stomach was cramping again. His chest was so heavy, he could hardly draw
breath. His temples pounded. He leaned against the corridor
wall, letting the cold of stone seep into him as he tried to
order his thoughts.

He had come to his mother's chambers thinking she would
test him and he would fail. But he had come to terms with
that failure years before. He had accepted it.

Now, instead of testing him with the horns, she had given
him another test, a test that might take him seasons to
complete—or to fail. And he didn't even know how to begin.
He had Nandyris' horn, but he didn't know how to use
it—nor how to teach himself to use it.

What had Amelyor told him? That perhaps in males the gift
for horns, if it was to develop at all, developed later and more
slowly than in females. *But if it was not to develop at all . . .*

And if it did develop, it would plunge him into the sea.
Torn, Keiris rubbed his neck. The sea . . . The sound of it
was suddenly loud in the corridor. Its pounding was insistent.
It made his head hurt, although it had not done so just a
moment before.

Maffis approached, one hand extended, but Keiris did not

want to speak to him—or to anyone. Turning, he ran down the brightly polished corridor, ran through successive wings of the palace, ran until he reached his own chamber. It seemed many hours since he had begun the day there. Yet the sun was still low in the morning sky as he stood listening to the hammering of his heart and thinking of the things—the impossible things—that were suddenly required of him.

THREE

Keiris stood at the sunset window of the landmost meeting chamber, gazing into the vivid colors of sunset, not seeing them at all. The voice of the sea was a whisper in the distance—a penetrating whisper, a small, hissing voice he could not escape.

Everything was done now. The effigy was complete. He had overseen the weaving of the cloth and the cutting of the pattern himself. He had gathered the symbolic objects required: Amelyor's amber bead to serve as the heart; the other stones, carefully polished, to represent the senses; the tiny, carved nuts and fruits to fill the belly and forestall hunger; and a tiny stone child to nestle deep inside the effigy to combat the worst kind of loneliness. He had not attempted to shape that himself. Those were carved at Sekid, and he had only selected the one he thought best.

Then, when he had stitched the effigy, he had gone to the library to find and memorize the words he must say for Nandyris.

Now there was nothing more to do until morning. He had an entire night to pass with no task. An entire night to pass in the company of his own thoughts, reluctantly, uneasily. He stirred restively, staring into the sun-shot sky.

"Young Keiris."

He turned, frowning. Norrid approached tentatively, as if he were uncertain of his welcome. "Yes?"

"Do I disturb your peace?" The old man spoke carefully, standing with heavy shoulders hunched, ready to turn away at the first sign that Keiris was displeased to see him.

27

"No. I thought of coming to you tonight," Keiris said truthfully. Norrid no longer had a place on the fishing crews, but he had sailed once and had a long memory and a treasure trove of tales to tell. If he had ever crewed with Keiris' father, if he would talk about it . . .

"To make knots with me? I came for that, to ask if you wanted to help tie a chart of your sister's days. The crews intend doing it tonight if you will work with us."

Norrid had come to invite him to join the crews in commemorating Nandyris? When he had never even been invited into the crew room before? When he had only paused outside the door, listening to the songs the crews sang? "Thank you," Keiris said, touched. "There are—there are some things we gathered on the shore. May I bring those?"

"Bring anything that has memory in it. We'll tie it into the chart. We've already cleared a space on the wall for it." Carefully the old man laid a huge hand on his shoulder. "And come to laugh, not cry. This will be a happy chart, Keir. Your sister had no sad days and she had no hard ones, not until the last. She had only good days."

Keiris nodded. It was true. Nandyris had not lived to know lonely nights on the dais, quarreling aides, or stillborn children. She had never been defeated by anything, until the last instant. "Let me look through her chamber," he said quickly. "There are things she would want tied into her chart."

"Fetch them. Then come to the crew room. I'll get down the cord. White because she sailed with the crews. Blue for the sea. And a strand of gold because she was our successor these two years."

"Yes." It would help to think about Nandyris a little longer. It would help to handle things they had discovered together. It would help to have company on his last night in the palace. Keiris went quickly to get what he needed.

He felt briefly awkward later when he entered the crew room. There was no trace here of the order that predominated in the rest of the palace. Here were no polished surfaces or tasseled cushions. The rough-hewn walls were hung with sea-wood and lizard hides. Discarded whites lay in heaps in the corners. The air held sea smells. The three battered worktables stood on long legs. One must stand to use them, or sit on tall stools.

Carefully, aware of the heavy-muscled men and women who moved aside for him, Keiris chose a place at one of the

tables and set out the things he had foraged from Nandyris'
chamber: shells, knots of wood, sea-scoured seeds and pods,
strange objects he could not identify. Tardis, master of the
fishing vessels, had brought mementos, too, small tools and
implements Nandyris had used. Some of them she had fash-
ioned herself.

There was food and drink, too, in quantity. Kristis exercised no parsimony when the crews came to the kitchen with
platters and pitchers. But no one ate or drank yet. The crews
waited silently for Tardis to begin.

When everything was arranged on the worktables, Tardis
strode heavy-footed around the chamber, assembling a selec-
tion of work-scarred gaffs and long-handled tools. "Choose
the pole, Keir," he instructed. The master of vessels was
taller than most Nethlor, his features blunt and unsmiling. His
eyes were the unreflective gray of clouds, and he moved with
slow-striding authority. "This one—Nandyris used it herself,
the day she gaffed the lizard. Had you seen her—"

"Yes. Yes, I'll take that one." Keiris could imagine how
Nandyris had looked as she faced the lizard. He could imagine her bared teeth and her reckless, laughing face. If he had
that much daring . . .

But he did not. Each time he tried to imagine himself at the
prow of a vessel, a lizard no more than a pole's length away,
he broke into a cold sweat.

He, Norrid, and Tardis took turns at first, winding the pole
that would support the knot-chart, then tying the row of
delicate knots that represented the first year of Nandyris' life.
After that, others took turns, too, remembering events and
creating knots to represent them. Gradually men and women
from the palace staff filtered into the room, bringing things
they said Nandyris had touched or used or admired, and the
crews tied and wove them into the pattern. The web of knots
extended. Soon there was laughter and the passing of platters
and pitchers.

Before too long, the people began to sing. Keiris had heard
the songs they sang from childhood, but he didn't understand
the words. They were old Nethlor, a tongue seldom used
now. They touched him anyway, long, variegated melodies
that spoke of love, joy, sorrow, and the coldness of ocean
depths. Listening, Keiris worked over the chart, he watched
others work over it, and he saw the completeness of Nandyris'
life grow from their many fingers.

Love, joy, sorrow—the coldness of ocean depths.

It was not until the tying was done and the knot-chart hung on the wall that Keiris realized that Norrid had remained at his side for most of the evening. Norrid did not sing the old Nethlor melodies. He sang something else, his husky voice low, the words repetitious. Occasionally, as he sang, he glanced at Keiris, as if he expected some reaction.

"Your song—what is it?" Keiris said, finally guessing that Norrid wanted him to ask. He had listened closely enough to tell that the language of the song was not classical Adenyo. Nor was it old Nethlor or common tongue.

A momentary slyness came into Norrid's eyes. "That I don't know," he said. "I knew a man who sang it once, though. He sang it when he went out with the crews. He sang it when he swam in the sea. Oh, he liked to do that—to swim in the sea. It's an old song, I think, in some Adenyo dialect almost everyone has forgotten. It occurs to me that if a person could learn which dialect, if a person could learn where, in all of Neth, people still sing in that tongue, one might find that man."

Keiris stared at him in surprise, licking his lips. What was Norrid trying to suggest? Something that could only be said indirectly; that was clear. And what could that be but . . .

Keiris frowned sharply at the old man. Had his father loved the sea so much that he swam in it? Keiris had never heard of anyone else who did. Few enough people went into the protected waters of the cove, even when the weather was warm. And the sea itself—that was to be respected, to be feared, but to be enjoyed? "At Sekid they might know the dialect," he said slowly.

"They might," Norrid agreed with a bob of his head, plainly pleased by Keiris' response. "And that might be helpful to a person who is searching for someone. Someone who isn't spoken of in our palace anymore."

It might. It might be the very clue that could lead him to his father. But Keiris hesitated, puzzled. "How did you know I might be hunting him?" How had Norrid guessed?

Norrid's slyness vanished. The old man met Keiris' eyes directly, frowning a little, his heavy face earnest. "There are things Amelyor finds shame in, although no one else who lives at Hyosis feels they are shameful. Still, she asked a long time ago that those things not be spoken of, so we don't speak of them. But we all know them, young Keir. We

know there is a last daughter. We know her father stole her.
We know we must have her back if there is the smallest
chance she can blow the horns. There are so few who can.
Fewer, even, than when I was young.

"And we know a few others things too. That your mother
called all her drawings and carvings of your father out of the
vault three days ago. That you have removed your personal
goods to storage trunks, as if you expect not to need them for
a while. That—what else can we think?—means you are
leaving us, and there can be only one reason for that. You are
going to find your father and your sister."

"Yes," Keiris admitted, humbled. He had thought he had
made his arrangements covertly, but obviously the people of
the palace knew everything. Obviously they had known everything for many years. He bowed his head momentarily.
"Can we go somewhere? I want to hear all the words of the
song."

"There are not many," Norrid warned him. "Just a few
phrases he sang again and again, as if he had learned them as
a child and then half forgotten them."

"Then I want those few phrases," Keiris insisted. At least
the song gave him a place to start: Sekid.

"There will be no one on the plaza. I'll sing to you there.
And if you find this man, I want you to remind him of the
afternoon I pulled him out of the water just ahead of the
whip-tail. He was a strange man, young Keir, but in the best
of ways. There are few Adenyo who can wield the tools a
Nethlor wields—and use the steering horn too. And few who
bring the mams gathering around our vessels to play in his
company, as he used to do. Even Nandyris never did that.
Nor did Amelyor before her. But the mams came to be near
your father, numbers and numbers of them. So many sometimes, it was frightening. But they seldom so much as rocked
the vessel.

"Then he left us, and it seems he did us a disservice when
he went. But there had to be a good reason. Everyone here
knows that.

"Come hear his song."

Keiris went, and when he returned to his chamber later, he
sang the fragmentary verses under his breath as he studied the
likenesses his mother had sent from the vault. There were two
carvings of his father, both in cool, white stone. He traced
their profiles thoughtfully with a fingertip, finding more in

them now than he had before—wondering when he might begin to find a man in them.

He studied the sheaf of drawings too. They were miscellaneous, made from many perspectives, by many hands. He saw little in his father's face that spoke of Nethlor heritage, however distant. Straight nose; wide, carefully made lips; broad brow; ears tucked back against an elongated skull—his features had none of the half-formed ruggedness of Nethlor features.

But his shoulders were broader and more heavily muscled than most Adenyo shoulders. There was power in them and in his arms and hands. And his eyes were obliquely set, giving his face a keenness, an alertness that was neither Adenyo nor Nethlor. He did not look like a man who had ever lingered long at an academy, committing words to paper or creating exquisite objects of stone or glass.

Sekid.

At least now he had a starting point.

Still Keiris did not fall asleep easily, nor did he sleep well. He turned restlessly in his bed, dreaming of strange places and deep waters—dreaming himself lost in them.

When he awoke, Systris had set. Vukirid hung low in the sky. It was time to take the effigy to the docks. Keiris pulled on his clothes and made his way to the path. He worked to suppress the cold promptings of apprehension as he went. He had never gone to sea before. He did not much want to go today. But neither did he want the crews to see that Nandyris' brother was afraid.

Tardis and the crew waited below. The vessel they were to take had been scraped and sanded. The setting moon painted its sails white. The crew stood silent in fresh-bleached whites as Tardis showed Keiris aboard and stationed him near the prow.

After a while the sounding horn wailed three times. The steering horn at the stern of the vessel answered twice, and the vessel moved away from the dock. By then Vukirid had set, and there were only stars in the sky. Keiris peered up, feeling suddenly very remote from the commonplaces of his life. Feeling that he was about to drift away from everything ordinary and familiar—whether he wanted to or not. He could distinguish only the bare outline of the columns that guarded the plaza. He could not see Amelyor, although he heard her horn call again.

Then he could see nothing at all as the vessel swayed from the darkness of the cove into the greater darkness of the sea. After a first moment of panic Keiris sat shivering in the prow, grateful for the darkness. At least no one could see how ill at ease he was on the water.

The vessel moved for a long time in darkness, or so it seemed. The wail of the sounding horn died behind them. Except for the occasional call of the steering horn, there was no sound except the slap of water against the sides of the vessel and the creaking of wood and ropes. The crew worked without speaking.

Then, slowly, sky and sea became diffused with gray light. The vessel entered an enveloping mist so dense, Keiris could no longer see the crew at their stations. He stared into the mist with a sick sense of unreality. Every creak of wood and ropes, every call of the steering horn was muffled. But if he listened, if he listened closely, beyond those sounds was another, and he wasn't certain he wanted to hear it. It was airy, it was whispering, it—

Abruptly Tardis loomed from the blinding mist and stationed himself beside Keiris, large and unsmiling. "The water's breath is persistent today. Slow to lift. It's seldom we hear the weed beds bubbling before the sky clears."

Keiris released a slow breath. So the sound he heard was only the weed beds releasing stored gases. Nothing terrifying at all. Weakly he found his voice. "How far must we go?"

"We'll reach the temple of waters before mid-morning. If all continues well in the area, we'll make the offering there."

For the first time Keiris felt excitement, excitement that overrode the terse lack of enthusiasm he heard in Tardis' voice. "Inside? Will we go inside the temple?" Norrid had told him of the temple of waters—a massive, hollow-chambered rock mass looming above the ocean's surface. Vessels had once slipped into its interior channels and glided through its vaulted chambers, exploring. But Norrid said they no longer went there; he said it had been decided decades ago that the danger was too great.

"Amelyor has asked that we go into the inner temple. It's an old custom that she wants renewed, at least in this case. And so we will." Tardis frowned, gazing into the undifferentiated silver of the mist without pleasure. "Look for sunlight soon," he said brusquely, before he moved away.

Keiris looked after him, puzzled by his mood. But before

long the disk of the sun burned through the mist, and he
forgot Tardis' terseness. Crew members began to talk and
laugh among themselves. Keiris looked across the sunlit water with fresh interest. Boundless, moving, blue—here was
the sea Norrid had told him of, the sea where legendary
creatures played. In the sparkle of sunlight he suddenly felt he
might see a sea-swallow leap from the water and soar on
finned wings, jeweled eyes glinting. He might see schools of
ghost-gillie dart past, glowing in bright colors, only to wink
out if he looked too closely after them. He might see a great
white rise from the depths, guided by a figure that rode on its
back.

That was an Adenyo legend, he remembered. The sea-
swallows and the ghost-gillie came from the Nethlor tradition.
It was the Adenyo who had come bringing tales of other
basins of the sea, where people and near-people—the tide
folk and the rermadken—rode the backs of the great sea
mams.

All the legends seemed to live this morning.

Then the temple of waters rose from the sea, an indistinct
darkness on the horizon. The vessel rocked forward, rising
and falling with the water, and after a while Keiris saw a
great multilobed dome of rock rising from the sea on columns
and pillars of black stone. It was large, much larger than he
had expected. Looking at it, he felt a coldness in the pit of his
stomach. No wonder vessels no longer ventured into the
temple. If they entered the interior maze and became lost, or
if some creature caught them in the narrow corridors where
they could not evade it—

Tardis was at his side again. "How did it get here? How
did the temple get here?" Keiris asked. Why had he never
heard? It seemed simply to have risen from the sea.

The question—or perhaps it was the temple itself—appeared
to displease Tardis. "The mams have stories of that," he
said, his blunt features unsmiling. "You would have to ask
your mother for those." His eyes narrowed, became challenging. "Pacys reports your mother's voice is clear and strong
today. You can take the steering horn if you want. To feel
how it blows."

Keiris darted a quick glance at the large shell horn mounted
at the stern. Pacys, the steering-hand who rode with them,
nodded formally, offering it. Keiris drew an unsteady breath
and touched the much smaller horn he wore at his neck. His

pulse pounded as if he were physically threatened. "No. No."

Tardis' eyes remained on him for moments longer, weighing. Then the captain of vessels strode away.

With the distinct feeling that he had failed a test, Keiris watched the temple grow closer, watched it grow larger, and felt his heart begin to press heavily at his ribs. Even the crew grew silent again. Tardis stood amidships, arms folded over his broad chest. He gazed at the massive formation with frowning gray eyes.

A few minutes and they slid into the shadow of the temple. The crew lowered sails. They locked oars into place. They bent over them. Still they were quiet, overawed.

The oars touched water smoothly, with scarcely a sound. Effortlessly the vessel glided into the channel the ocean cut through the arching cathedral of stone. Keiris gazed upward, holding his breath as they entered the first chamber. The smell of the sea was a concentrated tang here. Far above, the roof of the chamber was studded with bright-colored shells. As Keiris watched, the shells moved, creating a slowly evolving pattern.

Crawlers, he realized, shuddering—small creatures that salvaged empty shells from the ocean floor and wore them for protection against predators. Darting among the slowly moving shells were tiny creatures with faintly glowing eyes.

Star lizards. Harmless. Amelyor wouldn't have directed them here, after all, if there was anything to fear.

Keiris told himself that again as they entered the second chamber. Little sunlight penetrated here. Pale shadows moved in the water at either side of the vessel, and when he glanced back, the water itself glowed in their wake, lit by phosphorescent bubbles.

She would never have directed them here if there was anything to fear. But the crew was ill at ease, and increasingly Keiris could see that Tardis was displeased, even angry, that he had been directed to bring his vessel into the temple.

They passed through successive chambers, the oars cutting the water in disciplined rhythm. Some chambers were dark and echoing. Others were fissured and sunlit. Occasionally some creature screamed down at the passing vessel, or a streamlined shape arched briefly from the water beside them. Once a crawler dropped its shell, and it clattered to the floor of the vessel. One of the crew bellowed in alarm and then subsided into embarrassed laughter.

"You didn't want to come here," Keiris said when Tardis paced to the prow again. That much was clear. But would the captain of vessels tell him why?

"I like the open sea, where I can see what is before me," Tardis responded, scowling into the shadows. "I like to be able to take my vessel quickly in any direction. I like sunlight. But ahead—you will see what is ahead."

Ahead a narrow, dark passage cut through the rock. The ceiling hung low, barely high enough to admit the vessel. The only light within the passage came from the eyes of the star lizards clinging to the walls and from the vessel's phosphorescent wake. There was the stale smell of captive air. Keiris drew his arms close to his body, fully understanding Tardis' displeasure. The walls of the passage were very near. The vessel could easily scrape against them. And if Amelyor's voice should fail, if they should meet something in the passage, something unexpected . . .

After that it seemed to Keiris that they moved through stifling darkness for a very long time. He caught his breath and held it, trying to time their passage by the number of times he was compelled to release his breath and catch it again. Finally he saw light ahead, faintly. The crew bent over the oars, then lifted them as the vessel glided forward into a tall, domed chamber pierced at its summit by a circular orifice. Sunlight fell in a cylindrical shaft, describing a bright circle on the water's surface. Dimly Keiris saw that the dome of the chamber was crusted with slowly moving shells.

"Here," Keiris guessed, looking up into the light. This was the place they had been groping their way toward. It had to be.

"This is the place where Amelyor wants us to make the offering—the sun chamber," Tardis confirmed. He looked up into the sunlight, frowning. "Pacys . . ."

Pacys bent over the steering horn and sounded, eyes closed. The wail of the shell reverberated through the chamber. After an interval she blew again. Then she withdrew from the horn and opened distant green eyes. "We are safe here."

"We'll open the chests. Hepis, Finor . . ."

Two Nethlor left their posts and hurried to open the twin chests. As they did so, they glanced around uneasily, their heavy faces strained.

"We will offer gifts for the lost crews first," Tardis said. "We do that in silence. Then you can make your offering and speak the necessary words for Nandyris."

Keiris nodded and sat quietly while the crew members dropped the carefully assembled gifts into the dark water. Small carvings, polished stones, ropes of braided jewelry the dead had worn, carefully drawn portraits of families and friends, food . . . Pale shapes darted in the water, pressing curious noses to the offerings, then gliding away. Far overhead, several shrill voices screamed in chorus. Doggedly the crew members bowed their heads over each separate offering before consigning it to the water. Occasionally their lips moved, silently. Sometimes, despite themselves, they glanced around anxiously.

No matter what care they took over the ceremony, Keiris could see their uneasiness. He felt it himself. They had penetrated to the center of the chambered rock. Its weight hung over them. The long cylinder of sunlight illuminated very little. It served more to offer contrast with the surrounding darkness. Outside was light and warmth. This place was black and ancient and cold.

The temple was like a slow-beating heart of stone, and they had penetrated its innermost chamber. If the rocky muscle contracted before they escaped, they would be crushed.

Keiris felt that, but at the same time he understood why his mother had wanted them to come here. The sea was featureless, boundless. At least this place was marked. She would always know—just as he would always know—where he had made the final observances for Nandyris. The temple stood as a monument.

At last the offering chests were empty, and everyone turned to look at Keiris. He saw they were anxious to go. He shared their feeling. But he would not hurry. He promised himself that. He promised Nandyris that. He would not hurry the final observances.

Licking dry lips, he slipped the effigy from its protective silk. He looked down at it, frowning, momentarily dissatisfied. It seemed small. How could it possibly carry all the wishes he wanted to send with it? The wish that Nandyris remember family and friends; that she remember the good times of her life, even now that it had ended; that she be at ease with the brevity of her days. Could one small figure contain all those wishes—and so many more?

Perhaps not. But he had done his best and he would do his best. He touched the effigy's silk hair and closed his eyes.

There were words to be said aloud, and he said those almost without thinking. They had little meaning. They came from the library, not from his heart.

Silently he spoke simpler words, words he wanted Nandyris to hear.

Here we are, your family.

All of us in one figure.

Amelyor, your mother.

Kandris, your father.

Your sisters: Lylis, Pinador, Pendirys.

Me.

And the child you would have had one day.

We want you to have the child with you in the sea.

Give it whatever name pleases you.

If it is a boy, name it for me.

Did she hear? Did she understand? Keiris squeezed his eyes shut. Surely if he could make her hear him, she would understand what was in his heart. Surely if he could call to her in a voice penetrating enough, a voice that would reach her through fathoms of water . . .

Here we are, bound up in this figure.

We've come to be with you.

If you are cold, touch us.

If you are lonely, hold us.

Keep us close.

But how could she do those things when she was not here? When she had died in another place? He pressed the effigy to himself, crushing its heart to his, and spoke with as much intensity as he could summon—spoke wordlessly.

The shell horn dug his flesh, but he hardly felt that. Amelyor said he had a voice, however silent, however untrained. If he could summon it for just a few moments, if he could make Nandyris hear him, if he could make her understand why he must leave the effigy here instead of bringing it to the place where she had died, the unmarked place he didn't know how to find . . .

He was so lost in the effort that at first he didn't recognize the sound he heard as a human cry. It seemed thin, far away, and he let it pass without wondering. But it was followed by other cries, by the sounds of feet scuffling, by grunting breath. Then he felt strong fingers closing around his arm, shaking him. Numbly he opened his eyes.

"The effigy—drop the effigy." Tardis loomed over him, fear and anger in his gray eyes.

"Wh—"

"Give them the figure!"

Keiris blinked stupidly, then looked past Tardis. The other crew members had gathered at the center of the vessel. They hunched together in postures of fear. Their faces, in the dim light, were gray, frozen. Their eyes stared.

Stared past him. Stared at something at his back.

Slowly, so slowly he could feel the contraction of every separate muscle, Keiris turned.

For a moment he did not recognize what it was that loomed beyond the prow of the boat. The creature was too large, its presence too unexpected. It was so large, in fact, so near, he could not see it all at once, not from this perspective. It presented its face—mouth, jaw, eyes—but that seemed more like a steep wall of flesh. Its white skin gleamed palely in the dimness of the chamber.

A great white.

He saw it. Yet he did not believe it. Where had it come from? It could only have come through some uncharted underwater passage. Certainly it was too large for the channel they had come down. And now it floated so near, he could reach out and touch it if he wanted. He could touch its unreal flesh.

But this flesh—this mam—was very real. It looked at him with depthless eyes—eyes in which he fleetingly saw something he had seen in Amelyor's eyes a few days ago: a coldness, an age. His breath clutched in his chest. His heart did not want to beat.

The creature was silent. So silent. And it could destroy their vessel with a single flip of its tail.

"The figure!" Tardis hissed. "They want the figure. They've come to take it to her."

The white had come to take the effigy to Nandyris? Keiris drew a shuddering breath and tried to find his way past the paralysis of shock.

That was when he saw the others—the smaller mams. They glided soundlessly beside the vessel. He didn't recognize their breed. He saw only flashing gray skin and smoothly elongated bodies.

His mother had sent them, he realized with a shakily indrawn breath. She had sent the great white—was this the old friend she spoke of? No, that was a gray—and she had sent the smaller mams. To take the effigy to Nandyris. He drew a second, trembling breath and forced motion to frozen limbs. He raised the effigy and threw it over the side of the vessel.

One of the smaller mams rose smoothly and caught the figure before it touched water. Quickly the creature darted away with it. And while Keiris watched, expecting the boat to rock, to overturn, the other mams raced after the first. Only the great white remained, slowly gliding forward, circling the vessel, dwarfing it—then sinking silently into the water to disappear.

It took time for the crew members to find their wit again. For many minutes they simply stood staring at the water, ghost-pale, dumbstruck. Then, when the mams did not reappear, they returned to their stations, laughing raggedly at nothing, and dipped oars. Keiris could see the trembling of their lips, the pallor of their faces, as they nudged the vessel down the dark passage.

He saw something else, too, as they rowed their way back through the chambers of the temple. He saw the great white's eyes as it glided around the vessel. It seemed to watch him from the darkness even now. There was something old there, something that made him colder than he had ever been, as if the great white had drawn him with it to the depths of the sea.

As if he had offered an effigy and had been taken along with it.

The coldness stayed with him until they emerged from the temple, until sunlight sparkled from the water around them. Then, slowly, his hands warmed. His feet became flesh again. He looked around.

There were still marks of fear on the faces of the crew. Tardis' features were hard-bitten, frowning. He scowled back toward the temple as it slowly receded.

When that vanished, Tardis turned the same reflective frown on Keiris. Keiris endured his scrutiny uncomfortably. He did not try to speak to the captain of vessels until they reached land. Despite the warmth of the sunlight, he had intermittent periods of chill through the rest of the return voyage. He had moments when he felt that he had been drawn into the depths, that the weight of the water crushed him.

Finally they reached land and docked the vessel. Keiris waited on the pier until Tardis completed his duties and left the vessel. He paused, frowning again when he saw that Keiris had stayed behind.

"You thought the white would harm the vessel," Keiris said. It seemed necessary to say something. There was something unresolved between the two of them. He could not give it a name, but he saw it clearly in Tardis' frown.

"I thought it would drown us all," Tardis responded with open anger. "To call a great white into the temple . . ." He drew knotted hands into fists and pressed them together hard. "I am a Nethlor, young Keir. I am a fisherman. I care for my vessels and I care for my crews, and I can control those. I cannot control a white—or a gray, for that matter—and I do not want them near me."

Keiris flushed. He had not expected such clear-spoken anger. It almost seemed directed at him. "My mother—"

"I have no quarrel with the dais. I am pleased that Amelyor speaks with the mams and makes safe passage for us. Without that we would be poorer—much poorer. And we would have many more dead than just these few.

"I am pleased *she* speaks with the mams. I don't want to speak with them myself, and I don't want them so near my vessel that I can touch them. I have proper respect for them, but I want to respect them in their own place. Far from me."

Again the anger seemed directed at him. "I—I didn't know she was going to send the mams for the effigy," Keiris said stiffly. "She didn't tell me."

Tardis seemed about to speak back still more angrily but contained himself. Slowly he crossed his arms over his chest, barricading himself. There was bafflement and wariness in his expression as he studied Keiris. "Nor did she send them," he said finally. "Amelyor sent none of them. I have already asked her that, through Pacys."

"She—" Keiris stared at him dumbly and felt the cold of the ocean again. It made his hands heavy, it made his heart slow. It made his tongue thick, so that he could hardly speak. "*No*. If she didn't send them, if she didn't call them—"

"Then ask yourself who did."

"I didn't," Keiris said. "You can't think that."

"Who else rode in our vessel today? Do you think I called the mams? Do you think Pacys called them? They have never come to her before. I don't even want them near me, not in such a place as the temple. And there is only one other person who has ever brought so many mams crowding next to any vessel I have sailed in.''

His father. And now Tardis thought he had done the same thing, when he knew—knew in the pit of his stomach—that he was incapable. Keiris shook his head. "You're mistaken. I haven't even tested on the horns. I—"

"I offered you the opportunity to blow today."

"And I'm not ready. My mother told me that. She has summoned me to the dais, but I've never heard her voice. I've never heard her call." Didn't Tardis know even that much of how the testing was done?

"She has summoned you. I know that. Why don't you tell me—since we are speaking so freely—why you haven't heard?"

"Why? Why haven't I heard?"

"Tell me why you haven't heard," Tardis repeated.

"I just gave you the answer. I'm not ready."

"You are not ready," Tardis said, his gray eyes becoming distant. "We're seldom ready for the things we fear, are we?" He studied Keiris for a moment longer, then turned and strode heavily away. At the end of the pier he turned back. "Seldom, Keir."

Keiris stared after him, wordless. What was the captain of vessels trying to tell him? That he had not heard his mother's summons because he had not wanted to? Because he feared testing at the horns and failing?

That could not be true. He could not have screened out his mother's summons simply because he was afraid to hear it. And he could not have called the mams today. He had not even blown a horn. He had only tried to speak to Nandyris.

Tardis was wrong. Tardis was wrong in everything.

Yet Keiris felt the ocean as he made his way up the path. He felt the cold of it, the deep of it, and he felt the eye of the great white upon him. He began to run, trying to escape the pounding of the water against the shore.

FOUR

HE LEFT THE palace without speaking to anyone. He retrieved his pack from his chamber, slung a bedroll over one shoulder, and left, clattering down flagged corridors, running across the landward plaza. He didn't care who turned and looked after him. He didn't care who spoke his name. He didn't pause even when he heard Maffis call after him. Amelyor wanted to see him, of course. She wanted to speak with him. She wanted to question him about what had happened in the temple of waters.

But he had nothing to tell. Nothing. The great white and the smaller mams had not come to the temple of waters at his urging. He had not called them. How could he summon a creature as alien as the one that had risen from the dark water of the sun chamber? No, Tardis was mistaken. And if he felt cold, if the flesh of his arms was chilled, that was only because he had passed the morning on the sea.

Never mind that the sun had shone on the water. Never mind that the sun shone on him now. And never mind that what he felt was deeper than any ordinary cold, that he had the sense, even as he ran, of some alien medium licking at his boots.

His pack thumped against his back. He ran through the maze of workstations and trading stalls and down the lanes of animal pens beyond. From there a stony path led him down the rocky slope and conducted him toward the road that led to the Sekid.

It would be as near, he knew, to travel by the sea path at first. But that led beneath the seaward plaza, where Amelyor stood at the dais. And to look up, to see her there now, would only add to the confusion and fear he already felt.

Fear that despite his denials, he had—somehow—called the mams. Fear that in doing so, he had changed something. That he had somehow offered himself to the sea when he had intended to offer only an effigy.

No. Tardis was wrong. He had to believe that. To believe otherwise was to believe that the land could shift beneath his feet and become water.

He ran, breathlessly. The palace fell behind, and slowly the land widened under his feet. He passed boulder-strewn patches of farmland and occasional stunted orchards. The people who worked them raised hands to him as he passed, calling to him to stop and talk. Another day he would have done so, but today he stopped for no one. He could not pause if he was to outrun the sea.

Finally the land flared so wide, he could no longer hear or smell the water. Keiris veered off the road and followed a narrow path across abandoned orchard lands. The midday sun was warm. A few of the stunted trees still held their blossoms; they cast a thin fragrance in the air. Keiris threw himself down beneath them to catch his breath. Then he opened his pack and ate for the first time that day.

The rest of the day's travel was less a flight. He kept to the highest spine of the land, walking through stony orchards and steep-pitched grazing lands and across rocky wastelands, used for nothing. Sometimes he passed Nethlor villages and raised his hand to people who lived upon the land during the calm season, coming to the palace for shelter only during the worst storms. They called back, inviting him into their huts, but he refused and continued on.

He continued until dark, making his way along sheep trails and picking his way down narrow paths that led from village to village. As he walked, he was careful to think only of things that were immediate: the rattle of loose rock on the footpaths, the slow setting of the sun, the smell of turned soil when he passed occasional pockets of farmland. It was easier that way, easier not to think ahead to the later stages of his search.

When dark came, he made himself a bed in an empty herder's hut. He was sheltered by stone and thatch, but his dreams were rocking and wild, full of darting forms and mammoth shapes. He struggled against them, trying to wake.

Instead sleep carried him to a place deep and cold where he could not breathe—where half-glimpsed monsters hung suspended in some dense medium. It did not matter how he twisted and fought. He could not escape the glare of yellow eyes or the clammy touch of suckered appendages. Occasionally a human form rose on billows of phosphorescence—then turned a face to him that was not human at all.

Finally morning came, and he shuddered awake and escaped the hut. He stared around anxiously.

The land was empty. There was no one within sight, human or beast. The sea was a distant sheet of gray; featureless, unmoving. He heard not the faintest hiss of its voice.

It was the approach of drowntide that had brought the dreams, he decided. The moons were nearing their spring conjunction, making the tidewaters rough and tall. He had heard stories of people affected by the tides. It simply had never happened to him before.

Relieved to find a rationale for the night's dreams, he began to walk again.

The land narrowed again at mid-morning, becoming little more than a spiny ridge of stone. Twice, as he walked, he saw palaces in the distance, splendid expanses of gleaming pink stone. Instead of approaching them, instead of stopping to call, he set his route across the uppermost spine of the land, avoiding the traveled road, until the inhabited lands were behind him. By dark, his legs ached and his feet were blistered. But that night passed without dreams.

Finally it was evening of the third day and Keiris stood upon the cavern-pocked hillside above the Sekid quarry, looking down over the halls and plazas of the academy. Sekid appeared as it always did at this hour of the day. Gowned figures moved desultorily down broad thoroughfares. Statuary cast deepening shadows. The setting sun glanced off captive pools of water aproned by polished stone slabs. Occasional stone figures bathed in the pools, but no human ventured near the water. Beyond the academy, nearer the sea, he saw the huts of the Nethlor who served the academy.

He hesitated, studying the contrasting communities—the academy with its carefully laid thoroughfares and glistening halls of pink stone; the Nethlor village with its thatch-roofed huts gathered haphazardly along narrow, wandering lanes. Sekid was, as far as possible, a replication of the classical academies of the islands. The Adenyo lived here as they had

lived there, practicing the arts and customs of the islands,
carefully preserving a way of life tens of centuries old. By
convention, the Nethlor who cooked for the Adenyo and did
the heavy work of maintaining the academy's structures remained in their own village from early morning until dark, so
that only Adenyo walked the plazas and thoroughfares of
Sekid during daylight hours.

Keiris shifted unhappily, looking down over the academy.
He always felt ill at ease here, out of place among the artists
and scholars of Sekid. His clothing, his speech, his very
manner seemed wrong here—more Nethlor than Adenyo.
And his sisters would have heard of Nandyris' death by now.
If he went to them, they would insist upon following island
mourning customs, customs long abandoned in the palace,
where Adenyo ways were not so stringently kept. They would
demand his company at Sekid for days. But if he went to the
Nethlor instead of the Adenyo . . .

It was fitting, wasn't it? Hadn't his mother's revelation
made the Nethlor his kin by blood as well as spirit? Drawing
a deep breath, deciding, Keiris stood and picked his way down
the hillside toward the Nethlor village.

By the time he reached the village, the sun had set and
lanterns shone from thatched huts. Tracador, who worked
with Kristis in the palace kitchens, had kin here, a sister who
lived alone. Keiris asked up and down the wandering lanes
for her and finally found her hut at the northern edge of the
village. He rapped at her door, hoping she had not already
gone to the kitchens at Sekid for the night.

A stockily built woman appeared in the doorway and knew
him immediately. "Keir from Hyosis." She caught both his
hands and drew him into the hut. "We heard of your sister's
death. There was a messenger two days ago. Here, sit with
me. Have you eaten? What will you drink? Why have you
come? Your sisters, Lylis, Pinador . . ."

There were good smells in the hut, and he had not eaten
since midday. Sighing, Keiris gave himself to Naomis' hospi-
tality. "I don't want to stop with my sisters tonight. And I am
hungry. Please just give me whatever you have."

"What I have would be much better if I had known you
would come to my door," she responded immediately. "My
own sister—is that why you've come? Isn't she well?" Naomis moved quickly around the single room of the hut, offering him a stool to sit upon, pressing food and drink on him.

"When I saw her last, she had a swelling in her throat. Now—"

"Now she's fine," he assured her. "The crews brought in fresh burris-kelp pods, and Kristis boiled them down and bottled the liquor for her. She has had no trouble since."

Naomis nodded in quick relief. The table was rapidly set with food. She urged him to eat as she heated the pot for drinks.

"But you've come for a reason," she said when finally she settled herself on a stool opposite him. "There are three halls at the academy where you would be welcome. Your sisters—"

"I would be happier if they didn't know I was here at all," he said quickly. "My mother has asked me to perform an errand, and I have no time to stop. But I need to know something before I go on. If you will help me, if you will go to one of the history masters and ask . . . Can you go tonight?"

She agreed readily, and when he had eaten, he sang for her the few lines Norrid had taught him of his father's song. She sang them back to him, her voice husky.

Lantern light flickered across her thoughtful face. "Harridys will know what the words mean," she decided. "He's curator of the earliest collections. I have prepared many special dishes for him. He will complain, but I can ask this of him."

"Please—but I don't care what the words mean," Keiris said quickly. "I want to know what dialect they come from. I want to know where the people who spoke the dialect settled when they left the rafts. There is someone—someone who sings that song. I want to know where to look for him."

"Ah." Her eyes narrowed. "Then that is what I will ask. And you will find that person. You will go and find him, young Keir, and take joy back to your home."

Keiris sighed, recognizing her conspiratorial tone, guessing exactly what it meant. People knew, even here, what had passed in the palace at Hyosis seventeen years before. His mother's secret had never been secret at all—at least not from the Nethlor of Hyosis and their far-flung kin.

After she left, he glanced around the hut. He had intended to sit up until Naomis returned, although that might not be until the kitchens closed at dawn. But his stomach was full, the hut was warm, and his legs ached. Soon after she left, Keiris pulled off his boots and stretched out to sleep.

The fuel in the lantern had burned low and the hut had

grown cool when he awoke to the sound of rapping at the door. He rolled over, pulling covers over his head, then forced himself to get up and answer the door.

An attenuated Adenyo stood at the threshold, his hair dressed high upon his head, an elaborate gown draped in folds about his long-limbed form. His hair was silver, but his eyes were black and full of annoyance. "Keiris of Hyosis?"

Keiris stiffened at the peremptory tone. He had seen Harridys occasionally when he came to Sekid to visit his sisters—had seen him lecturing on the plaza outside the library or gathering students around him beside a captive pool of water. Keiris had wondered at the time why the scholar always seemed annoyed: with his students, with his followers, with his subject. Tonight he seemed more irritable than ever. "Yes. Will you come in?"

"We can talk in the lane," Harridys said curtly.

So it was beneath the scholar's dignity to step into a Nethlor hut. "Of course," Keiris agreed, stepping outside. The moons still hung in the sky, one trailing the other; it was earlier than he had thought. "My mother has sent me—"

"I heard your tale from Naomis," Harridys said impatiently. "I heard your song too. And if Amelyor has truly sent you on this errand, she is more foolish than I ever believed. To send you to find a person who sings a primitive ditty—"

"It is the only thing I know about the man I must find," Keiris said stiffly. "I have no other information."

"Then your search is useless and you may as well return to Hyosis. Or petition for admission here. It is time for that, isn't it? You've had nothing beyond a few years of tutoring. Not enough, obviously, to make a man of the Isles of you." His dark eyes flickered to Keiris' casual clothing.

Keiris drew a careful breath. Harridys was abrasive. Harridys was arrogant. Keiris wanted to respond to him with answering unpleasantness. But if he antagonized the only man who could help him . . . "I must complete this errand for my mother first," he said evenly. "She has especially asked this of me. When it is done, perhaps I can come here to study. If you can tell me the dialect of the song—"

Harridys raised both hands in a disclaiming gesture. "Of course I can tell you the dialect. And how will that help you? This is a tidelands ditty. This is a song once sung by the tide savages to their children—a night song. A lullaby." His eyes blazed from shadowed sockets. He tossed his silver hair irritably. Then, abruptly, he bared his teeth in a challenging grimace. "Does that help you find your man, Keir of Hyosis? This is a song of the tidal tribes, but there are no tide people now. There have not been since the cones fired. The tribes were not wise enough to take warning and build rafts, as our ancestors did. They had never weaned themselves from the sea; they cared more for their friends the mams than for their own kind. And so they had no culture, no civilization, nothing they cared for enough to salvage. They were savages. It was that simple. Our ancestors didn't even consider them human. In classical Adenyo they were the rermadken."

Keiris stared at Harridys. "No," he said, startled by Harridys' vehemence, surprised at what he said. Because Keiris was certain he was wrong. "I've heard of the tidal tribes. They're extinct; Sorrys taught me that. And I know the rermadken traveled with them sometimes, but they were something else." Something not human, something chillingly other—something alien, creatures more of legend than of history. To say that the tide folk had been the rermadken, to say at the same time that the song his father had sung was a tideland lullaby . . . He pressed his forehead, certain the scholar was wrong. "The rermadken—"

"You make the mistake of speaking when you know nothing," Harridys rejoined. "Give me your sources. What texts can you cite? What authors can you quote? And tell me, while we speak of it, how many years have you spent in the library vaults? How many nights have you burned the scholar's lantern?"

"I—"

"You have done none of that, have you? Because you care more for your own affairs then for our heritage. If it were left to individuals like you, our entire culture would be lost—as lost as the islands. Everything would slip away: our customs, our dress, our thought. We would lose ourselves among the Nethlor." He touched his carefully dressed hair, his eyes dark and bitter. "If you care to spend enough time in the vaults to substantiate what I've told you, it can be arranged. But you hardly want to do that, do you? You might discover just how mistaken you are in your assumptions about many things."

Keiris held his tongue again, forcing himself to speak evenly. "I have no time now. I must comply with my mother's wishes." Even as he suppressed his anger he was thinking. A tidelands ditty? Harridys seemed certain of his information. But how could his father have come to Hyosis singing a tideland song—singing it, Norrid had said, as an adult sang a song he had heard as a child? How could he have learned a tidelands song as a child when the tidal tribes were so long extinct?

Keiris frowned, pressing Nandyris' shell horn against his chest, reviewing what Sorrys had taught him of the history of the Adenyo. Originally all the people who would one day inhabit the Isles of Aden had lived in the sea as brothers to the mams, speaking to them both silently and aloud, following their cycles and migrations. Then slowly the more intelligent, the more advanced, the more forward-looking had emerged to build their palaces and cities and academies on land. Only the tidal tribes had remained in the water, riding the larger mams from shore to shore, touching land only to give birth to their young, to gather certain foodstuffs, and occasionally to ride out the most violent storms. While the Adenyo had abandoned the company of the mams, speaking to them only with horns, the tide folk had continued to live with the great creatures, had been carried and guarded and nurtured by them—savages of the sea.

Then the fire-cones had erupted, the islands had burst apart, and the waters had boiled. The Adenyo had cast themselves into the sea on hastily built rafts, eventually to be taken in by the Nethlor. And the tide folk had never been heard of again.

"You're certain of the dialect?" Keiris probed.

"Of course I am certain of the dialect," Harridys said curtly. "There were certain ditties the savages were heard to sing to their young when they came ashore. Both Pallis and Tiranidor recorded them. We've preserved them even though they are quite distinct from the music of our own ancestors— simpler, more repetitive, far more primitive, of course.

"If you want to find the man who sang that ditty, I suggest you go to the academies and ask for him. He can be nothing but a scholar. Who else would trouble himself to remember a song like this one? But he is a scholar, apparently, who has set aside his vocation for more frivolous pursuits."

Keiris bristled at Harridys' crisp arrogance. "Thank you," he said with cold formality. "Thank you for coming so far to tell me what you know."

Harridys seemed about to deliver some parting exhortation, but Keiris turned and stepped back into the hut.

It took minutes for his temper to subside. Then he began, haltingly, to think of what Harridys had told him, to study its implications.

It was not hard to discard the suggestion that his father had been a scholar. Neither Norrid nor his mother had mentioned any inclination to study.

No, instead they had said that he loved the sea. They had said that he spent as much time as he could near it. That he swam in it and that the mams gathered to him just to take the pleasure of his company.

They had gathered to him as once they must have gathered to the tide folk.

But how could his father be a man of the tides? None had come on the rafts. None had escaped when the fire-cones exploded.

Keiris rubbed the back of his neck, puzzling the matter. If the tide people had been on the islands at the time of the eruptions, they had not escaped on rafts. But wasn't it more likely that they had been at sea when the cones exploded? And if they had escaped the boiling waters on the backs of the great mams instead of on rafts, if the mams had brought them to some obscure shore of Neth . . .

Or if they had remained in the waters near the devastated islands and only ventured here later, perhaps many centuries later, perhaps only recently . . .

Keiris frowned. If that was the case, was that the alien strain in his father's blood? Not Nethlor but sea savage? Did his father perhaps even carry the blood of the rermadken? The suggestion terrified him. But if Harridys was correct, if they and the tide people had been the same, or if they had intermingled . . .

Was that why the great white had come to Keiris in the water temple? Because he carried tidal blood?

And if he did, what did it mean? What did it mean to carry the blood of folk wedded more to the sea than to the land?

He shuddered. What had his mother said? That she was afraid sometimes that the sea would steal her humanity? Keiris' fingers were cold again, so cold that they ached. He must find his father. He knew that with fresh urgency now. There was no other way he could learn what it meant to carry the blood of the tidal tribes. If, indeed, he carried it.

But how was he to find his father? He couldn't guess that any better than before. If the tide folk had come to Neth, where were they? What shore had then chosen? How much time did they spend there and how much in the sea? Why had no one seen them or heard of them?

Perplexities. He had come to Sekid hoping for information; instead he had only uncovered further perplexities. He stood frowning and still for a while. Then, almost without thinking, he went to the cupboard and took down a jar of dried willis-seed. He spilled the flat seeds on the table and began to form them into the shape of Neth, as he had learned it from Sorrys. The activity was automatic. His fingers worked, but he hardly thought of what they were doing.

The land took form quickly; long, narrow, twisting, like the spine of some half-emergent serpent. To the north were the spits, the serpent's many flickering tongues—uninhabited strands of land separated from each other and from the main body of Neth by the sea when the tides were high, joined when they were low. Below the spits lay the neck of the serpent, the narrow and treacherous northern lands where the people were as cold as the polar current that curled near their coast. Hyosis and the palaces and academies it held conventions with stretched along the ragged coastline to the south. Keiris knew each academy by name, but the palaces were more numerous. Still more numerous were the Nethlor villages the palaces served.

Keiris caught his lower lip in his teeth. If he had to go to each palace, to each village, and ask if anyone had heard or seen anything unusual, anything unexpected . . .

No, surely if the tidal tribes had come to Neth, he must look for them first among the spits, the isolated tongues of land that constituted the northernmost portion of Neth. No Adényo lived there—and, so far as he knew, no Nethlor. It seemed doubtful that the surly northerners who inhabited the harsh land of the serpent's neck took much interest in what happened in the spits. Certainly they refused to interest themselves in the activities of the other people of Neth, refused even to subscribe to the conventions of their southern neighbors. Wouldn't the tide people have chosen those deserted shores over the busier shores to the south?

But he knew nothing of the spits. Sorrys had shown him maps, but the spits had not been drawn with any attempt at accuracy. They had been drawn simply as furling, serpentine tongues, an artist's conception. How could he think of traveling among the spits when he did not even know how much of the land disappeared with each tide—and how much would remain to give him footing? The moons were nearing conjunction. It wouldn't be long before the drowntides, the tallest tides of the year.

He frowned down at his makeshift map, considering the undertaking. Would they help him at Kasoldys, the northernmost academy, if he went there and petitioned? Did they have maps there of the spits? Had they interested themselves to that extent in the land beyond their own cold-bitten shore? Would they offer him a guide?

He stared at the map he had made, then down at his hands. The fingers were blue, bitten with cold, as if the sea had overtaken him. *And what was to prevent it from doing so if he carried tidal blood?*

Suddenly it did not matter if the inhabitants of Kasoldys had mapped the spits or if they assigned him a guide. It did not even matter if they refused him the courtesy of a meal and a night's shelter. The question had become not just whether he could find his father. It had become whether he could safely establish his own origins—whether he could establish them firmly on land. And so he must go. Quickly, decided now, he swept the willis-seed into their jar and threw himself down on Naomis' mattress, then promptly stood and paced restlessly around the small room, indecisive again.

Because surely Harridys was wrong. His father had not been a savage or an alien. He had come to Hyosis and presented himself—successfully—as a son of the palace at Rynoldys. Could a savage do that?

As for why he had taken his daughter on the night she was born . . .

Keiris pressed his palms to his temples. Confusion was like a pain. His head ached with it. Perhaps he was building too much upon a few verses of song. Perhaps Norrid had remembered them incorrectly. Perhaps Harridys was not as learned as he thought. Perhaps his father was no more than a part–Nethlor who had studied briefly at some academy and then wandered away, singing as he followed the sea.

Or perhaps it was as his mother had thought. Perhaps there was an empty dais somewhere and his father had been sent to father a daughter and bring her back.

But who would send a part–Nethlor to father a daughter for the dais?

Who would send a tide savage?

Questions. Suppositions. Doubt. He examined them, and slowly one thing became clear. He would learn nothing here. He must go to the spits, whether or not he found help at Kasoldys. He must search the serpent's tongues, even though it meant confronting the sea at drowntide. Then, if that failed, he must travel the coasts. He must go from palace to palace, from village to village, asking for a man who loved the sea. He must listen—if he could teach himself to do so—for his father's voice.

He must do whatever was necessary. He must do whatever he could. Because unless he learned the truth, the ground would never be firm again. Wherever he walked, the sea would lick at his boots.

Tomorrow. He would go tomorrow. He studied that prospect bleakly as Naomis' lantern flickered and eventually burned out. When the hut was dark, he curled up on the mattress and slept.

FIVE

Suyolo, sulala, sutri
Miyoli, mibona, mitri
Tri-lili, tri-lili, trala
Bandansi, milu
Bandansi tu . . .

KEIRIS CURLED DEEPER into his bedding and covered his ears,
trying to escape the plaintive refrain of his father's song. He had
been dreaming before the song began. Dark, elongated forms,
pellucid water, swaying stems—drowsily he tried to call back
the elusive images, because for once they didn't frighten him.
For once they promised him some kind of understanding. But
the song, the persistent song, made the images flutter and
fade. The song dispersed them, scattering them more rapidly
with every note. Finally, sighing, he let the last waning image
go and shuddered fully awake.

It took him a moment to orient himself. He was in Naomis'
hut, tangled in the covers of her bed. The lantern was dark,
but the first faint light of dawn touched the interior of the hut,
turning shadows from black to gray. A stocky shape worked
over the table, singing huskily to herself.

Singing the words of his father's song.

Suyolo, sulala, sutri
Miyoli, mibona, mitri . . .

Sitting, Keiris rubbed one hand across his eyes. "Naomis?"
The Nethlor woman started, then peered through the dim-

ness at him, her heavy features contrite. "Did I wake you? I didn't intend it, young Keir. Here, let me cover the windows to keep out the light. And I'll be still. I'll—"

"No, no. I meant to awake," he assured her. "I want to go early."

"Ah. I thought you would leave today. So I'm preparing provisions for you to carry along. Tracador would not forgive me if I let you go empty-handed. If you will tell me what direction you plan to take, how long you expect to walk—"

"I don't know yet," he said quickly. Although why he bothered trying to keep secrets from Naomis, he didn't know. No matter how carefully he avoided any traveled road, she would hear soon enough that he had gone north. She would hear, just as any other Nethlor who was interested in his activities would hear.

"Have you a choice?"

"I—yes. Yes, I can choose. What Harridys told me—"

"It was no help?"

"He helped me," Keiris assured her quickly. "But nothing he said gave me a direction."

"Then travel south," she said positively, turning back to her work with fresh vigor. She had gathered bread and cakes and wrapped them in weed-fiber. Now she counted vandi-kernels out of a tall container, sprinkling them with salt. "There are so many more places where you can stop and ask after your father in that direction. And you know how unfriendly the people are in the north, Adenyo and Nethlor alike. Once you begin walking the neckbones, they'll neither feed you nor answer your questions. The wander-water makes them cold—not like us at all. And once you pass Kasoldys, there is nothing and no one. Why would any man go there?"

Why? Perhaps just because there *was* nothing and no one. Nothing but the narrow, barren land. No one but northern folk, hard-bitten and inhospitable, clinging to a damp-shrouded land, harvesting what they could from waters chilled by a cold current that coiled from the north to caress the line of their shore.

"If I choose that direction," he said carefully, "do you have kin near Kasoldys? Where I can stop?"

Naomis shook her heavy head. "No one, young Keir. Those are a people apart. They want nothing we have and they'll give us nothing of theirs—not even the pleasure of mingling with them. If you can call that pleasure. If you go north, you must save these provisions until you reach the neckbones. You'll need them then, more than you'll need them for the first dozen days of your journey when you'll find folk to feed you. It will take you that long to reach Kasoldys, you know—a dozen days. Longer, if there is a late-season storm.''

''I know,'' he said, shivering, thinking unwillingly of fogged crags and rough-gnawed shores. Thinking of the sea, stirring restlessly at the shore. Of drowntide slowly gathering.

And Naomis was singing again, her husky voice haunting the hut with his father's song.

> *Suyolo, sulala, sutri*
> *Miyoli, mibona, mitri*
> *Tri-lili, tri-lili, trala*

His nerves prickled with quick, involuntary doubt. Naomis sang the words, he realized, as if she had always known them. As if she had learned them as a child. Yet she had never heard them until the night before.

If she had learned them so quickly, if she sang them so easily, how could he be certain his father had not learned them the same way? Casually, from a passing acquaintance, from someone who sang the words just because he had heard them and they stuck in his memory? How did he know the song hadn't been passed from person to person just that casually for centuries? Perhaps even from the time of the rafts? Yet without the knowledge of scholars like Harridys, who insulated themselves in their libraries.

It was a question he must not pause to entertain. He could too easily dissuade himself from traveling to the spits.

Quickly Keiris stepped to the table. He took Naomis' hands, clasping them with feeling. ''Naomis, thank you for everything. I must go.'' Now, before he wavered. Now, before he persuaded himself he could as well search to the south as to the north.

''But wait—'' she protested.

''Now,'' he insisted. ''Just as soon as I have dressed.''

''Then dress while I pack these things for you. And remember what I told you. If you walk north, you must save every scrap until you near Kasoldys. You will need it then.''

''I'll remember,'' he promised, hurrying to his pack for fresh clothes.

Although he pulled on trousers and shirt quickly, he did not escape without promising Naomis the same thing twice again and without an anxious, parting embrace. But at least when he finally hurried down the winding path, he did not hear her husky voice singing his father's song after him. He heard only her last exhortation to take care. He turned once and waved. Then he ran, the bag of provisions she had packed bumping his back.

No, he did not hear Naomis singing after him. Still it seemed, as he left Sekid and made his way north, that someone sang. The words of his father's song, the plaintive words, followed him up the slope to the quarry. Before he had gone far, he found himself involuntarily echoing the repetitive syllables. Not aloud—he did not sing aloud. But the syllables sounded silently in his throat. They whispered in his mind. No matter how hard he pushed himself during the next hours, they would not be suppressed.

> *Bandansi, milu*
> *Bandansi tu . . .*

The words held no meaning; Harridys had not translated them for him. But when the sun set that evening, when Keiris settled himself in a half-tumbled herder's hut to sleep, the tideland song swelled and took possession of him. He closed his eyes and, half dozing, heard it sung in a voice of such piercing sweetness that the hut where he sheltered fell away. The land vanished from beneath him. The song cradled him in possessive arms and carried him into sleep.

And so it happened each night while he traveled north. The song came for him soon after dusk and carried him away. No matter how deeply he slept, no matter how vividly he dreamed, he heard it through the night. The syllables were clearest, he realized after the third night, when he slept near the sea. The song held him closest then. And the higher the tide, the more insistent the melody.

His dreams were more insistent then, too—when the sea pounded near. The yellow eyes that watched him were brighter, the suckered tendrils that reached for him more sinuous, his breath more labored. He had no more dreams like he had had in Naomis' hut—dreams that made him feel he was about to understand something. He had only dreams that made his pulse race with fear.

But those were night things: the song; the aching, half-familiar voice that sang it; the dreams. By day he had other preoccupations.

Leaving Sekid, he quickly established a discipline for his days. Each morning, whether he had passed the night alone or with a Nethlor family in their hut, he awoke with the sun and walked for an hour before he ate. Sometimes, if he had let his supplies run low and carried only the food Naomis had packed for him, he walked longer, until he reached a village. There was little to forage from the land, but there was food for him in any Nethlor settlement. He had only to stop, and he was offered more than he could carry: cheese, weed-bread, smoked fish and shellfish, every kind of sea fruit.

When he had taken his first meal, he walked until the sun stood overhead. Then he stopped and ate again, lightly, and slept for a while. After that he walked until dusk, when he began to think of a place to stay the night.

He walked until dusk, when the song returned.

Food, shelter, the distance his feet had carried him that day; he kept those things at the forefront of his mind for as long as possible. But when the sun glinted down over the sea and the water darkened, the alien words were in his throat again. He fell asleep with them sounding silently there.

He lived in two worlds, he realized as his feet carried him northward along the serpentine spine of the land. By day he lived upon the land, and it was familiar and firm. But by night he lived in another place, a place where glassy water immobilized him and dark shapes circled.

If ever he awoke and found himself still in the sea, if ever daylight came and he could not find land with his feet . . .

But he always did.

During the first ten days of his journey he passed palaces and villages almost every day. On his third day he passed the academy at Parlys. On his seventh, the academy at Nikkor. On his ninth, Pecidor. By then the land was already changing, subsiding, becoming bony and barren—far bonier, far more barren than the land to the south. The sea pressed close on either side as he walked. The sound of encroaching water became a constant. He seldom saw huts now, although he passed occasional bleak fisheries. There was no sign of orchards or fields; the land was too stony for that. At night he chose the highest spot he could find to sleep, uneasily aware that Systris and Vukirid, ever nearer their annual conjunction, drove the tides hard. He lay bundled in his bedding, staring wakefully into their enigmatic faces, wondering how he could be sure the spot where he had made his bed would remain above water through the night.

If the tide rose too high, would he even know, sleeping, whether the water that rocked him was real or a dream?

The nights became long. And he hadn't even reached the spits yet.

He hadn't even reached Kasoldys.

That came on the thirteenth day.

He walked most of that day in a cold mist. In late afternoon he passed a deserted fishery and a huddle of damp-stained huts. He walked along a narrow path that threaded among slippery sheets of stone—and in the distance he saw a massive structure of gray rock, its silhouette blocky and uninviting. It stood over the sea like a rampart, its sullen walls discolored with mosses and sea salts. Keiris paused, studying the forbidding structure, comparing it to the palaces and academies he knew in the south. Here were no broad plazas, no captive pools of water, no sign of huts and stalls standing separately from the massive main structure. Here were only rough-hewn gray walls looming from the mist.

Keiris rubbed his arms against the damp cold. The sea had grown gray and heavy. Mist hung over the rocky shore but did not soften its sea-bitten lines. He tried to guess why anyone, Nethlor or Adenyo, would choose to live here.

This could be nothing but Kasoldys, palace and academy, the place toward which he had directed his steps. The place where he must petition for information and perhaps assistance. Still he hesitated, shivering and reluctant, before walking slowly toward the forbidding structure.

Before he reached it, a Nethlor appeared from the mist, walking heavily, a net slung over one shoulder. Although his path carried him within a few paces of where Keiris paused, he did not raise his head or glance in Keiris' direction. When he seemed about to pass without acknowledging Keiris' presence, Keiris said sharply, "Kasoldys? Is this Kasoldys?"

The Nethlor raised a massive head and acknowledged him with a flicker of mist-cold eyes. "This is Kasoldys. But if you want food, you'll find nothing here." He paid the words out thriftily, in a rumbling voice.

"I've brought my own food," Keiris said quickly. "Will I find shelter here for the night?"

The sea-green eyes grew no warmer, the response no less grudging. "Within walls? You can ask."

"Who blows the sounding horn here?"

For a moment the man looked as if he would refuse to part with such precious information. "Diryllis. But you have no claim on her. No person from the south does, and anyone can see clear enough what you are. She'll not feed you."

"I'm not hungry," Keiris repeated with strained patience. Nor, he decided impulsively as the Nethlor turned and stumped silently away, would he ask for shelter at Kasoldys. But information—surely Diryllis would not begrudge him information, or perhaps even a guide. How could she if he spoke to her using his mother's name? If was not so much to ask, if anyone here knew the spits. Steeling himself, he continued toward the gray stone structure.

The entry, when he found it, was narrow and dark, as if to discourage visitors. It gave into a littered foyer where the air was damp and stale. Keiris paused, glancing around the deserted chamber, feeling less optimistic than he had just minutes before. He faced massive, crudely made double doors. To his left and right were dim corridors, their heavy doors standing open. If the plan was like that of most palaces, the public rooms lay directly ahead while the side corridors led to the more private areas. He hesitated, uncertain of which direction to take, then saw a long, knotted cord hanging against one wall. He tugged at it.

When he heard no sound, he pulled twice again. Still he heard nothing. "Hello?" he called.

No one came, although he pulled the bell again and called twice more. Finally, shrugging, he tugged at the heavy doors and entered.

He halted almost immediately, the doors groaning shut behind him, and caught a sharp breath. He had entered a long, narrow public chamber furnished with nothing but clumsily carved tables and benches—and shadow, banks of damp-smelling shadow piled deep in every corner. An elderly Adenyo with hair dressed high on his head faced him, hands thrust into the sleeves of his gown. The gown itself was as elaborate as Harridys' but soiled and limp. The Adenyo's expression was querulous. "What is it you want?" He placed himself before Keiris, frail and frowning, obviously displeased at the intrusion.

Keiris took an unwilling step backward. "I rang and I called," he said defensively.

"You were heard. What do you want?"

There was no mistaking the old man's repeated question for a welcome. Keiris frowned and spoke with what courtesy he could summon. "I would like to talk with someone who knows the land to the north. I plan to travel there, and it isn't so long until the drowntides. I want to know where I can safely sleep."

"You can safely sleep wherever the water is not," the Adenyo responded haughtily. "Even in the south they must teach you that."

Keiris drew a long, calming breath. "I would like to go to sleep and know the water won't rise to cover me while I'm sleeping," he said, measuring the syllables with careful patience. "I'm sure someone here has mapped the land, at least the nearest part of it. If I may study the map or ask someone to guide me—"

But the Adenyo had turned away. He called out a few incomprehensible syllables. Seeing motion in the shadows at the rear of the chamber, Keiris guessed he had sent a messenger to summon someone. A mapmaker, perhaps, or some other person who knew the land to the north.

Or perhaps he had simply called out an order for his dinner, because the Adenyo promptly vanished and Keiris found himself alone in the shadowed chamber. He drew a deep breath and gazed around. Light came faintly from narrow slits near the lofty ceiling. Otherwise the rough-hewn walls were unbroken by anything but patches of mildew and moss. The floor was as rough as the walls, ground by years of dirt—swept, apparently, but seldom swabbed. In one corner a droop-leafed plant bloomed unwholesomely. Keiris walked around the chamber, carefully avoiding the plant, wondering about the northern people and their ways. Why cling so stubbornly to the chilled margin of the sea when there were places to the south where they could live so much more comfortably? Simply because their ancestors had clung just as stubbornly in their own time? Or because centuries of hardship had weeded out any who saw the virtue of comfort?

Keiris circled the chamber, less and less certain anyone had been summoned to help him.

Then he started at a voice from the rear of the chamber. "We make no maps," the uncompromising words came. "And if we did, why would we give them to strangers? What fool would come from the south to fish the spits?"

A massive Nethlor padded toward him, his clothing stained and gray, a thick red beard masking the lower part of his face. A helmet of ruddy hair swelled upon his head. Keiris stared in fascination, wondering how he had grown so much hair—guessing from its color that the man had some measure of Adenyo blood, however small. "I haven't come to fish. I'm looking for someone," he said, "and I thought I might find him in the spits. Surely someone here has gone there. Surely—"

"Surely we tend our own nets in this corner of the world. Just as you should tend your own in the south. What is your palace? Or are you an academy sprat?"

Keiris looked more closely at the massive man and saw that despite his size and coloring, his features were Adenyo, well modeled, distinct. "I'm Keiris of Hyosis. My mother is Amelyor. She holds the dais there."

"And I am Rykiris, son of this dais. Who are you hunting in the spits?"

Keiris' eyes narrowed. This was Diryllis' son? Girth, stride, dress—despite his features, he appeared more Nethlor than Adenyo.

But, of course, things were not the same here as they were in other palaces, in other academies. The northern people went their own way, apparently even permitting the holder of the dais to dilute her blood—manyfold, to judge from Rykiris' girth. "I'm hunting a man who once lived in Hyosis and took something of my mother's when he left. I don't know his name, but I've been told he may have come from the tidal tribes." He offered the conjecture deliberately, testing the other man's reaction. If the tribes had come to the spits, if the northern people knew of it, surely Rykiris would betray something, however unintentionally.

But Rykiris' reaction told him nothing. "We tend our own nets here," he repeated, his voice flat and inexpressive. "And if you don't want to drown, you'll go back to your warm lands and your fine palace. Perhaps there the tides are tame at this time of year."

"No," Keiris said. "They are high in Hyosis, too, when Systris overtakes Vukirid."

"High there, too, you say?" The words were mocking. "Then let me tell you this: Whatever you call a drowning tide at Hyosis would be an infant tide here and in the spits. Do you know what lies under the water of our sea?''

"What lies under the water?" Keiris said blankly. The question was unexpected.

"Land—land just like ours. Hills and crags and hollows and valleys. That's what lies under there, and at drowntide our land drowns too. More than yours because we sit lower upon the sea. You call us the neckbone of Neth, as if we carried too little meat to bother with. Well, the neck washes in water in spring, while the body remains dry. And that's when we show what kind of meat we are. We stand our place and look the tides in the face—tides that would leave you southern folk fainting with fright. Oh, we know how you live in the south. We know about your fine furniture and your soft cushions. Ha! We learned long ago to live without all that. And you would, too, the first time the drowntide washed everything away.

"That's how it is here, where the strong are strong. And north from here, in the spits, the land drowns every day, even when the moons oppose and the tides are slight. If you want to walk there, you must know where the high points lie and you must plot your way among them carefully. Or you'll wash up on our shore one day like a waterlogged cushion, and just as useless."

Keiris drew a long breath. "I would like to know where the high points lie. That's why I stopped here, to learn about the spits," he pointed out carefully. "Whatever help you can offer, I will appreciate. If you don't keep maps, perhaps you could direct me to somone who knows the spits. Perhaps—"

"Can you talk to a drowned man?" Rykiris folded heavy arms over his chest. His eyes glinted with challenge.

"What?"

"He drowned. Farnilor drowned. Not so many months ago. He was map-keeper here. He was the one who knew the spits."

Keiris exhaled sharply. So there had been someone who had studied the spits, who had perhaps even kept maps. "Then—then let me talk to his successor. Or his apprentice."

"Drowned with him," Rykiris said tersely, gazing at Keiris over the mass of his beard. The challenge glinted more brightly in his rust-colored eyes.

Keiris frowned, weighing Rykiris' expression, growing skeptical of what he said. First there had been no map-keeper and no maps. Now there was a map-keeper, but he was dead. "Which of them? Which of them drowned with him? His assistant or his successor?"

"Both." Rykiris pronounced the word with crisp satisfaction.

Keiris met the obstructive gleam of his eyes and knew the big man was lying. Perhaps about the death of the map-keeper. Perhaps about the death of his successor and his apprentice. Perhaps in saying any of them had ever existed.

Keiris drew himself up and said formally, "I would like to speak with your mother. I would like to ask her permission to spend the night." Never mind his resolution not to ask. Diryllis could hardly refuse him. And she could hardly forbid him to look around the library when he had eaten his evening meal. If Farnilor or his predecessors had left maps (if indeed Farnilor had ever existed, if indeed he were dead) . . .

But Rykiris was shaking his massive head. "We have no bed for you. They're all taken."

"Then I'll just roll out my bedding on a floor someplace," Keiris said doggedly. If he spent much time here, he would become as stubborn as a northerner. "I won't take much room. I—"

"You'll have to take your bit of room in the entry foyer, then. We lock off everything else by night. You never know what might crawl out of the sea when it grows dark—or up the road from the south."

Keiris colored, his nostrils pinching angrily. "No one here is required to feed me or shelter me or answer my questions," he said sharply. "But as the son of Hyosis, I'm surely entitled to speak directly to the holder of the dais here. Take me to Diryllis."

This time Rykiris' eyes were bright with mischief. "That horn you wear—there, on the string."

Keiris frowned, touching the shell horn. "It was my sister's."

"Blow it for me, son of Hyosis."

Keiris hesitated. "All right," he agreed, putting the tiny horn to his lips. He blew a single shrill note.

"Now you have spoken to my mother, just as you were entitled to do," Rykiris said with a white-toothed grin. He drew a long key from his pocket. "You hear her answer, don't you? She welcomes you to Kasoldys, and since it is time for me to lock for the night, she bids you good journey as well. If she feels less weary later and wishes to receive you personally, she'll send someone to fetch you from the foyer."

Keiris flushed angrily as the big man bore down upon him, forcing him from the chamber. Rykiris closed the foyer door upon him, his chest rocking with silent laughter. Keiris glared at the heavy panels, hearing the key turn. He hesitated for only a moment, then went to the corridor doors that had stood open earlier.

They were closed now—and locked too.

All the palace was bolted against him—deliberately, he was sure. Whatever information it held was secured, probably for no reason beyond gratuitous meanness. If there were maps in the library, he would not see them. If the map-keeper did indeed exist, if he were still living, Keiris would not meet him. Not unless he took some other route into the palace—over the walls, perhaps, or through a drain passage.

He stood, considering that. But he guessed Rykiris had already anticipated him, and he guessed he would be intercepted. And he did not intend to make Rykiris a gift of his dignity. Turning sharply, he left the foyer and made his way out the narrow entry.

When he had walked a distance, he turned and looked back. He might as well not have stopped here at all, he decided angrily. He might as well have bypassed Kasoldys and not exposed himself to Rykiris' ridicule. But would he ever have come this far north if he had guessed that he would find no help here? Would he have dared, sitting in Naomis' warm hut, plot his journey this far if he had known what his reception would be at Kasoldys?

No. The undertaking would have appeared too large, the prospects of success too small. If he had guessed, twelve days ago, ten days ago, even two days ago, that he must face the spits without a guide, without a map, without any word of advice, he would have turned back.

But he had not guessed, and so here he was. He had walked up the neckbone of Neth and he stood near its bony brow. It was such a short distance now to the spits that he could not turn back.

He simply would have to build his schedule around the tides. He would have to remain on his feet during the hours of high tide and sleep when the water receded. And he would have to hope—hope hard—that the rising waters never caught him short of solid land.

He hitched his pack on his back and began to walk again.

For the first time since he had left Sekid, dusk came and he did not hear his father's song. He heard only the crash and clamor of the sea, rushing toward drowntide, and the lonely sound of his boots on the wet shale of the footpath.

SIX

KEIRIS HAD NEVER thought much about the complexities of the tides. That was a matter for the men and women who crewed the fishing vessels, or for the dock masters who tended the vessels when they were berthed. He knew they rose and fell because of the moons—knew the moons called to the sea and that the waters raced after them like wet lovers. He knew that when Vukirid sailed a certain distance ahead of Systris or a certain distance behind, the tides were slight, although they came more frequently. But during that period each year when the two traveled for a while in company, the tides ran high, and at Hyosis the dock masters hauled the vessels up the path and stored them beyond reach of the water.

He had never known anyone to drown during the tide season, but the tides were far more dangerous here on the narrow neckbone of Neth than at Hyosis. So for the next three days he watched water and land closely as he walked. If there were traces of sea-grass on the rocks, if there were freshly deposited shells, he moved on quickly. He only stopped to rest when he found a place where there was no recent sign of submersion, and he only slept when he saw the tides falling. That meant that sometimes he slept by day, sometimes by night. And sometimes, when the mist was dense, he could hardly distinguish the two.

Reality, dreams . . . Gradually, as he traveled north from Kasoldys, the two became confused. He dreamed that he walked. He walked in a dream. Not a bright dream, not a comforting dream, but a chilling dream of crashing breakers and slippery footholds. A dream of mist so dense, he thought it would drown him. A dream of light so diffused that some-times, at the beginning of day, at the end, he could not tell moonlight from sunlight.

And then, early on the fourth day after he left Kasoldys, the mist lifted and he walked for a while in sunlight as the tide slowly rose. Walked until he realized—unwillingly—that he approached the end of the land. Walked until the sea lay on either side—and ahead as well, the land in its thrashing mouth.

Feeling the first prodding of panic, Keiris turned and gazed back the way he had come. The water was still rising, and he realized he did not know when it would stop. Or where. If it came much higher, if it covered the path that had brought him here . . .

Keiris' legs began to tremble then. His entire body began to shake. Not violently, but he felt the tremor and his breath came hard. He had come to land's end, and he felt a fear so potent that it was like a physical blow. He sat heavily, not even noticing where he sat, and stared at the lashing water.

He wanted to get up. He wanted to run. But he could not permit himself to do either of those things. Because if he turned back now, he realized grimly, he would turn back all the way. He would never come this far again, because he knew now what waited here: fear and an angry sea. And what could he say—to Naomis, to Norrid, to his mother—if he turned back? How could he explain his failure to pursue the search? What could he say to himself? He imagined Rykiris' laughter and shivered miserably.

He must go on. At least there was no sign of fresh sea-grass on the rocks where he sat.

But how much did that mean at this time of year, when the tides ran higher each successive day?

It meant little. The water had not overrun the rocks yester-day. That did not mean it would not overrun them today.

Still, he forced himself to sit. Slowly the mist returned and tucked damp fingers around him. Then it darkened from silver to leaden gray. Sunset? Or a deepening of the clouds that had already deadened the sky? He couldn't tell. Finally, when the urge to turn back had ebbed, he opened his pack and ate. Then he slept.

When he awoke, the mist had lifted again. The sun stood low in the sky, staining the sea copper. And now there was land ahead, a beckoning bridge of it. It was narrow, it was slippery-wet, it was littered with sea vegetation, but it was land.

Stiffly he stood. He turned and looked back, offering himself a last chance to default. Then he walked ahead, putting boot before boot, testing each foothold as he went.

It seemed to him that he spent the next months, the next years, the next centuries of his life that way, testing his way from rock to rock or along smooth-washed strands of sand, sleeping when he could, eating when hunger became a hard pain, watching the constantly changing tides with an anxious eye. Much of the time he walked in a shrouding mist. Sometimes the sun struck through, showing him land and sea in bright colors. Occasionally he came to a broad prominence of land and fell into a stupor, sleeping for hours without thought of the tides. Other times he miscalculated and found himself stranded on a shrinking rock or sand spit as the tide rose. When that happened, he sat stiffly for hours, every muscle aching as he waited for the water to recede again—as he waited and hoped that this time, this one time, he had not made a fatal error. If the water rose higher before it fell again . . .

But it never did. Each time the tide finally pulled back and he walked again.

Two days, three days, four . . .

Or perhaps it was longer than that. The song no longer came to him at night. He no longer dreamed of tentacles and yellow eyes. But neither did he move entirely within the realm of reality, waking or sleeping. Its edges were blurred—by exhaustion, by fear, by the persistent pounding of the water.

The edges of reality were so blurred that he thought he was dreaming the night he found the cove. It was near dusk, and although the tide was high, he walked on a broad prominence of land, the sound of the water no more than a hiss in the distance. The mist had burned away hours before and not returned. The air was warmer than it had been for many nights. The stars etched bright patterns in the sky. Keiris sat to his evening meal with an unfamiliar sense of well-being. When he was done, he spread his bedding on dry ground and stretched out.

And the song came. Bright, sweet—it wasn't plaintive at all tonight. It flowed like water; not like the water of the sea but like the quieter water of a spring, crystal and clear. Keiris pulled his covers nearer, lulled by the cascading syllables.

Suyolo, sulala, sutri
Miyoli, mibona, mitri
Tri-lili, tri-lili, trala
Bandansi, milu
Bandansi tu . . .

Familiar words. Words he might have known from childhood—would have known from childhood if his father had
remained in Hyosis.

But then the voice continued and there were other words,
and those words were not familiar at all.

Natolo, natila, nata
Chondolo, chondona, chonda
Mi-lili, mi-lili, mila
Mondusi, milu
Mondusi tu . . .

The words came in long, rippling streams, so sweet, so
liquid that it was a long time before Keiris cast aside their
spell and threw off his blankets, his heart pounding hard
against his ribs.

Someone was singing. Not from a dream but from the dark
somewhere ahead. Someone who knew more than a few lines
of the song. Someone who knew verse after verse.

Someone . . .

As he hesitated, the voice wavered and grew faint. The hiss
of the sea briefly drowned it. But then it rose again, soaring.
Keiris shivered and stood. There was no need for a decision.
He had no doubt what he must do. Taking up his pack and
bedding, carrying them, he followed the song.

By then both moons were in the sky. They lit his way
brightly. And he didn't have far to walk before he reached a
slight prominence and looked down over the cove.

Even by moonlight he could see that the sheltered water
was quiet. It described a wide curve, an arc marked by a
broad, sandy beach. Just beyond the beach, sheltered by a
stand of trees, were huts—not planked huts but huts made
entirely of thatch. They were small. There were perhaps two
dozen of them.

On the beach, gathered near a driftwood fire, were as many
people: perhaps two dozen adults, most of them women with
infants in arms. A very few older people completed the

group—and they were much older. Keiris could see their frailness even from where he stood.

It took Keiris several minutes to pick the singer from the group. She sat with her back to him. She bent over an infant, he realized, cradling it in her arms as she sang. She rocked gently, the sweet syllables rising with no apparent effort.

Keiris stood watching and listening, and slowly the hair rose on his arms, on the back of his neck. The people below were not Nethlor. He could see that by the light of fire and moon. He could see the slender length of their limbs. He could see their smooth, dark hair. They were not Nethlor at all.

But who were they? Had he found the tide savages? Or simply an isolated band of northern Adenyo, living far from any palace?

Were there any such? He had never heard of them.

Below, the first singer rocked back on her heels and became silent. Another woman raised her voice in a different melody. Keiris stood without moving, trying to think what he must do.

Go down and ask these people who they were? Or move closer and study them before approaching? He could see no harm in them. He could see no harm in anyone who sang as they did. But would they understand what he said if he did approach? Would they understand common tongue? Classical Adenyo? Certainly neither of those was the language of their song.

Perhaps they would be frightened if he approached them.

Or perhaps he would find them as inhospitable as the inhabitants of Kasoldys. And he was reluctant to meet a disappointment of that order when he had come so far, when their song was so inviting.

Torn, he hesitated too long. The second woman finished her song and everyone rose. Quietly the women and the few elderly folk made their way to their separate huts, leaving the fire to die untended.

Sighing, Keiris squatted and rocked back on his heels. He waited until there had been neither sound nor movement below for a long time. Then, moving as quietly as he could, he rose and made his way to the dying fire.

Water lapped gently at the shore of the cove. There were footprints in the sand, a few sticks of unburned wood—nothing to tell him definitively who these people were. He weighed a twisted length of driftwood in one hand and gazed toward the trees that sheltered the huts. Their species was unfamiliar. They grew in clusters, each fat trunk capped by a spread of coarse, stiff foliage. The foliage rattled with every breeze.

There was no other sound except the quiet sound of water upon sand.

Keiris squatted by the fire until it died to embers, watching the huts. The night was warm. After the cold of the last few nights it felt balmy. No one stirred. No one moved. Finally he made his way into the trees and laid his own bed. He would decide tomorrow how to approach the women of the settlement.

He did not hear his father's song as he fell asleep. Nor did he dream.

He did not dream unless the woman who knelt over him sometime later was a dream, and he thought she was not. The surprised rush of her breath when she discovered him was too distinct. The heat of her thigh as she knelt beside him was too real. He even smelled the scent of her skin as she bent over him. Rousing himself, he opened his eyes and gazed up into her face.

It was an Adenyo face but with several differences. Her forehead was not just high but boldly curved. Her eyes were striking, very dark, and set obliquely above high cheekbones. Her lips were wide, like his mother's, but full, as his mother's were not. Even her hair was different—thicker, glossier. She wore it combed down over her shoulders. He did not recognize the fabric of her shift. Nor could he be sure of its color by moonlight: silver, white, gray.

She didn't appear afraid. She simply knelt over him, studying him. Keiris licked his lips, trying to awake himself fully. But before he could do that, before he could speak, she stood and moved silently away. He rolled to one side and looked after her. Then, too drowsy to take his feet, to follow, he settled back into his bedding.

When he awoke in the morning, the huts were empty. He got up, pulled on his last fresh change of clothes, made his way through the trees—and found, with sinking heart, only the silence of a deserted settlement.

The women, their infants, the frail, elderly people who had joined them around the fire—all of them were gone. Their huts stood empty. There was no sound beyond the crisp rattle of stiff foliage.

Distressed, dismayed, Keiris hurried among the huts, looking for some sign that the women had abandoned their settlement in haste. But there were no forgotten possessions. There was nothing tossed aside in panic. There was nothing to indicate that they had gone because he had discovered them.

All he found, as he broadened his search, was an orderly row of footprints leading into the water of the cove.

For a moment he stared down at the smooth-washed sand and did not believe what he saw. The tide was low. The water had groomed the sand to a smooth sheet. The footprints stood out clearly, leading down the beach and into the water.

Slowly Keiris raised his head and peered across the cove. The sky was clear. In the distance he could see the rocks that guarded the cove. The water was lightly ruffled by the morning breeze. Sunlight glinted upon its quiet surface.

There was no sign of the women, not in the water, not upon the distant rocks. Nowhere.

Nor did he find sign of them anywhere else upon the sandy beach. They had gone into the water and they had not come out.

He had no doubt now that they were tide folk. Who else would walk into the water and not emerge? But his glimpse of them had been so brief. He had watched them around the fire. He had heard them sing. Briefly one of them had knelt over him. But now they were gone.

He closed his eyes, calling back the sound of the song he had heard the night before. Calling back the contours of the woman's face as she knelt over him: oblique eyes, broad cheekbones, gleaming black hair. Pressing his eyelids tight, he even called back the fresh scent of her skin.

Then he choked with something that was more like grief than anger. He had found the tide folk, but they had slipped away. They had eluded him. They had slipped into the water where he could not follow.

He sat, his legs drawn up, his forehead pressed to his knees. The strength of his feeling surprised him. But to travel so far, only to find himself alone again on an unchartered beach . . .

But he was not alone. He realized that slowly, with the stirring of some sixth sense. There was something in the water, something swimming near. He became aware of it without raising his head, without opening his eyes. He felt its presence.

Finally, unwillingly, he raised his head.

A sea mam circled slowly in the water, its long, dark body sliding effortlessly through the shallows. When Keiris looked up, it began to swim more rapidly. As he watched, it disappeared beneath the water, then reappeared, arcing smoothly into the air. It was larger than the gray-beaks that had brought Nandyris' horn. Its flesh was darker, almost black, with a pattern of white on its belly. Each time it circled, it hopped briefly from the water, studying him with unwinking eyes before sliding back under the surface.

Instinctively Keiris knew the mam had not come by chance. Instinctively he knew it was not simply playing, enjoying itself in the sunlit cove. It maneuvered with too much precision for that, circling, breaking the surface, studying him, sliding under the water again. It had come for some reason.

Simply to do what it was doing: to observe him? To study him? Perhaps to convey some message to him—a message he didn't understand because he had not learned to speak with the mams?

Or to carry him away?

That thought struck like summer lightning, stunning him. But he saw the validity of it immediately. The women had walked into the water and disappeared. Surely they hadn't swum, encumbered by infants and the elderly. Surely, if they were tide folk, they had simply ridden away on the backs of mams.

And they had sent this mam back for him. He couldn't guess why. But the women had known he was here. One of them had seen him. And here was the mam, leaping and plunging, beckoning him into the water.

Beckoning him to take his place on its back.

How else was he to find the tide folk again? He stood hesitantly. The mam immediately swam nearer and hovered in the shallows, its tail flukes slowly wagging. Keiris studied it: its smooth, dark hide; its scarred dorsal fin; the single eye that peeked from the water to study him.

Keiris studied the mam and realized this was not the time to hesitate. This was not the time to weigh and evaluate. This was not the time to pose himself questions he could not answer.

This was the time to act—quickly, before the strange, crushing breathlessness he felt turned to fear. For what was it but fear momentarily forestalled? And once it declared itself, he would not be able to act at all.

Moving woodenly, he slipped off his boots and stuffed them into his pack. He secured his bedding and his pack to his back. He stepped into the water.

It was easier than he had expected to seat himself on the mam. He waded waist-deep into the water, and the big creature drew near and hovered just beneath the surface while he slid one leg over its sleek body and gripped its fin to pull himself into position. Then, slowly, it began to swim again, making a wide circle in the shallow water. Keiris slipped at first, unsure of his balance. But he soon learned to lie forward against the smooth body and to grip with his knees. The mam's skin was silken to the touch, cushioned by fat, but he could feel smooth muscle beneath it. It propelled itself easily, barely burdened by his weight.

When he was more certain of his seat, the mam described larger circles in the water, carrying him farther and farther from the beach, until finally they were coursing toward the cove's rock-guarded inlet.

Water washed over the mam's back, soaking him. It was not as cold as Keiris had expected, not within the cove. But when they slipped past the rocks and into the sea, the wander-water was icy. Keiris hugged the mam's back, shivering violently. His eyes stung with salt. He rubbed them—and almost lost his grip on the mam. His entire body prickled with alarm as he floundered. He caught at the creature's dorsal fin with icy fingers, clamped his knees to its sides, and regained his balance.

He didn't dare think, at first, where the mam was taking him. If the creature carried him so far that he could not see land . . .

But the mam did not take him out to sea. Instead it swam northward, gliding effortlessly through the rough water parallel to the shore. Still shivering, blinking salt water from his eyes, Keiris stole anxious glimpses of the land as it slid past. Beyond the cove, tall croppings of rock towered from the water. Rugged islets jutted out. The sea slashed at them with white-capped frenzy, and the sun reflected from the water in sharp yellow needles. The morning mist was thin, little more than a haze upon the water's surface.

Numbness, surprise, a detached sense of disbelief . . . Gradually Keiris passed beyond those to fear. His fingers had grown icy cold. His body was rigid, every muscle locked. He gritted his teeth so hard, his jaws ached. The mam's motion was smooth, effortless. But the water was rough. If he let his attention waver for just a moment, if he slipped . . .

A sudden vision of a drowned land came to him. Hills, crags, hollows, valleys; he saw them just as Rykiris had described them. Trees with floating limbs, weeds that bent to the motion of the water . . . and walking among these things, he saw himself, water-blinded, strangely pale, his hair billowing around his head. Bubbles rose from his mouth, from his nose.

He gasped, suddenly starved for air, and drove his knees hard against the mam's sides. *Land.* He had to put his feet on land. Rock, soil, sand—it didn't matter which, so long as it was not the drowned land of the seabed.

And there was land ahead, jutting into the water. Squinting the salt water from his eyes, he could make out its dark lines. He could make out . . .

The lines of a palace.

He stared, surprised, for a moment forgetting his panic. A low prominence curved into the sea ahead, a narrow strip of sand aproning it. Upon it, sitting close to the water, was a palace of black stone. Its seaward plaza stood just above the tideline. Behind it, the structure stretched long and low.

Keiris sucked a whistling breath. A palace—and the mam was carrying him toward it. The mam was carrying him toward the narrow strip of gray sand that lined the shore.

Had the women come here? And then sent the mam back for him?

Why?

And if they had come here, were they really tide folk, after all? Or were they some forgotten group of Adenyo?

He couldn't guess. But the mam glided closer to shore, as if guided by his urgency. He clung to its back until they reached the shallows. Then he slid off the creature's back and stumbled through the surf.

The water was deeper than it had appeared, and the feel of land beneath his feet was not as reassuring as he had expected. The current was strong. It tugged and buffeted at once, and the sand shifted under his feet. The mam pursued him through the shallow water, squeaking and whistling urgently, nudging him, trying to guide him to its back again.

But the shore was so near. Keiris fought the current, fought the frothing breakers that pushed and pulled, fought his way from the water.

Exhausted, he threw himself down on the sand, struggling
for breath. The mam lingered in the shallows, darting back
and forth in apparent agitation, squeaking and whistling. He
stared at it blankly, shivering, trying to rub life back to his
fingers. He had no intention of returning to the water, no
matter how loudly the creature cried to him. He had no
intention—

He caught the first hint of motion in the sand from the
corner of his eye. Startled, he turned his head and recoiled—
uselessly.

The thing that flapped from hiding beneath the sand had
wings of toughened flesh; a long, curving tail; a squint-eyed,
toothy face. Keiris saw neither legs nor feet. It spilled damp
sand from its spreading wings and sailed at him with an angry
chatter. As it soared past, it flicked its tail at him, catching
the flesh of his upper arm. And then it was gone, gliding over
the breakers.

Keiris turned numbly and looked after it, clasping his arm.
Slowly he became aware of heat against the palm of his hand.
Puzzled, still numb with surprise, he rolled up his sleeve and
stared at suddenly inflamed flesh. At the center of the inflam-
mation was a tiny slash wound.

Keiris swayed, dizzy and hot, his thoughts becoming disconnected. Could such a small wound infect him with this
sudden fever? With this roaring light-headedness? With this
painful, churning nausea, as if his stomach and intestines
were turning in upon themselves?

Such a tiny wound, yet he felt all those things. Dazed, he
realized the mam was still whistling, slapping the water insis-
tently with its flukes. Keiris glanced at it blankly. Muzzily he
knew he had to have help. He could not guess if he were
poisoned or touched with some swift-moving infection, but it
was clear he could not help himself. He could hardly stand.
And it had been no more than a minute or two since the
creature had caught him with its tail.

The palace. It was not so far to the palace. Drawing a
shuddering breath, he gazed at the dark structure. Then he
launched himself toward it, staggering.

Half a dozen paces, a dozen, two dozen . . . His feet grew
heavy, his legs numb. There was a sound in his ears like the
ringing of a hundred bells. His head seemed to have swollen.
It throbbed almost as much as his arm.

Then, abruptly, the throbbing ceased, and that was worse.

Because now he felt nothing—in his arms, in his legs, in his feet. His limbs, his extremities had lost all sensation. He tried to reach out to steady himself. He tried to take another staggering step forward. Instead his knees buckled and he sagged to the sand.

He lay there, hardly feeling the sand against his cheek. He lay there and stared with blurring eyes at the breakers, realizing with sudden and useless clarity that the tide was coming in and he could not move. He sent messages to his muscles. They did not respond. He could not lift a hand or a foot. He could not even raise his head. The sound of the water had become distant, but that was deceiving. Everything had become distant: the black palace, the squeaking mammal, his own useless limbs.

The last thing he heard before he lost consciousness was not the sound of the water, not the mam's squeaking cry, but another cry. It seemed to him, momentarily, that he heard his own voice calling out. But he knew that could not be, because he no longer had strength or will for that. He could not even close his eyes to shut out sight of the encroaching sea.

SEVEN

KEIRIS GROPED BACK to consciousness slowly, with pain. He lay in a bed—he knew that. Someone came and went at regular intervals, pausing to tend him, to touch his face with a damp sponge, to brush light fingers at his hair. Sometimes she poured something warm into his mouth and it found its way down his throat. If he choked, she patted him and waited before giving him more. Whoever she was, she seldom spoke, but occasionally her hair touched his cheek. She had an elusive scent, one he could put no name to.

He knew from the echo of her footsteps that the chamber where he lay was tall-ceilinged and spacious. He guessed from the changing sound of the sea that more than hours were passing, that tides were rising and falling, that days were passing while he lay trying to open his eyes, trying to speak—failing. Always failing.

Then one day, when she had fed him and washed him, when her footsteps had slapped lightly away, his eyelids responded. Keiris opened his eyes and blurrily gazed around.

The chamber was as he had thought, tall and generously proportioned. It was dim, too, the walls made of dark, porous stone, the windows high and narrow, admitting only a weak band of sunlight. Keiris rubbed his eyes, trying to clear them. There were smudges of green on the walls, irregularly shaped, irregularly placed, as if something grew there. A heavy chest of dark-grained wood stood at one side of the chamber. And in the dimmest corner of the chamber . . .

He drew a slow, hissing breath. In the corner stood a carving: a woman, a very young women, twined in ropes of

sea-grass, her hair streaming across her breasts. Her face . . .
But his gaze barely skimmed her face. For, looking more
closely, he saw that the ropes that coiled around her arms,
around her neck, around her small, well-shaped breasts were
not sea-grass at all. They were serpents, their carved bodies
intertwined, their many heads staring at him with a single
blind gaze.

He gasped and, looking up, met another blind gaze—hers.
And that startled him more than the snakes. Every carved
detail of her was so tenderly made, so real, that the shadowed
emptiness of her eyes caught at him. He glanced away, then
forced himself to look back, to study her face, her disturbing
face: broad, curving brow; widely spaced eyes so large that
they were like heavy drops of darkness in the pale stone of
her face; fine-lined eyebrows; shallow nose with rounded
nostrils; lips that described not an arc but a slightly flattened
circle. How would those lips look smiling? Would they pull
wide and turn up at the corners? Or would they pull back
from the teeth evenly, describing a circle? Even her hair was
strange. It sprang crisply from her curving brow, then fell in
undisciplined curls and tendrils around her slight shoulders.

He shivered. She was formed like a woman. Two arms,
two legs, two breasts; eyes, nose, mouth . . . Yet there was
something not human at all in her carved features, in her
eyes, in the way she stood poised and unshaken while serpents coiled around her.

Human yet not? Keiris drew another hissing breath, push-
ing himself up in bed, standing—weakly. At first his legs
were reluctant to bear him. But he put one dogged foot before
the other, moving unsteadily across the floor, until he could
place cold fingertips against the stone flesh of her cheek. The
features were as strange to his fingers as to his eyes.

Stranger were the vestigial membranes that joined her fingers. Keiris touched those and knew finally, unmistakably,
what she was. She was a rermadken, one of the legendary
creatures who rode the mams, just as the tide folk did.

At least he had always thought the rermadken were more
legendary than real. But he saw clearly, from the tiny, jagged
scar on this one's chin, from the careless way the locks of her
hair curled, from the lips poised as if to speak, that the
sculptor who had created this piece had not worked from a
legend or from his imagination. His model had been flesh—as
much flesh as Keiris was.

Keiris stared at the stone flesh, frowning, trying to under-stand. His thoughts were in confusion, but one thing stood clear. This meant—surely—that Norrid had been right and Harridys wrong. This meant there had once been two breeds of people in the sea: the tide folk and the rermadken. Two breeds who were not the same at all. Because this woman and the woman who had bent over him as he slept near the cove shared likenesses, but there were profound differences be-tween them too.

So his father, if he were one of the tide folk, was simply a man who lived in the sea. He wasn't alien. He wasn't rermadken. The blood he had passed to Keiris was human—entirely human.

Keiris felt tensed muscles uncurl, as if he had passed a test.

But that was only the first test, he realized, gazing weakly around the chamber. He had found the tide folk—he was certain of it now—and he had established, for himself, that they were simply human, of Adenyo stock. But he had not found his father. He had not found his sister.

He still had the spits and all the sea to search.

He retreated to the bed and sat down heavily. All the sea . . . Closing his eyes, he lay back, a sick sensation in his stomach, and tried to imagine how large the sea might be, how far it might stretch.

Immeasurably large. Immeasurably far. And in all that expanse he must find one man and one girl.

Unless they were here—within palace walls or somewhere in the spits.

That seemed unlikely. The women sheltering at the cove, burdened with infants and elderly folk, must have come ashore during the storms of late winter to wait for the weather to settle. But why should his father and his sister linger ashore? His mother had said that his sister was frail. Was she that frail?

Had she even survived, if she was so much frailer than the other tide folk?

Keiris opened his eyes and gazed at the high ceiling, then around the chamber. The green blotches he had noticed earlier, he saw now, were living plants. They grew from crevices in the walls, craning upward toward the high windows. He studied them, waiting for the sensation of sickness to pass, then stood again.

Someone had laundered his clothes and folded them neatly

on the chest. He selected shirt and trousers and pulled them on. When he had done that, he felt weak again and sat for a while. Then he pulled on his boots, slipped the shell horn around his neck, and left the chamber, looking for someone to answer his questions.

The corridors were long and dark. They smelled as damp, as brine-steeped, as the foyer at Kasoldys. Plants grew from every crevice, sending long streamers after the distant sunlight. Furniture was scant and poorly carved, as if no one had cared enough to lavish workmanship on it.

As if beauty captured in permanent form had little value.

But someone had lavished skill on the carving of the rermadken—and on the other carvings he saw as he wound through the deserted corridors. Those were of rermadken too. They followed his progress with blind eyes, draped and twined in snakes, hair streaming over their breasts. After he had examined several he began to be saddened by them. There was something melancholy in the care lavished upon them, something wrenching in the emptiness of their eyes, as if the person who had carved them had offered all his skill to make them live and had failed.

Nor did the corridors of the black palace live. Keiris made his way from one empty hall to another. Sometimes the sea sounded near. Other times it grew distant. Once he paused at a broad, tall window overlooking the sea. It was oriented neither to the sunrise nor to the sunset, and that puzzled him.

There were many things to puzzle over in the black palace. Several times he heard voices in the distance, but when he made his way toward them, there was no one. Once he found a table where someone had recently eaten. But he never found the kitchens, nor did he find private chambers that appeared occupied.

And to enter the seaward plaza he did not pass through a large, private suite like his mother's. He simply opened one door like many others—and he looked out upon the plaza. Startled, he backed quickly away, hoping he had not been seen. It was a fundamental violation of courtesy to step upon the seaward plaza without a summons from the dais. And the man who stood upon this dais, the man who turned with white hair billowing, certainly had not called him there.

"No, don't go." The command came distinctly over the sound of the water. The white-haired man stepped from the dais, moving toward him.

Keiris froze, holding the heavy door back with one hand, waiting for a reprimand.

But there was no anger in the man's face, no annoyance in his dark eyes. He was tall and long-limbed, like an Adenyo, but more strongly built, his tread lithe for a man of his years. He wore a close-fitting gown that once had been white. His arms were bare, heavily muscled. His lips were full, his eyes dark and oblique. He was clearly of Adenyo stock, but no one would have mistaken him for one of Harridys' colleagues from the library at Sekid.

"You were a long time waking," he said. "The sand-bat has a nasty sting."

The thing that had stung him was called a sand-bat? "The bat—I've never seen anything like it," Keiris said.

"They nest here in the spits, in certain places. You won't find them in the south at all. But how are you now that you've awakened? Your father will be here with the tide tonight. Do you feel well enough to meet him?"

"My father?" Keiris said blankly, totally unprepared for the question. His father would be here—and did he feel well enough to meet him? His first thought was that the white-haired man mistook him for someone else, his second that he had not really awakened from his stupor, that he still lay in bed dreaming—but with a particular vividness.

His father would be here.

"Yes. You were asking for him, were you not?"

"Since I came here?" He was not aware that he had spoken, but perhaps he had. Perhaps he had spoken to the woman who cared for him.

"Several times. And before, of course. Along the coast."

Keiris licked his lips with a rapidly drying tongue. The conversation was moving too quickly, its direction completely unexpected. Perhaps the white-haired man simply misunderstood who he was. "I-I've come here to find my father, yes. My name is Keir of Hyosis."

"Of course. I know. Your mother is Amelyor. I've heard of her, although we have never met. But forgive me: I am Nestrin on the land. I am the spanner here at Black Point during the months when we have people living ashore in the spits. And I've walked lower Neth, although not recently. I satisfied my own curiosity there when I was much younger."

He was the spanner? What was that? He had walked lower Neth when he was young? And his name, Nestrin on the land

. . . Keiris hesitated, balancing several questions uncertainly on the tip of his tongue. How did Nestrin know his name? How did he know he had come looking for his father? Keiris was certain no one had preceded him from Kasoldys.

Could the news have come through the mams? But through mams his mother had spoken to? Through mams Diryllis had spoken to?

He had spoken to no mams. He was certain of that. In all the days he had walked near the sea, he had not even seen a mam, not until he reached the cove.

"How did I get here after the sand-bat stung me?"

"We sent men for you, of course, when we heard the cry."

The cry? Had he managed to call aloud for help, after all? He tried to remember, but the effort only drained his sparse store of energy. He touched his forehead with shaking fingers, suddenly wishing he were in bed again. His legs were still weak and his head had begun to ache again. "I think—"

"I think you need someone to help you back to your chamber," Nestrin said. "And to fetch you a filling meal. Then you need to sleep so that when the tide comes, you will be stronger."

"Yes," Keiris agreed weakly. That was exactly what he needed. To rest, to eat, to be stronger. If matters were to continue to move so quickly, if his father was to come tonight with the tide, he needed to be strong.

"Let me call." Nestrin turned back to the dais and raised a long, spiraling shell horn, a horn like Keiris had never seen before. It wailed thinly when he blew.

The woman who responded was not the woman who had knelt over him when he slept near the cove. She was younger, her skin darker, her eyes narrower. Nor, he knew when she spoke a few incomprehensible words, was she the woman who had tended him while he was sick. Her voice was not the same.

Nestrin spoke with her briefly, then turned back to Keiris. "I've told her to guide you back to your chamber and feed you. She will fetch you again when the tide is up."

"Thank you," Keiris said.

He cradled his own shell horn in one palm as he followed her down long corridors. When they reached his chamber, the woman gestured to his bed with one hand, inclined her head slightly, and withdrew. A short time later she returned with a tray of food, then disappeared as silently as she had before.

The food was familiar: weed, sea fruits, sea nuts, fish. It was flavored differently than Keiris was accustomed to, but he hardly noticed. He had not realized how hungry he was until the food sat before him. Then he ate voraciously, barely tasting what he swallowed.

His father was coming with the tide. When he had finished eating, he repeated the words softly to himself. "With the tide." And he had not even thought to ask his name.

And there were so many other questions. How long had the tide folk been coming here to weather winter storms? How many of them were there? Why did no one in the southern palaces know of them? Why had no one even guessed that they had survived the destruction of the Isles of Aden? Simply because no one had been interested enough to give thought to the fate of savages? Or because scholars like Harridys, arrogant, prideful, wanted to distance themselves as far as possible from the tidal tribes?

Nestrin did not seem a savage. Nor had the woman Keiris had seen singing on the beach.

And this palace . . . Had the tide folk built it here? Or had it been erected by some early band of Adenyo and then abandoned?

There were no answers. Lying back, Keiris fell asleep again.

He did not wake until the woman returned and touched him lightly on the shoulder. Then he sat, startled and disoriented. "What—?" It was dark. Moonlight threw narrow bands of light through the high windows. The sound of the sea was loud, intrusive, as if stone walls had become a fragile barrier.

The woman stepped back, speaking rapidly, incomprehensibly. Since he had seen her last, she had coiled her hair and bound it to her head. She wore not the close-fitting fabric gown she had worn earlier but lizard-skin trousers and a closely tailored, long-sleeved tunic of the same material. In one hand she carried a spear much like the spears the fishing crews carried when they set out for the wild waters. She retreated, beckoning distractedly.

"Is my father here? Now?" Surely she would not summon him so unceremoniously to meet his father—his elusive father. Surely there had to be more sense of event, of occasion than this. Surely there had to be something more than a hurried odyssey down salty-smelling corridors, the stone rermadken staring blindly as he passed.

But there was not. When she saw that he followed her, the woman neither slowed nor spoke again. She only hurried ahead of him and threw open the door that led to the seaward plaza.

Keiris caught the door in one hand, his heart suddenly racing. He forced himself to pause for a long, steadying breath. Then, with a jarring sense of unreality, he stepped forward. The sound of the sea was overbearing. The water seemed to surge just beyond the plaza wall. The moons stood close together in a lightly clouded sky. Their light silvered the wet flaggings of the plaza. The dais, Keiris saw, was empty. Near the wall a man stood, turned.

Moonlight carved his features from shadow, and they were unmistakable. Keiris stared, unable to move, as his father approached.

He was taller than Keiris had expected. He was strongly built, as Amelyor had said. Although he was not as muscular as a Nethlor, there was sure strength in every limb—and the grace of an Adenyo, besides. His features were well modeled, but the eyes were more obliquely set than Keiris had expected, his lips fuller. Several things showed in his face that had not shown in the sketches and carvings Keiris had studied before leaving Hyosis: intelligence; authority; a dry, challenging humor. "Keir of Hyosis—so you've come all this way to find me," he said. "It's been a very long time."

Keiris' face reddened. His father spoke lightly, almost playfully, as if Keiris' journey and the reasons for it were not to be held seriously. Stung, Keiris spoke his business immediately, bluntly. "I've come for my sister," he said. "My mother sent me. She asked me to tell you that you took what is hers according to the conventions. Now you must return it. In exchange—" Keiris broke off, frowning. *In exchange he could keep what was his.* That was what Amelyor had said, and Keiris had not realized until this moment what she meant. That his father could keep him, if he wished. Because by convention a mother was entitled to her daughter, a father to his son.

That was the message she had sent him with, that she offered a son for a daughter. Keiris' cheeks burned. Why hadn't he understood that before?

His father raised dark brows, questioning Keiris' sudden

silence. "So that's what you've come to tell me," he said when Keiris did not continue. "I suppose we must speak of it, although the time is not good. Tell me, do you suppose Amelyor thinks I can really do that? Do you suppose she thinks I can simply send Ramiri back to Hyosis after all these years, when she has no memory of anything there? When she is one of us—not one of you at all? Not in any way?"

"I—that is the message Amelyor asked me to bring you. The conventions—"

"We aren't bound by the conventions of lower Neth. We never have been. A few of us winter here sometimes, but that means nothing. No more than a handful of your people have even guessed that we still exist, and they're afraid to say it aloud because the scholars will denounce them. I can speak of it with you, can't I? Surely if you've come this far, you know what we are. Surely you've guessed."

Keiris exhaled heavily. "I know. You're tide savages." The harsh word crept out without his full consent.

Instead of frowning, his father laughed. "Tide savages . . . nothing changes, does it? You call us savages still, and we have names for you land folk that aren't any sweeter." His eyes narrowed and become measuring. "How did you enjoy your ride here?"

How had he enjoyed his ride on the mam's back? Keiris stiffened at the open challenge in the question. "Did you send the mam for me?"

"No, no—I was in another basin of the sea at the time. Nestrin sent her for you after the women reached Black Point. Had you been to sea before? Do you serve on a crew? This . . . ." Lightly he fingered the shell horn, but his eyes were still narrowed, intent.

Why did everything he said seem a challenge? Even when he spoke lightly, with a smile. "It was Nandyris'." Keiris drew a deep breath and issued a challenge of his own. "I've guessed what you are, but I don't know your name. The name you gave my mother was false."

"Ah, it was." If he recognized any accusation in the statement, he did not let it disturb him. "But a name is only an arbitrary syllable or two. It has little to do with the person, does it?"

"You have the syllables of my name," Keiris said stiffly. "I've never had yours."

"Then call me Evin."

"Is that your name?" And why did he persist in playing with him? Teasing him with light words but watching his every reaction with a finely honed gaze? Was he deliberately trying to anger him? Or was he simply trying to take his measure? If he was, what standards did he measure by?

"If it's important, yes, that is my name on land: Evin. How important is it that you take Ramiri back to Hyosis? How important to you?"

"It's important to us all." Keiris drew a second deep breath. "Amelyor is beginning her cessation. And Nandyris is dead."

Evin's dark brows drew together in a quick frown. "Ah. I didn't know. I didn't hear. And I know how Amelyor treasured her. I'm sorry for it."

"It happened . . ." Keiris hesitated, realizing he didn't know anymore how long it was since he had left Hyosis. "It happened near the beginning of the season. She was my mother's successor, although she hadn't taken the dais yet. Now there is no one else to blow the horns."

"Not your other sisters? Pendirys? Lylis? Pinador?"

"They can't use the horns. They've gone to live at Sekid."

"Amelyor's sister—she had daughters?"

Keiris shook his head.

Evin paced away toward the dais, then turned and gazed into the moons. "Not yourself?" he said carelessly, stroking the spiral horn.

Keiris felt his face blaze. "Would I have come this far for my sister if I could blow the horns? Would my mother have sent me?" He spoke with a low, bitter anger and was immediately embarrassed that he had betrayed himself so completely. But what was he supposed to feel? It was a question his father need not have asked.

His father paced back immediately, studying him critically, with no trace of humor. "I asked you before how you enjoyed your ride on Soshi's back. You never answered me."

"I was afraid. And cold." Keiris bit the words off crisply. If his father must know all the ways in which he was lacking, then here was another.

Evin nodded. "Yes, you would be. Raised in a palace, never stepping into the water without a boat's hull between you and the waves. In all the time I spent upon lower Neth I never met a man or woman who was not afraid of the water."

"Nandyris wasn't afraid," Keiris said quickly, defensively.

"She wasn't? Think again, Keiris. I remember how she dared her fears, even when she was a small child. Some children like bright beads. Some like sweets—or bitters. Anything to challenge their senses. Nandyris liked to make herself afraid. She found spice in that."

Keiris frowned, confused. "She—"

But his father gave him no time to think more about Nandyris, about her laughing recklessness and its causes. "Come. Let me show you something that is beautiful to me. Tell me if it can ever be beautiful to you." Quickly, taking the spiral horn, Evin approached the plaza wall.

Keiris followed, puzzled. The crash of the water grew more shattering with every step as they crossed the wide plaza. Then they stood at the wall and Keiris caught a sharp breath.

"The drowntide," Keiris said, peering over the wall. "The drowntides have come." The sea had risen so high, the palace seemed to float precariously upon it. Systris and Vukirid hung close together in the dark sky, their faces full. Their light created moving peaks and valleys in the thrashing water. Keiris wanted only to turn, to find higher ground, before it rose farther.

"People who are afraid of the water call it that. We call it the gather-tide. And if you want to take Ramiri back to Hyosis with you, you must come with us to the gather. Because that's where you will find her, and that's where you can put your questions to her—if it is important enough to you to ride the water again."

The gather? Ride the water . . . to the gather? "What—"

But his father had already put the horn to his lips. He blew a long, wailing note that made Keiris' spine tingle.

The note had not died before it was answered. A hundred bodies rose from the sea, wailing, booming, squalling, chattering, howling in response. Or perhaps there were more than a hundred. Perhaps there were a thousand. Stunned, Keiris stared down at every kind of mam he had ever heard of—and more. Grays, whites, blacks, mammoth creatures, all spouting, casting up tall flumes of water vapor. Gray-beaks, yellow-fins, white-tails, darting and bobbing, leaping, slapping the water with broad flukes. There were mams with humped backs and mams with backs that dipped; mams with tall fins, short fins, straight fins, drooping fins. There were mams with smooth skin, mams with mottled skin, mams with skin warted and tumored. There were mams who stood high in the water, others who sat low, showing only a watchful eye. Their din drowned out the sound of the sea. Keiris pressed his hands to his ears, backing away from the wall.

His father sounded the horn again and every voice died. The leaping mams, the spinning mams, the darting and bobbing mams stood still in the water. "Will you ride?" his father demanded. "It's the only way."

Keiris stared at him dumbly. Would he ride where? To the gather—but where was that? How far? The water was rough and high. Surely he would drown if he tried to ride a mam tonight. Keiris frowned anxiously at his father and saw the challenge in his father's eyes. It was keen and direct now. No humor masked it.

"We can't wait while you think about it," Evin said. "Everyone who wintered in the spits has been called. This is the hour."

Keiris turned and was startled to see that the plaza was filling with people. Men, women, children, they ran across the rough flaggings, laughing, shouting at each other. They were all dressed as his father was, in closely tailored lizard-skin trousers and tunics. The women had bound their hair tightly to their heads. Some of them carried infants. Others carried spears. Many of the men carried young children. The older children ran with the others.

"Please . . ." If his father would just explain some of this to him. Why everyone was running to the edge of the plaza. Why men and women were helping children and older people to the top of the wall. Why they were jumping from the wall into the water—tossing themselves casually into the thrashing water. Laughing as they did it.

Why they were pulling themselves to the mams' backs, gripping the slippery skin with tight-pressed knees, clutching tall fins.

Why . . .

His father explained none of it to him. He had stepped to the top of the wall too. He was turning, bending, diving with beautiful precision into the water. He cleaved its whitecapped surface and briefly disappeared. Keiris held his breath, his lungs aching, and searched the water for him.

When Evin reappeared, it was beside the largest of the mammoth whites. He bobbed up from the water, shook his head briskly, and immediately began to work his way to the creature's back. He did so expertly, as if he had done the same thing many times before, as if he habitually rode astride the mammoth creature. When he had his seat, he turned and waved one hand to Keiris, beckoning, challenging.

Frozen, Keiris stared at him, at the others—stared as the mams began to bear their riders joyfully away. There was no one left on the plaza. Everyone was in the water. Everyone but him. Keiris pressed himself to the wall, a plea forming in his throat, pressing at his vocal cords. All he wanted was to understand what was happening. But who would hear his voice over the crash of the breakers?

If he jumped—with the thought that was taking form in his mind, his heart began to pump so rapidly, the blood rushed in his ears—if he jumped, how could he even be certain he would gain a mam's back? How could he be certain he would not simply drown in the confusion of the tide?

If he did not jump, he would never find his sister. He knew that with grave and total certainty. His father had offered him a challenge; everything in his manner told Keiris that. If he did not take it, his father would not turn back for him. And Keiris would never find him again, no matter how far he searched.

Keiris stared down at the water, agonized, thinking of all the questions he had not asked his father. Thinking of all the things he would never learn from him if he remained behind. Counting the regrets he would live with as he walked south again, alone.

Regrets as numerous as the waves.

Keiris' feet were heavy, his legs numb. It seemed the greatest effort he had ever made, to climb the low plaza wall. But the effort that followed was a hundred times greater. Closing his eyes, holding his breath, he hurled himself into the sea.

EIGHT

FIRST CAME PAIN, when he slammed so hard against the water that it knocked his breath away. Stunned, for a moment he felt only that and the sudden, paralyzing emptiness of his lungs. Then he was beneath the water, staring helplessly into the opaque dimness he had dreamed of, his mouth open in soundless terror. Reflexively he inhaled, and water rushed into his lungs. Choking, he managed to thrust out arms and legs, struggling to brace himself, to put his feet down. But there was no solid place to put them. There was neither handhold nor foothold. No matter where he reached, his hands came back empty and his legs thrashed uselessly. He tumbled in the water, nose and throat burning, every nerve shrieking.

If he could just find the surface and fill his lungs. Or if he could find the bottom, if he could press his feet against it and push upward— But his arms and legs were thrashing now as if they had a life of their own. He had lost control of them, just as he had lost all sense of direction. Only the gradient of light told him he was falling away from the surface of the water, rolling and tumbling toward the darkness of the sea bottom.

He shouted again—uselessly, since there was no air in his lungs. He tried to turn himself, tried to propel himself back into the lighter regions of the water. His arms beat against the water, but every motion seemed to send him in the wrong direction. And he was growing weak. If only there were something to cling to, something to dig his fingers into . . .

When one hand touched flesh, he didn't recognize immediately what it was. He only recognized that here was some-

93

thing his hand did not slash helplessly through. Here was something solid, and he scrabbled at it, sobbing with frustration when his hand slipped helplessly off its resilient surface. Then he felt an entire long body slip beneath him, buoying him. He recognized the familiar touch of flesh and fat and muscle. His hand found a dorsal fin bearing a familiar slash of scar tissue.

Soshi . . . That was what his father had called the mam. He caught her in a panic-hold, his heart, his lungs bursting. He clung so tightly—with arms and legs, with knees and elbows, with fingers and toes—that muscles knotted and cramped everywhere. His mind, he recognized, was slowly darkening toward unconsciousness. His thoughts ran at half speed, sluggishly. If his fingers slipped, if he lost his grip on the mam's fin, on her slippery back . . .

Before that could happen, they broke the surface and he was coughing and vomiting salt water and struggling for breath. His clothes clung heavily to his arms and legs. His boots, filled with water, weighted his feet. He didn't dare reach down to pull them off. He had too little control of his muscles. If he bent to one side, to the other, he might slide back into the water. He could only cough the last salt water from his lungs and sprawl forward on the mam's back, shivering and gasping, and hold tight as she began to swim.

At first, as the mam surged through the water, Keiris shuddered and trembled with cold and exhaustion. His muscles cramped so sharply, it brought tears to his eyes. His throat and lungs burned. But after a while pain ebbed away, to be replaced by an exhaustion so profound that it left him numb. He lay weakly against Soshi's back, keeping his place without even thinking of it. He raised his head only twice to look around. He and Soshi were alone on the sea. There were no other mams, no tide folk near, no land within sight. But he was too numb to feel more than a faint stab of panic. After a while the mam's rhythmic movement lulled him and his eyelids slipped shut.

He didn't realize until he awoke that he had slept. Then he started upright, alarmed, disoriented, and nearly lost his balance. The sun flashing on the water, his wet boots clinging heavily to his feet, the mam . . .

A hand steadied him, and he looked in confusion into the face of a girl two or three years younger than himself. She rode beside him, astride a second mam. "What—" His throat was raw, his lips caked with salt, but he did not feel cold, even though his clothes were heavy with seawater.

The girl gazed at him with momentary concern, her hand on his elbow. She was slight and sun-browned; her hair coiled into a glossy black cap. When she saw that he was steady, she touched her chest and said with a flashing smile, "Nirini."

He looked at her uncomprehendingly. Nirini? Was it her name? Or was it a greeting of some kind? Did she expect him to answer? Keiris licked crusted lips and gazed around, uncertain how to respond.

The mams, he saw, had spread themselves across the sea in all their numbers and all their variety. Gray-beaks swam together in small groups, weaving and darting, racing among the others. A massive white glided silently. White-tails, buglers, great grays, a dozen breeds he couldn't give a name to—all swimming together, eastward, slipping carelessly above and beneath the surface as they went. Some moved silently. Others uttered strange, squeaking cries or loud whistles. Listening, Keiris heard the booming voice of one of the larger mams and heard an answering boom from somewhere behind.

He didn't see his father. He didn't see Nestrin. The only person who rode near him was the girl, and their two mams coursed together as if paired. They were of the same breed, he saw, with dark skin and white undersides. Their eyes were round and small, but their mouths were wide and up-curved. They seemed to grin with broad good nature as they swam. Keiris sighed, settling back on Soshi's back, deliberately relaxing cramped muscles. It was difficult to remain tense when Soshi and her companion swam so cheerfully in the sparkling sunlight.

When Keiris glanced the girl's way, she tapped her chest again with slender fingers. "Nirini." Her smile was bright, engaging.

Nirini—surely it was her name. "Keiris," he offered, touching himself. "Where—where are we going?" Would she understand common tongue? His father had. Nestrin had.

She answered with an incomprehensible question, and when he shook his head, she shook hers in imitation, laughing softly.

"Where is my father?" he persisted. "Evin? Where is Evin?"

The name seemed to stir no recognition. With a liquid flow

of syllables she asked him a second question of her own. Again she laughed and shook her head when he shook his. Then she touched her mam's dorsal fin and uttered a soft squeak.

Immediately the creature disappeared beneath the surface of the water. When it emerged again, it leapt brightly in the morning sun, Nirini laughing and shaking the water from her hair. She looked back, and Keiris could not tell whether the words she uttered were an invitation or a challenge. He tensed his grip on Soshi's fin and flanks, half expecting her to dart beneath the water. But she continued to course at the surface of the water.

Nirini called to him twice, then turned back to rejoin him. She rode beside him silently, watching him with open curiosity, the two mams matching their paces expertly. Keiris wiped his crusted lips distractedly, wondering how long the mams could swim, how far they must go. Wondering why Nirini seemed so fresh and bright when he was beginning to ache with hunger and thirst.

Tentatively he called her name and touched his stomach. He raised his brows in question.

She raised her own brows in imitation and patted her own stomach uncomprehendingly.

"Aren't you hungry?"

"Nungry?" she echoed imperfectly.

"Hun-gry."

"Nun-gry." Then she raised her brows again, as if in sudden comprehension. "Priliki-ka," she said, slapping her stomach hard.

Keiris hesitated. "Priliki-ka," he agreed, copying her gesture.

She laughed aloud and then, before he understood what she intended, she slipped off the mam's back and disappeared. She slipped so smoothly beneath the water, she hardly disturbed the surface. Bubbles streamed up, brightly sparkling.

Keiris caught a startled breath, staring at the place where she had disappeared. He clutched Soshi tightly as she began to circle with the other mam, relieved that at least the mams did not seem disturbed. They did not squeak or whistle.

Still Keiris paid out his breath slowly, determined not to breathe before Nirini reappeared. And if she did not . . .

A moment later she came arrowing out of the water so swiftly that he started. Water spilled from her clasped hands, from her head and shoulders in sparkling streams as she shot into the air, then arched back, and finally slipped effortlessly aboard her mam's back. Over one shoulder she carried a strand of fruit that looked almost like reef-apples. She broke one free and offered it. "Priliki-ka," she said, smiling in bright anticipation of his pleasure.

Relieved, Keiris hesitated for only a moment, then accepted the fruit and bit into it. It was crisp and cold, juicier than a reef-apple and sweeter. Nirini nodded happily at his expression.

The mams swam slowly as Nirini and Keiris ate. When they had devoured the last fruit, Nirini slapped her mam's side sharply and addressed an incomprehensible question to Keiris. He nodded tentatively.

Immediately Nirini uttered a high whistle, and both mams arced out of the water, then slid smoothly beneath its surface. Keiris only had time to seize Soshi's fin and to close his mouth on an involuntary cry. Then he was clinging to the mam's back as it darted underwater, swimming briskly after a school of large yellow-striped fish. He stifled the reflexive urge to draw in a deep breath. Instead he searched the water for Nirini, and when he realized from the stream of bubbles flowing from her nostrils that she was slowly exhaling, he did the same.

The hunt was brief and swift. The two mams surfaced three times to permit their riders to breathe, then darted underwater again, racing through growths of underwater weeds, past submerged boulders, over shadowy sand beds, until they had their catch. Then they returned to the surface and glided sedately in the sun. Touching Soshi's smooth sides when he had stopped shaking, Keiris could almost feel her full-bellied satisfaction.

He learned many things over the next few hours. He learned that if his fingers were cold, he could warm them over the single round orifice at the top of Soshi's head. He learned that if he watched, he could see her breath puff out there in a wispy plume. He learned that if he pressed his knees more tightly to her flanks, she swam more quickly; if he rubbed her head, she whistled with pleasure; if he tried to imitate the sounds she made, she answered him with more complex sounds.

He learned, when he and Nirini sped ahead, that the number of mams traveling together was more than he could count.

Once he glimpsed his father, far ahead, still astride the mammoth white.

Once, turning carelessly when Nirini called his name, he slipped from Soshi's back into the water. The mam dived after him, and he was astride her back again before he had a chance to be frightened. They surfaced together, and Nirini laughed as he poured water out of his boots and tugged them back on.

A short time later Keiris was aware of a change. Soshi shuddered, and Keiris glanced over to see Nirini and her mam briefly dip under the surface of the water. When they emerged, Nirini's lips were drawn into a tight grimace. She called back a few incomprehensible syllables as her mam began to course swiftly ahead.

Keiris pressed his knees to Soshi's flanks, but she had already begun to speed after her companion. Glancing around, he saw that other mams were swimming more rapidly, too, with none of the playful darting and bobbing he had noticed earlier. The entire group was gathering in, pulling close together. He clung to Soshi as the water grew thick with moving bodies.

He saw other riders now. He saw men, women, children, grim-faced, hugging the streamlined bodies of their mams, fitting curve to curve.

"Nirini—what is it?" He mimed perplexity, indicating the anxious people, the swift-moving mams.

Nirini stretched low on the back of her mam, fitting her body to its smooth curves. "Hiscapei," she hissed. "Hiscapei."

The word was endowed with more fear than meaning. When he only looked at her uncomprehendingly, she urged her mam near and touched him on the wrist. "Hiscapei," she repeated, making a sinuous motion with one arm, the hand rising as if to strike.

Keiris chilled. "Lizards?" But the writhing of her arm, the motion of her hand, was more the motion of snake than lizard. "Sea snakes?" he demanded, tense muscles relaxing. He did not want to encounter a nest of snakes, but surely they were less threatening than lizards.

Whatever the danger, it passed. After a while the mams drifted apart, spreading themselves wide across the sea again. Nirini urged her mam into a series of leaps, laughing each time the creature curved through the air, then carried her briefly under the water. Finally, shaking herself, she addressed an incomprehensible observation to Keiris, ending with the query, "Priliki-ka?" She slapped her stomach sharply.

He hesitated over his response. He was hungry again, and
Nirini was obviously no longer afraid. Still, he was reluctant
for her to dive when he didn't know what had frightened her
and the others. He shrugged, feigning indifference.

"Reri-ka?" she demanded in response. "Hechili-ka?
Lisana-ka?"

Was she offering alternatives to the fruit she had brought
him the first time? He frowned and shook his head.

"Wasono? Mesoki? Rerinana?" She stroked her mam,
slowing it, making it circle. She pointed to the water, then
threw up her hands in a gesture of helplessness, as if faced
with a guest who would not be pleased. When he did not
respond, she shook herself and drew her hands across her
face. When she drew them away, they left behind an expression of self-disgust. She bowed her shoulders, as if under the
weight of his disapproval, looking at him sideways from eyes
half teasing and half watchful.

Keiris drew a long breath. "Priliki," he said finally,
capitulating.

Nirini nodded briskly and disappeared into the water.

By the time they had eaten again, it was early afternoon.
The sky was clear, the air warm. Golden needles of sunlight
danced on the water. Nirini settled herself upon her mam's
back, draping arms and legs casually, and dozed. Soshi
slowed to match the other mam's pace. Finally Keiris lay
against her smooth back, knees lightly gripping her flanks,
one hand loosely clasping her dorsal fin, and slept too.

It was mid-afternoon when he awoke to the insistent prodding of Nirini's fingers at his ribs. He opened his eyes and
brushed at them with one hand, alarmed. "What is it?"

She laughed at his expression, then pointed to the distance.
Her eyes darted back to measure his reaction.

He looked and saw a dark blur: clouds, perhaps; a storm.
He glanced back at Nirini, only to see her slip from her
mam's back and begin swimming toward the storm, tossing
her head and calling back to him. He clutched Soshi's fin,
startled. "Nirini . . ." If she expected him to swim after
her . . .

That was what she expected. She made that much clear to
him, circling back twice, tugging at his leg. Then, with an
impatient shake of her head, she upended into the water and
swam away without looking back.

It was minutes longer before he understood her excitement.

That was when he realized that the darkness on the horizon was land, an island, and he felt a surge of relief as keen as the excitement he had seen in Nirini's eyes. As they drew nearer, the details became more distinct: a broad beach of black sand; lush trees laced with scarlet-and-white blossoms; a single, tall, dark-shouldered peak densely grown with vegetation standing as a backdrop to beach and trees. The water washed the shore gently, sending runners of white foam across the black sand. There were people in the water, emerging from the sea, and others on the beach, laughing and calling. Those on the beach had wrapped themselves in bright cloth: scarlet, sun-yellow, vivid green.

Nirini circled back and paddled beside Soshi, occasionally tugging at Keiris' knee, urging him into the water. Finally, when he saw the water was shallow, he tugged off his wet boots and slid gingerly from Soshi's back.

The sandy bottom was soft, the water current gentle. Keiris padded easily after Nirini, holding her hand. Looking closely, he saw thatched shelters among the trees and on the slopes of the rocky peak. The trees themselves grew luxuriantly, cloaking the island with shade. "Nirini . . ." What place was this? Had they reached the gathering? Was his father here? His sister? But she couldn't answer his questions.

People were summoning from the beach, but Nirini halted abruptly at the line where water met shore and stood gripping Keiris' hand tightly, a sudden, troubled expression on her face. "Keiris . . ." she said uncertainly, gesturing back toward the water. Then she gestured ahead to the land and raised her eyebrows, asking a silent question.

What did she want to know? He raised his shoulders, miming puzzlement.

"Keiris, Nirini," she said again, gesturing to the water. This time when she gestured to the land, she said, "Talani."

"Talani?" he echoed. Was that the name of the island? But why was she suddenly troubled? Why did she seem hurt that he did not answer her? What did she want him to say? Why did she gesture to the land again, naming it Talani, then drop his hand and run ahead without him, leaving him standing alone at the edge of the water?

"Nirini—wait!" he called, running after her.

She led him up the beach, toward the trees. He called her name again, but she only glanced back and ran on, dodging between the people who gathered everywhere, laughing and talking. She was not trying to evade him, he realized as he ran after her. She did not run that quickly, and she kept glancing behind, to be sure he followed. Nor was she teasing him. There was no laughter in her eyes. But where was she leading him . . . ?

She led him beyond the beach, through the shadowy trees with their nodding blossoms, and up the slope of the black peak that dominated the island. There, beside a freshwater stream, a thatched structure stood on a stilted platform. Vines coiled around its supporting beams, and blossoms peered from the thatched eaves, scarlet and white. Quickly Nirini scaled a makeshift ladder.

Keiris hesitated, then climbed the ladder after her.

He stopped short at the top of the ladder. His father had stepped from the shadowed interior of the hut, wrapped in a length of bright green cloth, his shoulders bare and brown. But he gave Keiris only a passing glance. Nirini seized his wrist and spoke rapidly, nodding her head emphatically, gesturing to Keiris. Keiris was puzzled to catch a note of distress in her voice.

"If I did something wrong . . ." he said uncertainly.

"No, no," his father said when Nirini paused in her discourse. "You simply failed to give her your land name. Or so she thinks. So, of course, she's hurt." He took both the girl's hands, pressing them between his own hands, and spoke to her in a reassuring tone.

Keiris glanced from one to the other, confused. He had failed to give her his land name? Did his father mean he should have given her his palace as well as his bestowed name? But what would that mean to her?

His father listened while Nirini spoke again. Then he took one of her hands and quickly pressed it into Keiris' grasp. "I've explained as well as I can that you have the same name—just the one name—for land and sea. That you didn't mean to be only a sea-friend when you refused to give her a second name. That you will be her land-friend as well."

Keiris touched his lips with the tip of his tongue, aware that Nirini was watching him closely, a slight frown on her face. "I don't understand," he said.

His father clasped their hands more tightly together. "I asked Nirini to be your sea-friend when we left Black Point, and so she stayed with you through the night and gave you her sea-name when you woke this morning. When you reached the shore, she offered you her land-name—she is Talani upon the land—but you did not give her yours. So, of course, she thought she had done something wrong.''

"She—she didn't do anything wrong," Keiris said.

"She stayed beside you all night and all day?"

"Yes."

"She saw that you ate when you were hungry?"

"I don't know what I would have done without her," Keiris said truthfully. If he had awakened alone, if he had clung to Soshi's back through the day with no companion, no one to reassure him with her lighthearted company . . . The sea had become less frightening to him today; Nirini had made it so.

Evin spoke again to the girl, then released her hand and stepped back. She immediately took Keiris' hand and began speaking excitedly.

"I've made her understand that your name is the same on land and sea. And I've explained that she did well and you want to continue as her friend. So now she wants to take you to the bathing falls. Then she'll see that you have fresh clothes and that you have plenty to eat and land-friends to spend the evening with."

She had already begun to tug eagerly at his hand. Keiris held back, frowning, reluctant to have his father so quickly dismiss him when he had come so far to speak with him, when he had dared the sea itself. "Evin . . ."

"You have questions. Of course. Come to me tonight, after the singing. Oh, something you should know . . ." He studied Keiris with a half smile. "Things are different among us than in the palaces of Neth. Our customs, our ways of doing things, even ordinary things—you'll find some of them strange."

Keiris tensed. "Yes?" From his father's expression, apparently he referred to some particular custom, and apparently he was half amused by it. Or half amused by the reaction he expected from Keiris.

"I can see Talani has more than a friend's interest in you. If you want her only as your companion, don't let her string flowers for you. You can let her pick a blossom for her hair and one for yours. But if she reaches for a third, slap her hand away. Or she will consider you her mate as well as her friend for the summer."

Keiris felt his face redden. "She's too young for that," he

said incredulously. She was only a child, two, three, perhaps even four years younger than he was.

"Is she?" Evin raised questioning eyebrows. "In the palaces she would be. And in the palaces you would expect her kin to come with genealogies. You would expect them to sit down with your kin for several days, discussing the match. You would expect the match, once it was made, to last for a very long time. You'll find that some things are far more casual here. I should tell you, too, that she isn't permitted to pick the flowers except in your presence—unless she sees a blue-wing."

"A bird?"

"A bird. If she sees a blue-wing, then she's permitted to slip away and string flowers without telling you. And if she does that, you're obliged to wear them. You should know, too, that sometimes girls Talani's age see things that aren't there. Especially blue-wings."

Keiris glanced at Talani uneasily. She listened with smiling attention to the words she couldn't understand, watching his face. "Can't you just tell her that I said she's too young?"

"But, of course, she isn't too young," Evin said firmly. "She knows that very well."

"Her family . . ." Surely they had something to say.

"They haven't arrived yet. Talani traveled with my pod because she had heard stories of the palace at Black Point and she wanted to see it. That is something very strange to our people, structures like the palace, built to last forever, to contain a people from season to season, generation to generation. Our people wonder what holds the Adenyo and the Neth in their palaces, what makes them stay when the sea is just beyond. I should tell you that Talani is all the more curious about you because you came from a palace, because your mother is a spanner. And she is of an age where she's eager to make her first alliance. Unless you want to obligate yourself, I would advise you not to let her out of your sight until the sun sets."

"And then?" Keiris said weakly.

"Then the flowers close. I think you'd better go. Come to me tonight."

Keiris glanced around and was alarmed to see Talani scampering down the ladder. He swung back to his father, wanting to protest. He hadn't thrown himself into the sea, he hadn't ridden so far on the back of a mam, only to be dismissed. He had questions for his father. Many questions, urgent ones. Urgent to him.

"You'd better go," his father repeated.

"But . . . is this the gather?" Surely his father would at least tell him that much.

"Not yet. Not here."

"Then my sister—"

"Tonight. Come to me tonight and I'll tell you what you want to know."

Reluctantly Keiris turned away.

The rest of the afternoon passed in confusion. Talani led Keiris up a slope of vine-choked rock, and they bathed together in a waterfall. Then they ran down the slope to a long, thatched shelter where fruits and fish were set out on long tables. Everywhere they went, Talani found people Keiris must meet, and there was much clasping of wrists, much nodding and laughing, much talk he didn't understand.

Somewhere along the way Talani found lengths of scarlet cloth for them both. He gave up his clothing reluctantly and wrapped himself. Afterward, his shoulders exposed, his legs bare, he felt self-conscious and awkward, since he was neither as muscular nor as brown as the other men. Somewhere else—he did not notice when it happened; he thought he had watched her every moment—she picked two flowers and tucked one behind her ear, one behind his. The gleam in her eye was mischievous, a veiled, half-teasing threat.

She was far too young. Her energy, her ceaseless, laughing activity told him that. Taking a mate was a serious matter, a matter for long consideration, and Talani only wanted to run and laugh and talk. After a while she didn't even seem to mind that he didn't understand what she said to him as they made their way around the island. She clutched his arm and drew him along with her from place to place, pointing out things to him, offering him strange fruits and berries, introducing him to friends who either studied him with frank curiosity or greeted him with a single word and then forgot him completely. After a while he couldn't have said which response made him more uncomfortable.

No one seemed to notice that other girls as young as Talani were bestowing strings of scarlet flowers on boys barely older than themselves.

No one seemed to notice that children two and three years old played at the edge of the water unattended.

No one seemed to notice that high on the slopes of the black peak, wisps of steam came from the earth.

No one seemed to notice that just before sunset, the earth moved. Keiris was the only one whose blood rushed from his face, leaving him pale and shaken, when it happened. Afterward he tried to tell himself that he had imagined it. But the motion had been distinct, a sharp motion followed by a gentle rolling of the ground. Yet the others either did not notice or were so little alarmed, they didn't even pause in their conversation.

Then the sun sank into the water, the flowers closed, and there were fires on the beach. People gathered around the fires in circles, singing songs like the ones Keiris had heard when he first saw the tide women at the cove. Talani chose a circle and pulled Keiris down beside her, nestling against him.

Sweet songs. Lingering songs. Songs that sometimes were plaintive against the sound of the sea.

Talani pressed a warm thigh against his. One arm rested against his arm. Her hair touched his shoulder. Keiris sat as the songs continued, trying with increasing difficulty to stifle his response to the warmth of Talani's skin, to the scent of her hair. A child . . . She was a child, and he could not exchange the stringency of his conventions for the laxity of hers so easily.

He could not. But there was something in the air, something melting and fragrant, something compounded from the perfume of flowers and the tang of salt. Something . . .

He dismissed it, that tantalizing promise, and almost immediately he began to feel an increasing sense of disorientation. He listened to the songs the people sang, some bright and laughing, others sad. He watched the stars slowly declare themselves against the increasing blackness of the sky. He watched the moons rise, and slowly he realized a terrifying thing. He did not know where he was. He was on an island somewhere, an island that steamed and shook. But how far did it lie from Neth? In what direction? They had traveled to the east and slightly to the north for much of the day, but there had been occasional shifts in their direction. And he could not be at all certain what direction they had traveled while he slept.

He sat among a strange people in a place he didn't know and began to ache for the solidity of Neth's soil beneath his

feet. Began to ache for the palace, for the faces of people he
knew. He ached to hear words spoken that he could understand, songs sung that he could sing too. He clutched the
shell horn that still hung at his neck, but that gave him no
comfort. At the bottom of his unease was a simple fact: He
had come far and did not know how to return. Even if he
went into the water and found Soshi, he had no way to tell
her to take him back to Neth. He had no way to make her
understand.

His father . . . He looked around, but his father was
nowhere on the beach. He wasn't a member of any of the
circles of people. In fact, Keiris had seen him only once, at
the hut Talani had taken him to earlier.

Was he still there? Carefully Keiris moved so that Talani's
thigh no longer touched his. He wriggled to one side so their
arms no longer pressed together. She glanced at him, but he
looked quickly away, avoiding her eyes. Finally, moving
slowly, moving gradually, he extricated himself from the
circle and slipped away.

He padded up the beach and into the trees, picking his way
silently.

The thatched hut where they had found his father earlier
was deserted. He found nothing but a tiny ground-lizard in its
two rooms. Disappointed, Keiris stood for a while on the
raised platform, looking down over the firelit beach, trying to
make sense of everything that had happened in the past two
days. He had jumped into the sea. He had ridden Soshi's back
and learned to fear the water a little less. He had come here,
where the tide folk were so intent upon their celebration that
they hardly noticed a stranger among them.

He had come here, and now, standing alone on the platform of his father's hut, he felt as overwhelmed by the
strangeness of the land, of the people, of the language, as he
had felt by the sea.

And the singing . . . As he stood there wishing for Neth,
wishing for his own familiar chamber, his own familiar bed,
the singing became like the sound of breakers. It rose and fell
relentlessly; swelling, receding but never dying.

Suddenly cold, frightened again, disoriented, Keiris retreated into the hut. But its thatched walls held back none of
the sound.

How long would the singing continue? When would his

father come? He sat in the corner of the single room, hunched, pressing his palms to his ears. The singing swept over him, a drowntide, until finally he curled up in a corner and escaped into sleep.

NINE

HE SLEPT AND the song came to him from a dream. It was not a simple song. There were no freely flowing notes, no repetitive melodies. Instead it was webbed and layered with subtlety, a song at once like bright stones and dark mosses, like shadow and light and the misted sea. And it carried other images and impressions too. It carried colors and scents and the fleeting impression of unfamiliar flavors. It carried glimpses of a clouded sky, the tang of dried salt on warm skin, the vividness of the equatorial sun. All these impressions and more hovered at the edge of Keiris' consciousness as the song unfolded, flirting with him, teasing him—eluding him each time he tried to capture them, to test them.

It was their very elusiveness that finally brought him awake. *White sands, green depths, dancing women with hair that curled over their shoulders* . . . His dreaming mind struggled after the vagrant images, struggled so doggedly that finally he was no longer sleeping but awake, staring wide-eyed at the ceiling of the hut where he had come to meet his father.

Puzzled, disturbed, he sat and rubbed his eyes, then pressed his fingers against the lids. When he did that, the song returned faintly and wound its way through his mind again, teasing him with images and sensations that evaporated when he tried to bring them to clearer focus. *Schools of translucent blue fish flashing from underwater warrens, fountains of ash against a red sky, the taste of unfamiliar fruit* . . .

Confused, frightened, Keiris stumbled from the hut to the edge of the platform it stood upon. Below, the beach was deserted, narrowed to a strand by the tide. Systris and Vukirid stood at a quarter angle to the horizon, silvering the foam the sea cast against the black sand. Vukirid's chase was almost over; he rode a bare few degrees behind Systris tonight. The tall waves they raised together caught at the ashes of the fires where the tide folk had sung earlier, dispersing the last embers.

No one sang on the beach now. But someone sang in Keiris' mind. He recognized that slowly, with chilling reluctance. The song he heard when he pressed his eyelids was not a lingering dream, not a persistent carryover from sleep. Nor was it a song from the beach below or from one of the thatched huts. No, someone cast words and images at him, words and images he could only imperfectly grasp—yet they had penetrated his dreams, and now they breached his waking mind as well.

He could dampen the song, he discovered, by clutching the rail of the platform tightly with both hands. He could dampen it by closing one hand so tightly around the shell horn that the scalloped rim of the bell cut his flesh. He could dampen it by squinting his eyes shut and gritting his teeth. But each time he relaxed, the song returned.

His father . . . His father would know what was happening.

But he had not heard his father return to the hut. Frowning, Keiris entered the shadowy structure and called his name. There was no answer.

There was no answer but the song plying itself softly against his mind. And then not so softly as he closed his eyes and exhaled, relaxing tensed muscles, deliberately letting down the barriers of resistance. Immediately images and impressions grew sharper, clearer. *The sea curling against sand so white, it hurt his eyes to see it. Fire belching from a black cone and raining down on blossoming trees. A palace much like the one at Hyosis but placed differently upon the land. Reysis? Socires? Was it one of those? Next a woman who might have been his mother, her face soft, joyful—younger, less guarded than he had ever seen her. Then a place undersea where mōss-grown rocks formed a tall arch and tiny fish with winking eyes swam. The water was shot with sunlight. Grains of sand floated in it like gold. A girl swam nearby, but he could see only her shadowy silhouette in the water. He could see only her slight limbs and her flowing hair. . . .*

Then those images were gone, replaced by a single bright image, a small fire laid on some rocky surface. It licked hungrily at sticks and moss, crackling as it devoured them.

The sound of the sea was near, but Keiris caught not the smell of salt but the stale odor of stagnant air. Frowning, he recognized that these images, these impressions, were different. They were more immediate than the others, more concrete—not something remembered but something seen now. He drew a cautious breath, steadying the image, and somehow—he wasn't sure how he did it—managed to widen the range of his vision.

The song had receded into the background now, even as the visual images that accompanied it grew more distinct. He saw cavern walls. He saw moss and lichen growing on damp stone; the moons, one pursuing the other toward the horizon; a lone trailing vine; a hand—

He caught a startled breath, and for a moment the image wavered. When the image steadied again, he was looking down at a human hand, spread, palm up. As he watched, the fingers curled, beckoning.

For long moments he could only stare blankly. Then a hot flush began at his hairline and spread, washing down his temples, flooding his cheeks, making his entire face and neck burn. Because now he understood. He understood the song. He understood the impressions it carried with it. He understood the beckoning hand.

"Come to me after the singing," his father had said. And so, misunderstanding, Keiris had come to the hut. He had come here and waited.

This was not where his father had intended him to come at all. His father had intended him to come to some other place.

His father had intended him to come to a cavern above the sea, where a small fire burned.

And the song he heard was his father's voice—the same singing voice his mother had described. His mother had summoned him to the dais and he had never heard her. Now his father summoned—and he heard clearly.

Shaken, he stepped back to the platform and gazed down at the overgrown slopes below, at the tide-washed beach. Then he turned and gazed up the side of the dark slope. He heard the summons, but he saw no tongue of flame anywhere.

Perhaps if he went to the beach and gazed back up at the darkened slope of the hillside from there . . . He waited for a moment, for several moments, and no better idea suggested itself. Frowning, uncertain, he descended the ladder.

The ground seemed more rugged, the shadows deeper,

more forbidding than they had earlier. The trees and vines seemed to crowd more closely together. Foliage hid the stars. Keiris caught only a distant glimpse of Systris and Vukirid as he picked his way through the trees toward the tide-washed beach.

The song returned as he made his way through the dense growth. It wove patterns in his mind, patterns of thought that clearly were not his own. He found himself thinking of people he did not know, remembering faces he had never seen, looking across lands and waters that were strange—yet with a haunting sense of their familiarity. There were memories at the back of his mind of paths he had never walked, of stars he had never seen, of foods he had never tasted. If he did nothing, if he simply made himself receptive, they flickered there brightly. But when he tried to grasp them, to examine them in detail, they swiftly evaporated, leaving him with nothing.

No one stirred in the thatched huts nestled among the trees. A warm breeze ruffled the heavy foliage of the trees. There was no other sound except the pounding of the tide.

The beach where the tide folk had sung earlier was awash now. Breakers rolled across it restlessly, leaving behind foam and streamers of uprooted sea-grass. Keiris hesitated at the edge of the sand, wondering which direction to take, wondering where his father called from.

A cavern above the sea where a fire burned. Turning, he peered back at the dark slope again. Again he saw no wink of fire anywhere.

A cavern above the sea where a single vine intruded. But there were vines everywhere.

A cavern above the sea . . .

At least he knew the cavern lay on this side of the island. His father could not see the setting moons if the cavern were on the far side of the island. The bulk of the rocky slope itself would block them from view.

Instinctively he turned and began walking to the west, toward the setting moons, picking his way along the edge of the beach.

Breakers cast foam at his bare feet. From the trees a bird called, then was still. Once he stopped, breath held, when the sea itself seemed to utter a series of booming cries. He stared across the water, dumbstruck—and saw nothing. He waited, but the sound did not recur. Uneasily he walked on.

After a while he knew that he walked in the right direction because the song had become more intense, the images and impressions it carried more vivid, more detailed. The fire, his father's hand—he saw them as clearly as if he stood at the mouth of the cavern. His father threw a handful of sticks on the fire and Keiris felt the heat on the back of his hand. His father popped a tiny, sour fruit into his mouth and Keiris' tongue curled. His father whistled softly to himself and Keiris felt air rush across his own lips.

Another bird called, uttering a single strident cry. This time, Keiris realized, he was hearing it twice, once nearby—and again faintly, from a distance. He stopped, drawing a shaky breath, realizing what that meant. He was near his father's hiding place now, near enough that his father heard the same call he heard but more faintly.

He paused for a moment, looking up through the trees at the dark flanks of the hillside, seeing nothing. Then, thoughtfully, he placed the shell horn to his lips and blew a single note.

Strangely he felt the muscles of his father's face form a smile. At the same moment he heard the note of his horn as his father heard it—a fragile sound from somewhere below and to the east, almost lost against the sound of the surf.

Keiris peered up again, then began running along the narrow beach, pausing occasionally to put the horn to his lips. Each time he blew, he heard the second note more distinctly, until finally he looked up and saw a small orange tongue of flame directly above.

For a moment he saw the same flame through his father's eyes. He felt a small sound of approval in his father's throat. Then the connection was severed, and the song that had receded to a faint melody died. "Evin?" he called as he began to climb. "Father?"

His father met him at the mouth of the cavern, his eyes glinting. "You found me more quickly than I expected," he said, gesturing Keiris to join him beside the fire. The cavern stretched behind him, a shadow-choked tunnel. Evin wore the same length of vivid green fabric he had worn earlier. The flicker of firelight highlighted his cheekbones, his obliquely set eyes.

"Why didn't you tell me?" Keiris demanded, glancing quickly around the rocky chamber, wondering how far into the hillside it extended. "Why didn't you tell me you wanted me to come here?"

"What would you have done if I had told you that? If I had told you how I intended to guide you?"

Keiris frowned down at his feet, reluctantly recognizing what his response would have been: to sit rigid and wakeful through the night, afraid both that he would hear his father's summons and that he would not. "I would have listened for you," he said. He would have listened so tensely, with such anxious concentration, that he would have heard nothing.

But his father hadn't told him how he intended to call him, and now he was here. And all the questions he had wanted to ask earlier were still on the tip of his tongue. "Will you tell me—"

"I can tell you very few of the important things," Evin warned. "You must discover those for yourself. Just as you discovered how to find me."

Keiris hesitated, frowning. "You can tell me where we are. What this island is called. You can tell me when I'll meet my sister. You can tell me—"

"We call this place Fhira-na. Properly it is one of the Adens, but you won't find it on any of the charts in your libraries, because it had barely crested from the sea when your folk took to their rafts. My people have known of it for a very long time, of course. We knew of it long before it emerged."

Keiris looked at him blankly. "Emerged? This is one of the Isles?"

His father laughed at his bewilderment and drew him back to the mouth of the cavern. "It's one of the group."

"But the Adens are gone," Keiris said. At least he had been taught that, although he was beginning to doubt some of the things he had learned as a child.

"No, they're not gone at all. The Adens lie at the southern extremity of the fire belt, so they sometimes rise and sometimes fall. That is their history, their geological nature. The ones your folk fled fell. They're still beneath the surface. But just now Fhira-na has risen." When Keiris still looked at him uncomprehendingly, he said, "Look there. Look out there at the sea, Keiris, and tell me what you see."

"Water," Keiris said. What other answer did he want?

"Yes, but beneath the water there is an entire land. Mountains, valleys, chasms, furrows. And none of them are forever. Not at all. Our world is an active one, in some places extremely active, in other areas—the seas around Neth, for one—quieter. Its features come and they go. Not within the space of years, certainly, but sometimes, in the fire belt, within the space of generations. There is a great heat within the earth, and that creates great pressures. Within the fire belt there are hundreds of places where molten materials are forced from the earth's interior to its exterior. It mounds up there and a cone rises; eventually it rises all the way out of the sea and becomes a land to live upon, as Fhira-na has done. Later, of course, if the vent closes over and too much force builds inside it, the cone may shatter and flatten itself beneath the surface again.''

''The Isles of Aden—''

''They had been quiet long enough that your folk forgot what they were. In fact, your folk had so insulated themselves from the sea around them, from the nature of the world beyond the shores of Aden, that they forgot land could be anything but forever. The Isles are under the sea now, the ones your people lived on, slowly building their way toward the surface again. If you swam very deep, you could see them.''

Keiris nodded. It made sense to him that if islands could explode and disappear beneath the surface, they could rise as well. But what had happened yesterday . . . ''Yesterday,'' he said hesitantly, ''I felt this island move.''

''Yes, it does that. Its foundations shift and rub. It's something that begins very deep in the earth. Not on the ocean floor but far beneath that.''

''But how do you know that?'' Keiris demanded. Certainly he had heard nothing about the earth shifting from Sorrys. Nor had he read of any such thing in the library at Hyosis.

Evin raised questioning brows. ''Ah, have the scholars persuaded you that everything worth knowing is to be found in a library somewhere?''

''No, but—''

''You'll learn much more than any library—or any scholar— could teach you when you learn to listen to the mams. Their memory is long—longer than any written history. And they don't exclude facts and events because they are uncomfortable with them, as your scholars do.''

When he learned to listen to the mams? Keiris glanced up sharply and saw the familiar, testing expression in his father's eyes. He pulled himself erect. "I won't learn that," he said stiffly.

"Ah? Because you refuse to learn it? Or because you don't think you can?"

"I—"

"Did you think, when you left Hyosis, that you would ever hear a call like mine tonight?"

"No," he admitted.

"But tonight I called and you heard."

"This time. I heard *you.*"

"But you don't ever expect to hear a mam? Because you are afraid to listen closely enough, carefully enough?"

Keiris felt his face drain. "I—"

"You've come telling me that you want to take Ramiri with you to Hyosis. You want her to live on the land like a Nethlor, like an Adenyo. But you don't even know who she is, and now that you're here, you're afraid to learn. Keiris, Ramiri isn't a child of the land. She's a child of the sea. And you will never know her, you will never understand her, you will never understand what you ask of her, unless you open yourself to the sea. Because she has been shaped there. She has been made there, even more than I have. She—"

Keiris drew back, disconcerted by his father's intensity. "But she's half–Adenyo," he protested. "Just as I am."

"And who are the Adenyo?" his father demanded.

"They—"

"They are only tide folk who retreated from the sea. You know that. Even your scholars admit it is true."

"It's true, but—" But he had not heard it in just those terms. He had heard that the Adenyo had emerged from the sea, not that they had retreated from it.

"It's true, but you admit it in the same spirit that your scholars do. You give it lip service, but you're afraid of the meaning behind the words." He gazed briefly over the moon-lit sea. "Have you ever cut your finger and sucked the wound to make it clean?"

Keiris frowned. "Yes," he agreed with instinctive wariness.

"What did you taste?"

"Blood."

"Yes, but what did you taste in the blood? Let me tell you—you tasted salt. You tasted the sea. Your blood is a tiny sea, contained by your flesh, and that is one thing that has never changed, not in all the history of our race. Your folk have lived on land for centuries, many centuries, but they still carry the sea in their blood. Their hearts still pump it through their veins. The sea is in them, and they will never completely expunge it, no matter how much they fear it.''

''The Adenyo don't fear the sea,'' Keiris said quickly—too quickly, because he knew he didn't speak the truth.

''Do they not? Do *you* not?''

''I'm—I'm only one person.''

''You're one of many persons who is afraid to listen to the tides that beat in your own body. Why do you think the Adenyo have such difficulty finding spanners to blow the horns? Hyosis isn't the only palace where the dais is in jeopardy. There are others—more than there were even a century ago when my grandfather visited Neth.''

''Your grandfather?''

''He spent three winters in lower Neth. A certain number of us do that, you know.''

''I—I didn't know.''

Evin shrugged. ''We like to see how it goes with our distant kin. And we look enough like you to pass.''

That was true. The tide folk looked enough like Adenyo or part–Adenyo to pass if no one expected to meet them on the land, if everyone accepted the fact that they were long extinct. But if anyone had been watching for them . . .

But the other thing his father had said was more urgent. ''And the other, the horns—''

''It's true—there are fewer women developing the gift than there were just a century ago. And there are no men at all. Study the records when you return to Hyosis. The longer the Adenyo live upon the land, the more they fear the sea, the more they close themselves off from it. Your mother has closed herself from it. Your sisters. You.''

His mother? ''No, not my mother,'' Keiris objected. ''She goes to the plaza every day. She listens. She—''

''I know how she listens,'' Evin said. ''Carefully. Cautiously. With fear. She speaks only to a few of the coast mams, her special friends, and they protect her. They shield her. They never take her too deeply into themselves. Because they love her and they know she is afraid of their strangeness. So they gather information for her from the sea mams, but—''

''No. It's the sea mams she speaks to.''

Evin raised his shoulders in a shrug. ''We call the mams your spanners speak with coast mams because they remain

near the land year-round. They don't swim in our migrations.
They never breach the fire belt to feed in the northern seas in
summer. They're a very small subgroup of the true sea species. Even their numbers are small. And when your mother's
friends speak to her, they don't carry her too deep or too far.
They gather information from the sea mams to pass to her—
but they speak to her carefully, so that she never touches the
deep sea herself. It's the same with the other spanners who
work from Neth. A few have voices powerful enough to call
far across the sea—as I do, as the other spanners of the tribes
do. But they never cast their voices far from land. And they
close themselves to the voices of all but their traditional
friends.

"But here is what I'm trying to tell you, Keiris. You've
come for Ramiri, but you don't know who she is because you
don't know the sea. We come among you, but you never
come among us. And so you don't know us. You don't know
Ramiri and you don't know me."

Keiris sighed deeply. "I don't," he admitted. His father
looked like an Adenyo. He spoke common tongue as well as
anyone. Keiris could talk to him here, now, and forget that
they were strangers. But tomorrow on the beach, with the
bright-garbed tide folk gathered around, laughing, chattering
incomprehensibly, their children rollicking heedlessly in the
waves . . .

His father would be a stranger again then, a man of the
tides, shaped by experiences Keiris could not imagine, formed
by depths he was afraid to touch. How could Keiris know
him, how could he know Ramiri when he met her, if he
refused even to learn to listen to the sea mams?

"My sister—will she come with me?" he asked. "When I
ask her, what will she say?" It seemed presumptuous, suddenly, to ask Ramiri to leave her people, to leave everything
she knew, when he had never spoken with her, when they had
never laughed together or shared a meal, when the only bond
between them was birth. He was her brother, but what did
that mean? He remembered what Nandyris had wanted of a
brother: someone to share her exploits, someone to laugh with
afterward, someone to reflect some of the day's sunlight back
to her when it was night. What would Ramiri want of a
brother?

Someone, surely, who could share the things she knew.
And the thing she knew was the sea.

There was some minute change in his father's eyes, some tiny shift in his expression. "I can't speak for Ramiri. Your sister—"

Evin broke off, and for a moment Keiris saw something entirely unexpected in his father's eyes, something very like helplessness. Because he thought Ramiri might answer Amelyor's summons and go with Keiris to Neth? Might leave him for her mother?

"Your sister . . . ." Evin said again, and his voice trailed away. He stared out over the sea. Then he turned back and took Keiris' hands in both of his. "I'm glad you came," he said unexpectedly, clasping Keiris' hands. "I've wondered about you over the years. I've thought, many times, of return-ing to Hyosis. Briefly, just to see you. I was sorry—I am sorry—for what happened. It was unexpected."

"It was unexpected that you—that you had to leave?" Keiris said, surprised by the strength of his father's grasp, by the warmth of his hands.

"Everything was unexpected. That I heard your mother's voice one day when I was swimming near the shore. That I was drawn to her. That I felt about her as I did. That we had children together. You. Your sister." Again, mention of Ramiri seemed to bring some shadow to his eyes.

Keiris hesitated, then said boldly, "Will you tell me why you took Ramiri and left me behind? If you are a spanner, if men can learn to do the same things women do . . . ." Was he correct in assuming that his father's position among his people was much the same as his mother's? That his duties, his responsibilities, were the same? To listen, to gather infor-mation, to warn?

"Ah." Evin shook his head. "You'll know soon enough why I couldn't leave Ramiri at Hyosis. But you? I left you because it seemed fair. I left you so Amelyor would have a child too."

Keiris frowned, wondering. Hadn't his father guessed Amelyor would be little pleased with a son when the conven-tions said she was entitled to her daughter instead? "She told me she found dyes in your chambers after you left—for your hair and skin."

"And you've seen I don't need those things to pass myself off as an Adenyo." Evin frowned and shrugged. "I thought she would feel better if she thought I had left because I was sorry for the deceit—the deceit of passing myself off as an

Adenyo when I was a part–Nethlor instead. And I thought it would be best, too, if she made any search for me, that she ask for a part–Nethlor.''

So that her chances of finding him would be that much smaller. ''You could have stayed,'' Keiris said, issuing a challenge of his own.

Evin raised his eyebrows. ''Ah? Couldn't it have been the other way instead? Your folk think more in those terms—of permanent bonding between mates—than we do. Couldn't I have brought Amelyor with me?''

Taken her away from Hyosis? To sea? ''She had a family. She had responsibilities—to the people. To the dais,'' Keiris protested.

''And I had a family and people and responsibilities too. Things I had neglected for too long already. A father whose voice was waning. A brother who had difficulty finding his voice; he has since been lost on migration, in the fire belt. No sisters at all. And then, finally . . . Ramiri.'' He frowned, momentarily lost in his thoughts, his dark eyes narrowed. Then he broke free of his thoughts and pressed Keiris' hands firmly between his. ''All those things, and together they made me think I would never see you. They made me think we would never be father and son, not in the way we should be. But here you are. You've come far—too far to go back without learning what there is to learn. Keiris, will you let me show you my land? My wet, watery land?''

Keiris sighed, doubt seeping away—doubt he had hardly admitted to himself until now. Because from somewhere his father had found words Keiris hadn't even guessed he wanted to hear: ''I'm glad you came. I wanted to see you.''

''I thought you were displeased to see me,'' he said huskily. ''At first. At the black palace.''

''And I thought that if I didn't prod you, you would remain behind there when we left. I was afraid you wouldn't find the courage to follow me if I didn't nettle you into it.''

Keiris laughed softly. ''I didn't find the courage. I followed you, anyway.'' At least he didn't feel any more like a person of courage than he had felt when he left Hyosis. He felt just as lacking, just as reluctant, just as afraid. Except that now he had dared the sea. He had plunged into the water and ridden a mam to an uncharted island somewhere in the middle of the ocean.

And now, he knew, he was about to venture even farther. ''I'll try to learn what you want to teach me.''

His father smiled, obviously pleased. "The learning will be yours. I can't teach you. But I can guide you. And if you want it, I will."

"I want it," Keiris said, with a firmness that surprised him. Because while he did want it, while he did want to share his father's world, he couldn't look out over the sea without feeling fear rise in him, a fresh tide in his blood, as potent as it had ever been.

Evin's dark eyes glinted. "Tomorrow night, then. We leave here then and travel south for the gather, before we make our way north again. I'll ask Nestrin to span for me. He is capable. And you and I will drop behind the others and take sea sleep together."

"Sea sleep?" Keiris said uncertainly.

"It is like a long dream—and an exploration. It will enhance whatever sensitivity you have. It will bring it to the surface, at least for a while. Long enough for you to begin to understand some things you'll understand no other way. I'll guide you, and when you awake, you'll be better able to hear what the sea has to tell you. Meet me at the shore at moonrise, when the others gather." He turned back and knelt beside the fire, his gaze becoming remote, as if his thoughts had already moved ahead to the next evening. "Till tomorrow, Keir."

He was being dismissed. "Tomorrow," Keiris echoed weakly.

Tomorrow he would take sea sleep and begin to learn his father's world. And if he could not learn it, if it simply swallowed him up, if he failed ineffectually and lost himself in the sea . . .

He left the cavern and picked his way down the hillside toward the beach. The moons were near setting now, and the tide had begun to recede. When he reached the beach, he paused. Then he began to circle back around the island.

He had not gone far before he saw a small shell, much like the one he wore at his neck, nestled in the sand. He paused and touched it with his toe but did not pick it up. Instead he turned and peered up to where the fire flickered. He did not see his father. Nor, when he closed his fingers lightly around his own shell horn, did he hear his song.

He listened instead to the sound of the sea as he made his way down the beach toward morning.

TEN

When finally he slept, Keiris had dreams, but he did not realize until he stood on the shore the next night that they had been prophetic. He dreamed that the sun sank so heavily the next evening that it flattened itself for a time upon the horizon and lay there egg-shaped and swollen. He dreamed that it dyed the sea molten colors and that the sky grumbled when finally it slid underwater, lightning darting like snake's tongues from a distant bank of clouds. He dreamed that Talani was a woman in that strange light, a slight child-woman with wise, laughing eyes and warm flesh, which she pressed against him. He dreamed that when she did that, Fhira-na shifted on its foundations so sharply that he knew the land itself would be offended if he let himself be beguiled by a child.

He dreamed that then the moons rose, silver and silver, lovers very near union, and that the people shed their bright cloth for lizard skins and disappeared into the sea. He dreamed that he was among them, on Soshi's back—but that when he nudged and coaxed Soshi ahead, that when he called up to his father where he sat high on the giant white—"Evin! Father! Evin!"—his father did not glance back at him. He simply crouched against the white's resplendent flesh, a stranger called by the sea.

And so it happened, much as he had dreamed. The sun set, Talani laughed and pressed warm, bare arms and thighs against him, the moons rose, and the tide folk swam away on the backs of their mams, Keiris among them. And when he found his father and called up to him—"Evin! Father! Evin!"—a stranger looked back.

But only momentarily. Then both Evin and Talani laughed, and Talani leaned over to slap at Keiris' wrist and said, "Rudin, Keiris. Nirini *ca* Rudin."

"I'm Rudin in the sea," his father reminded him, calling the words down with a laugh. Although the white swam with most of her bulk beneath the water, Rudin sat high above Nirini, and Keiris on their far smaller mams. "And this is Pehoshi, my moonsteed: my finest sea-friend, my teacher, and the maker of songs you'll hear soon, songs that go long and deep. Where I need to go, Pehoshi carries me." He stroked the flesh of the white, then spoke in his own language to Nirini, gesturing to the tide folk who rode ahead of them.

Whatever he said displeased Nirini. She grimaced in protest and shook her head, arguing back with him. Then she turned to Keiris, grasping his wrist, speaking heatedly to him.

"I don't understand," he said helplessly. He touched his lips, his ears, then threw up his hands, miming his incomprehension. "I don't understand what you say." But he did understand the hurt in her eyes when she spoke again, more softly, then looked from him to his father in injured frustration. He glanced up to his father for explanation.

"I told her that you and I were going to the sea pools, that she must go ahead with the others. She feels that if she hadn't failed as your land-friend, we would invite her to come with us."

If she hadn't failed? "She didn't fail," Keiris said baffled. If anything, she had worked too hard at being his friend. She had stayed with him every moment of the day, chattering, laughing, touching him as she showed him favorite places, favorite foods, favorite games. Several times he had tried to slip away, but she had caught at his arm, detaining him, and hurried to show him some new thing.

His father shook his head. "She is certain she did because she reached for the third blossom four times today, and you refused her each time."

Keiris turned from his father's smiling glance in discomfiture. He stroked Soshi's dorsal fin, his fingers tracing the scars there. "I tried to tell her why." He had tried clumsily, with gestures, pointing to small children who played in the surf. Even more clumsily with figures drawn in the sand.

"Ah, and she wonders why you would find it so repugnant to have a child with her. She thinks it's because you're the son of spanners and she has very little voice for the sea."

Keiris sighed. She had misunderstood him entirely. "If you would just tell her that she is too young . . ." But his father didn't have to tell him again how that argument would sit with Nirini. She had pointed out several couples to him that afternoon, children, laughing as they disappeared together into the trees. If he asked his father to tell her he had refused her because their families had not met and exchanged genealogies, that would only confirm the argument she had just made. And if he told her that any union he made must last for more than an interval, that he could not father children and leave them behind, if he told her . . .

He bowed his head. There was nothing to tell her, really, that she would not turn into a hurt. "Can we take her with us?" he asked finally. "To the sea pools?"

"We can do that," his father agreed.

"Would I be—would I be obligating myself if she came? Is there anything I don't know?"

His father lifted his shoulders in a light shrug. "She would have greater expectations that you would let her pick the third blossom the next time. But she has to accommodate herself to you, doesn't she, in some things? Just as you have accommodated yourself to her in others."

It seemed fair. "If you would tell her, then—"

"You can do that, can't you?"

He could. He turned to her, reaching to touch her wrist as she had so often touched his. "Come with us," he said. He didn't know how to word the invitation in her tongue, but he thought she would understand.

She insisted that he repeat the invitation twice. Then her eyes glinted with pleasure, and she leaned forward and whistled to her mam. The creature immediately plunged ahead, thrusting itself into the air in long, curving arcs, then disappearing beneath the surface, Nirini clinging to its back. Each time they curved through the air Nirini laughed, beckoning to Keiris. Pearl droplets of moisture rained from her upraised arm.

"Play for a while," Rudin said. "Quilin has taken the span from me. We can drop away now."

"Quilin?" But he could guess; Nestrin must be Quilin upon the sea. "Father—"

"Later," Rudin said. "There is something below that appears tasty to Pehoshi. If we're separated, listen for me." And before Keiris could ask more, he and the great white sank beneath the surface, leaving behind nothing but a patch of still water.

Disconcerted, Keiris hesitated for a moment. Then he whistled softly against the side of Soshi's head and set her leaping after Nirini's mam.

They traveled through the moonlit night together, the mams feeding and playing. Soshi and Kasha, Nirini's mam, whistled and squeaked to each other sociably. Pehoshi swam in massive silence, her white flesh ghostly by moonlight. Occasionally she bore Rudin beneath the surface. Sometimes he still clung to her back when she surfaced, blowing loudly. Other times he bobbed to the surface before her, alone, and swam beside the two smaller mams for a while.

There was room for two on Soshi's back, but Rudin only laughed when Keiris suggested they ride together while Pehoshi fed. And so Keiris sat rigidly, clutching Soshi's fin until the white surfaced and his father mounted again. And he tried not to think what things might be hiding in the opaque water, what things might turn yellow eyes on his father and see prey.

They traveled until the moons had passed their zenith and begun their decline. The stars wheeled as they traveled, and sometimes, strangely, Keiris heard a bare wisp of his father's song. Occasionally he thought he heard an answering song as well, but the voice was so deep, so oddly resonant, he could not be certain it was a song he heard at all. It seemed more like something that jarred deeply inside him. It seemed like something that vibrated in his stomach, in his chest, in the joints of his largest bones: hips, shoulders, thighs.

Then Nirini leaned to clasp his wrist and began to talk excitedly, nodding to the sea ahead. And Pehoshi disappeared for a moment and surfaced with a resounding release of vapor from her blowhole. Rudin slipped from her back, just as Nirini slid from her own mam.

Keiris glanced anxiously at them bobbing in the water. "What is it?"

"The sea pools are ahead. The mams won't carry us any farther. They don't swim where sleep grasses grow."

Sleep grasses? And did they expect him to join them in the water? Keiris licked his lips. "I—I don't swim," he pointed out.

"We'll help you. It isn't far to the rims. Here, slide down. I'll catch you under the arms and we'll swim together on our backs. All you have to do is lie on the water and kick your feet."

Keiris hesitated. There was something in his father's voice, something hurried, distracted, and Nirini was kicking impatient circles around them both. Her eyes glinted eagerly. Biting his lip, Keiris slid from Soshi's back.

Nirini was beside him immediately, patting his arm, holding him soothingly by one wrist. His father quickly slipped his hands into Keiris' armpits, and Keiris found himself lying on his back, buoyed and supported by his father's body, gliding backward in the water.

"Relax—relax your arms, your legs. You're stiff." Rudin's words were encouraging, but again they seemed hurried, distracted.

Keiris nodded and tried to comply. Still his legs trailed rigidly, and he held his hands wide, ready to snatch at the water if his father sank from under him. Once, at his father's instruction, he kicked experimentally, but the motion disturbed his balance and he stiffened again. He thought, as they swam, that he felt things trailing against him, stroking his feet, his legs. He tried to raise his feet, but then his hips sank and he floundered momentarily.

"Not far," his father reminded him.

And all the while Nirini paddled easily beside them, cooing to him reassuringly, as if he were a child.

Embarrassed, Keiris put his feet down with relief when his father released him and said, "Here we are. Solid rock. Here—come up here and choose a pool."

Keiris caught his balance and picked his way after his father up a low wall of rock that jutted from the water. At the top of the wall he paused and stared across the water in surprise. There were rims of black stone protruding above the sea's surface, craters filled with still, silver-washed water. Some were no more than a few paces wide. Others were larger. Keiris could not count how many there were. He thought there were as many as forty or fifty, perfectly circular, their walls joined.

He glanced at his father in astonishment. He had a dozen questions. What had made the craters? How long had they been here? Why wouldn't the mams bring them this far? Must they go into that still water? But something in his father's manner, something in the distracted glint of his eyes, told him his questions would not be answered. "What—what must we do now?" he asked, and flushed at the openly anxious note in his voice.

Rudin spoke to Nirini in their own language, then turned to Keiris. "Nirini has been here before. Watch what she does."

Keiris nodded and watched as Nirini scampered lightly around the rocky rims and selected one of the smaller pools of water. She shed her lizard skins, flashing a bright, pleased smile at Keiris, and dived cleanly into the silver water, making it shimmer. Keiris caught his breath, following his father around the rocky rims until they stood beside the pool where Nirini had disappeared.

She surfaced slowly, lying upon her back in the water as if supported there, her arms and legs spread. She dipped her head back, so that her hair was submerged and the water touched her eyebrows. Her eyes were closed and her expression so blissfully expectant that Keiris shifted uneasily.

Then he tensed as he realized that green tendrils reached up from the pool and were curling slowly around her outspread arms and legs, that thicker tendrils reached across her bare abdomen and encircled her chest. He turned to his father, expecting to see alarm in his face. "Father—Rudin—"

His father smiled absently. "All you have to do is put yourself into the water. The grass will take care of the rest."

"But what—" The tendrils were wrapping themselves ever more securely around Nirini, some at her neck, others reaching from the water and snaking across her face. Instinct told Keiris that one of them should plunge into the pool after her. One of them should pull her free of the strangling grass. But his father only stood gazing, and on his face was not alarm but anticipation. "Father, I don't think I can do that," Keiris said in a shaken voice. "Rudin—" Suddenly it seemed difficult to find a name for the stranger who stood beside him watching Nirini strangle in green tendrils, doing nothing.

His father turned back to him, moonlight pooled in his eyes. "There's nothing to fear, Keir," he said. "The grass will breathe for you when it takes you under. And I'll guide you into Pehoshi's song. All you have to do is listen for my voice."

Keiris stared at him, stunned. The grass would breathe for him? When it took him under? He shook his head violently. "Father—" But his father seemed unconscious of his fear. Keiris turned back to the pool.

Nirini's face had no discernible expression now. It was lashed over with green tendrils, and with horror Keiris saw that some of them reached for her open nostrils, that some forced themselves into the corners of her mouth. Then, with horror, Keiris saw that the grass was slowly curling in upon itself, dragging Nirini beneath the water. For a moment she was a stain of white just beneath the surface. Then she was a pale glimmer. Then she was gone.

And still his father's face held only an expression of distracted expectation. He turned to Keiris with a bright, meaningless smile. "Which pool do you want?"

"I—" Keiris stared at him blankly.

"Choose any one. No need to share. There are only three of us."

"Father—"

"Do you want me to go first?"

"*No!*" It took Keiris the barest fraction of a moment to weigh those two terrors against each other: the terror of stepping into the water himself and letting what would happen, happen; the terror of watching his father dragged down as Nirini had been, green tendrils curling into his nose and mouth, and then standing there alone, on a rim of rock, in the middle of the sea. "I'll go." His hands had begun to shake violently.

His father nodded absently. Moonlight made frosted mirrors of his eyes. "Any pool, then."

He seemed not to notice how long it took Keiris to select a pool. He seemed not to notice how stiffly Keiris picked his way around its rocky rim. He seemed not to notice how long it took Keiris to peel off his lizard skins and step slowly into the water. Rudin stood like a blind sentinel, erect, alert, seeing nothing.

Then Keiris was in the water, dizzy, nauseated, trembling. He felt the first trailing touch at his ankles, at his calves, as he waded slowly toward the center of the pool. The water reached his thighs, his hips, his waist—

And suddenly there was no longer a bottom to the pool. He took one last, cautious step forward, and there was nothing beyond that. No rocky strata underfoot. No foothold. Only water and the grass that stroked at him so tenderly.

He hesitated there and then, because there was nothing else to do, he crouched and lay forward against the water, holding his breath.

It was not as he had expected. He sank briefly, the water closing over his back and shoulders. Then he was gently rotated in the water and buoyed back toward the surface. His

arms, his legs, his torso, his head . . . It was as if a dozen
inhumanly pliable hands raised him and supported him. Then
it was as if the fingers of those hands began to stroke and caress
him, sliding velvet-soft across his bare skin. The water was
warm. So were the moving fingers. And where they touched
him he felt his skin begin to glow with a special, inviting
heat. Surprised at his own reaction, he melted against the
water, letting his head drop, arching his neck so the caressing
fingers could better reach his chest, his throat, his chin.

Sensitive zones, all those, and the grassy fingers touched
and pleased. Keiris' flesh began to tingle, at first superfi-
cially, then in deep places where nothing had ever touched
before. His skin seemed to swell and throb with pleasure, as
if it had become an organ separate from him, aching with its
own sensuality. The sensation reminded him of dreams he
sometimes had in the early days of spring, dreams of pleasures
he could not name. Sighing deeply, he closed his eyes and let
breath flow into his lungs, forgetting where he was, forgetting
that he had been afraid just moments before. Moonlight penetrated his eyelids, shedding a brief interior light.

He hardly noticed when the tendrils made their way into his
nostrils. He hardly noticed when they pressed into the corners
of his mouth and reached down his throat. But after a while,
hanging there in the water, his body coursing with pleasure,
he did notice that his chest no longer rose and fell. He did
notice that air no longer whispered along his air passages.

The plants will breathe for you when they take you under.

Suddenly he wanted very much to fall all the way into
those velvet hands. He wanted to fall all the way into pleasure. He wanted to learn what lay beyond.

He opened his eyes and saw the moons, clear in the sky,
keeping their silver vigil. Then they rippled and dimmed, and
he knew that he had his wish. The grasses had taken him
under.

He did not begin to dream immediately. For a while he
simply hung in the water, aware of the tiny currents that
disturbed its stillness, aware of the occasional breezes that
rippled its surface, aware of the slow transit of the moons.
His flesh pulsed and throbbed with unidentifiable sensations
while he hung suspended. His blood flowed warm and thick
through him. He felt its scarlet richness against the interior
walls of his blood vessels. His eyes, whether he opened or
closed them, told him of brilliant colors.

Hanging there, he wondered distantly what made those things happen. He wondered what intoxicating substances the grassy tendrils breathed into him. He wondered what kind of strange, watery drunkenness this could be. He wanted to celebrate like a fisherman who had taken too much brew. He wanted to bellow with laughter and cry sweet tears. He wanted to sing—loudly, so everyone could hear.

For a while it seemed to him that he did. It seemed to him that he sang, not rowdily as he had thought he might but in some unearthly voice—sang a song that was only his, full of joy and sunlight and orchards and a palace sitting high above the sea. He sang of friendly Nethlor faces and a table set with thin-shelled platters and a sister who laughed and swung over the sea on a rope.

A sister who swung over the sea . . .

A sister . . .

Then the first dreams began, dreams of another sister. This one did not swing over the sea on a rope. She swam instead. She coursed beneath the cloudy water, a shadowy figure with streaming hair, and try as he might, he could not make the water clear. He could not bring sunlight deep enough into it to see her as he wanted. He knew she was Ramiri, but he could not see the shape of her brow, the depth of her eyes, the breadth of her cheekbones. She was only a shadowy figure moving pensively through the dull water, grasses coiling around her.

Grasses? Were they grasses? Keiris stirred, for a moment uneasy, and tried to distinguish detail. Then lethargy and pleasure overtook him again, and he watched uncritically as the sister of his dreams moved in the depths.

She did not sing as she swam, or if she did, he could not hear her. And he was sorry for that because if he could hear her songs, he would know what things she carried in her mind. Hadn't he seen what things his father thought of, what things he remembered, when he had listened to his song: *White sands, green depths, dancing women with hair that curled over their shoulders . . .*

Again uneasiness stirred him. He opened his eyes and for a moment gazed toward the surface of the pool. The moons had set. (When? Had he been under the water so long?) There was no light. There was only grayness. He could not distinguish the margin where water and air met. He could not tell how deep he lay.

Shuddering, he remembered his father's promise: that he
would guide him, if Keiris would only listen.

Surely it was time to listen. Instinctively he closed his eyes
and let his limbs lie limp against the supporting tendrils
again. After a moment the warmth and the stroking pleasure
returned. Brilliant colors fluttered on the inner surfaces of his
eyelids. And finally he heard his father's song, subtle, distinctive, reassuring. Without effort, as if the two, song and
memory, were separated by only the thinnest membrane, he
passed from the song into his father's memory.

*A boy swimming one night far from land, searching for
something he couldn't name; a great white shape rising from
the water nearby and spouting; the boy, awed into stillness,
feeling droplets of vapor on his face and shoulders, a chris-
tening, an invitation—or a summons; the boy hesitating, then
swimming toward the great creature, expecting it to slip
beneath the surface and disappear at any moment; the white
creature waiting there instead, waiting patiently while he
swam inquisitive circles around it, waiting while he touched
its resplendent flesh with diffident fingertips, waiting while
he climbed to its back for the first time; a boy sitting high on
the white's back and knowing he had been greatly honored,
knowing that this was his moonsteed, come to carry him
wherever he most needed to go. . . .*

But beyond his father's memory there was more. There
was another membrane, and although it was resistant, Keiris
pressed through it and slipped into another memory, a far
deeper one. He slipped into the memory of the great white
who had honored his father as a boy, who honored him now,
who was his most special friend and companion.

He found . . .

. . . memories that seemed to come from times so distant,
there was a mist upon them; memories stored in sensory forms
so alien, he could not be sure he understood them at all;
memories he probed and explored, anyway, carefully at first,
feeling his way, then with abandon.

Memories . . .

*A place far distant both in time and space. It had the name
Urt among men. Among mams its name was different.*

A sky that held one moon, so small, so white.

*A sea that fumed and burned with poisons. It had been
different once, that sea. It had been a cherished home.*

No more.

Living in it or near it two kinds—human and mam—who had painstakingly learned to speak with each other after centuries of ignorance and pillage.

And so they spoke with each other, awkwardly, often uncertain of their understanding even now.

But certain of one thing, their mutual yearning for a home like theirs once had been: clean and welcoming.

Urgency, need, anguish—shared by those wise ones of their two kinds who saw what was being so irrevocably lost.

Then a flashing silver body, not flesh but metal, hurled against the winking stars, darting past the tiny moon, challenging the darkness beyond.

Another sea, unspoiled.

Hundreds of bodies, human and mam, released into it, leaping and celebrating and making sounds of joy—while on isolated pieces of land other humans, those who chose not to dwell in the water, celebrated their new homes too.

Then, in the sea, the discovery of a great strangeness.

A strangeness entirely unexpected.

A strangeness that was almost human in form.

The strangeness came for a time among those humans who lived in the sea. The two kinds mingled and then parted, leaving behind a hybrid people who carried bits of strangeness in themselves.

Leaving behind a hybrid people who heard voices they had never heard before. A hybrid people who heard what their friends the mams had to tell without the clumsiness of the language their two kinds had so painstakingly devised.

A hybrid people who heard danger as well, calling from the depths of the sea, touching their deepest fears.

Danger they had been deaf to before, before they had mingled the strangeness into themselves.

Years.

Centuries.

Aeons.

Time passed. Humans and mams made the new sea their own. The mams discovered their own voices, some of them faint, tenuous, others deep and far-reaching. The strange returned occasionally and grew less strange—but the dangerous became no less so. It lay in certain vital zones of the sea, calling them, making an end of many who were not wise enough or wary enough.

Making an end of many whose hybrid blood made them vulnerable to its summons.

Movements. Migrations. Great routes established from basin to basin.

More years.

More centuries.

More aeons.

Changes. Many changes. Peoples and mams coming and going in great waves. Fires spouting from the seas. Land rising and falling. Those beings considered strange finally grown so familiar that they were mourned when their numbers began to wane. They were invited to come among the people and make their slow multiplication there, while the people multiplied ever so much more quickly around them. The two bloodlines intermingled again, and children who were at once both and neither swam in the sea.

And still the deep danger, calling, sending compelling summonses to every sensitive mind.

Briefly Keiris stirred. Was it daylight now? Did he really see the sun hanging brightly over the water? Or was that just another part of the dream? Of the exploration? Because the two songs continued, his father's and the other, deeper song, and together they guided him to places he had never imagined.

Deep places.

Far places.

Places for feeding.

Places for breeding.

Places for birthing.

Places for gathering and joining songs.

Places for parting.

Places for dying, alone or together.

Places even for madness.

Keiris went to all those places. He saw them. He knew them. Or so it seemed to him. As he saw them and knew them he marveled at the way such varied memories and impressions were stored in the song of a sea mam. He marveled that so much of their strangeness translated itself into forms he could understand—yet remained strange. Strange and haunting.

Other memories, other impressions, were not so easily translated. Their colors, their content, remained enigmatic and troubling, their meaning obscure.

Then the moons were in the sky again and the grasses were

raising him—tenderly, gently—to the surface. He lay blinking and confused on the surface of the water, wondering drunkenly why pleasure no longer wrapped velvet fingers around him, wondering why he must work so hard for breath when before it had been given him. Wondering how he could have passed both a night and a day under the water and not been afraid.

He lay against the supporting grass for a while longer. Then, carefully, he groped for the bottom of the pool and made his way to the rim. He pulled himself out of the water and stood weak-legged, panting, on the rocks. There was no sign of Nirini, of his father, and for a moment he felt afraid.

But that was only for a moment. Because, turning, he saw that he stood in a sea of light. The still surface of every pool caught the two moons and reflected them. Their light threw a hundred brightnesses around him. The lesser brightnesses of the stars threw a thousand more. He stood there, dazed and dazzled, his mind full of brightnesses too.

There were pinpoints of knowing everywhere. There were sparks of understanding in hundreds of places where there had been only darkness before. There were empathies it should have taken him a lifetime to develop. There were memories it had taken a thousand men and a thousand mams to amass. All of them, mysteriously, were his now.

Some of them he fully understood. Others were simply there, so alien in form and content that they lay beyond his conscious comprehension.

Dazzled, groping, he found his lizard skins where he had thrown them down the night before. He pulled them on absently, turning unsurprised at the touch on his shoulder a few moments later.

Nirini had emerged from her pool. She stood naked in the moonlight, gazing up at him, and he saw immediately the truth of what she had been trying to tell him all along: that she was not a child. She was a woman, small and young and driven by bright, laughing energies—but a woman. And she knew the same things he knew. Her mind brimmed with the same long memories, the same deep song. Her skin had warmed and tingled under the same velvet touch. The grasses had breathed the same strange ecstasy into her as into him.

Some of the ecstasy lingered. There was a pulse at Nirini's throat. Or was she Talani, standing upon the solid rim of rock? It didn't matter. Seeing her pulse, Keiris felt his own speed to match it.

They began talking at once, he in his language, she in hers. They began touching, and for the first time she was not the only one who pressed flesh to flesh, offering warmth. She dipped her head back and laughed aloud when he bent to peer down at the moons in her eyes. Then he dipped his head back, and she peered gravely into his eyes. Finally they ran together across the joined rims of the sea pools and slipped into the sea itself. There Keiris had no difficulty at all learning what Nirini wanted to teach him.

Afterward, in the last, lingering aftermath of the long ecstacy, he found he had learned to swim as well.

ELEVEN

EVERYTHING WAS DIFFERENT by daylight, of course. Nirini was a child again, the woman only glancing from the corners of her eyes at odd moments. The sea was no longer an enchanted place, and the two smaller mams were only mams, whistling and squeaking playfully as they swam.

Still Keiris retained some of the euphoria of the night. And mingled with it was a bright-minded forgetfulness. The things he had learned in the sea pool—the hundreds of things, the thousands of things—were no longer discrete particles floating in his mind, brilliant and distinct. Instead they had begun to merge: with each other, with his own memory and experience. And he guessed that if he did not disturb the slow process of digestion by probing at it, by dwelling on it, soon all those bright motes of knowledge would fuse and simply become a part of the matrix of his own experience. Many, in fact, had already slipped into the lower ranks of his memory. They lay there all but forgotten, heirlooms stored in a trunk.

And he had learned to swim—not strongly, not fearlessly, but he could slide off Soshi's back and keep himself afloat for as long as he needed, bobbing on the water. It came so naturally, it almost seemed as if swimming were a skill he had acquired as a child and was just now remastering.

That confounded him. He could accept the rest: that he had spent a night and a day lying under the surface of the water, that he had found the woman in Nirini, that he was somehow incorporating experiences taken from his father's mind and Pehoshi's into his own memory. *Another world, a dying sea, metal vessels flying against the fuming sky* . . . But which of them had taught him to swim—his father, Pehoshi, or all those others whose memories were encapsulated within theirs? Which had taught him to relax against the water? Which had taught him the growing ease he felt there?

He swam with Nirini and his father and wondered.

He rode and swam with Nirini and his father for a day, for two days, traveling east and sometimes north. As the hours slipped past, the sunlit water sparkled with hypnotic intensity, and occasionally, absently, Keiris wondered other things. He wondered where the first humans and the first mams had entered the water of this world. Was the place near or far? He wondered what the two kinds felt when they first learned to speak with silent voices. Pleasure? Or fear at the sudden closeness that was thrust upon them? He wondered if he could hear Nirini's voice, however faintly, if he listened closely enough. He wondered if Soshi had a voice, if Kasha had one. And during that brief interval when he had imagined that he, himself, sang, had his father heard his song? Or was his voice as imperceptible as Nirini's?

But there was danger in those latter questions, he knew, because beyond them were other questions, questions he was not ready to examine.

And so he did not pursue them. He rode with Nirini and his father, hugging Soshi's flanks when the water was rough, sliding from her back to swim when it was still, letting the process of forgetfulness proceed without interference.

They saw many things during those two days. They saw fish that leapt from the water and made rainbows in the air. They saw gray-beaks traveling without riders, sporting cheerfully, leaping and diving—hundreds of them. They saw a lonely gray, and Keiris heard its song when it passed. They saw a place where tall stalks grew from the floor of the sea and reached high into the air, their tips fleeced with something very like wool. They saw other sea pools, and they saw a black lava peak that had barely tipped above the water.

"Is this the fire zone? Here?" Keiris asked when the emergent peak was behind them. It was near evening of the second day, and he guessed from his father's sudden air of distraction that something lay ahead: the group they had parted from, land, something. They had changed course just minutes before, shortly after his father had first begun to frown and glance uneasily across the water.

"We're at its edge," Rudin said. "We won't enter the

most active area until after the gather, when we begin our summer migration.'' He glanced narrowly at Keiris and briefly seemed about to say more, then did not.

''Do you travel through it each year?'' Keiris pressed when his father did not continue. He was puzzled by the weighing quality of his father's glance, by his distracted frown. He seemed to listen for something as they spoke. But what?

His father nodded, still studying him narrowly. ''All the tribes travel through the zone each spring on their way to the northern feeding grounds.''

The feeding grounds: *boulders of ice rising blue-white from the water. Rugged mountains marching into the sea, not fire-cones but mountains of a different kind, mountains that looked as if a segment of the earth itself had tipped up and reared out of the water. Rivers of fresh-melted ice pouring from sheer faces of rock. Feeding beds, rich with food-species for every kind of mam. The brisk contrast of clear, sunlit skies with the chill air that rose from water.* He knew about the feeding grounds. The images rose sharply, clearly, from the back of his mind.

And, he found, surprised, that he knew about the fire zone too. He knew enough to feel the sharp slash of terror when the first stored images sprang to the forefront of his mind: *exploding rock, boulders flying in the air, a sky dark with ash, bright ribbons of fire running down black slopes to the water* . . . Abruptly the last, lingering euphoria of his mood turned brittle. Had those fiery terrors implanted themselves in his mind while he lay in the sea pool? He had not been aware of them before this moment, not at all. Was it possible the process of storing away particles of experience had begun even before he left the sea pool? Had the most frightening sunk to the floor of his mind before he ever became aware of them?

Or had he buried them there, unconsciously protecting himself?

But more disturbing, he quickly recognized as the ashen images blazed past, that they weren't fully responsible for the terror he felt. There was something beyond those, something that had begun to keen distantly at the edges of his awareness. He shook his head and pressed himself close to Soshi's back, wondering what it was he heard. Its voice was like the beginning of pain: faint, ominous, swiftly intensifying.

To Keiris' surprise Soshi began to tremble beneath him.

Then, startled, he saw Nirini clutch at Kasha, pressing herself tight against the mam. He turned sharply, alarmed. "Father—"

His father darted a narrowing glance at him, frowned, and slid abruptly from Pehoshi's back into the water. He surfaced at Soshi's side and pulled himself up, wrapping one arm around the mam's curving body. "Do you hear it?" he demanded. "Keir—you hear it. Don't you?"

Keiris' mouth had gone dry. The voice had come nearer. It was inside his head now, quivering there, as if it danced upon exposed nerves. "I hear something," he whispered, shrinking from the intensity of his father's gaze. "I don't know what it is. I—"

"Hiscapei!" Nirini hissed, guiding Kasha near. She reached to touch Rudin's shoulder. "Rudin—hiscapei!" Fear was clear in her eyes.

Rudin spoke to her briefly and patted her hand reassuringly. Then he turned back to Keiris, his eyes narrowed. "Push the voice back," he said. "Whatever you have to do—don't listen to it. If you do that—"

"What?" Keiris demanded. What would happen if he listened? And how could he push the sound away? How could he close his ears to it when it didn't reach him through his auditory system at all? When instead it reached him through the branching tracery of his entire nervous system?

In fact, if he concentrated, if he narrowed his attention, if he heeded only the voice, he could plot its route from fiber to fiber. He could—

He cried out in startled pain as his father brought his open palm sharply against his cheek.

"Keir, *don't listen to it*. We've already changed course. We'll be beyond range in just a few minutes."

Keiris clutched his stinging jaw. "It's—it's dangerous?" A mindless question but his thoughts had become numbed, slow, as if he had been injected with paralyzing venom. The hiscapei, whatever it was, was the voice he heard in his mind. It was the pain that raced along the passageways of his nervous system. And certainly it was dangerous.

A danger that called from the depths of the sea. A danger that had destroyed so many who were unwise or unwary. A danger . . . He had an inner glimpse of a gray-beak struggling against something he could not see, then of a pale body curled tight in a nest of wavering white arms.

What did it mean? And if this was the voice of the deep

danger from Pehoshi's song, why did *he* hear it? He was no hybrid sea-child, touched with strangeness.

Was he? He shook his head again, sharply this time, and glanced helplessly at his father.

"Yes, it's dangerous. But we'll leave it behind. We're leaving it now. Here—do this. Does this help?" Rudin rasped his nails roughly against the flesh of Keiris' arm, creating a gash of white. "Grit your teeth. Count. Count aloud and backward. Put up every barrier you can. I should have warned you. I didn't guess—"

He should have warned him, he hadn't guessed—what? That somehow, by letting his father and Pehoshi into his mind, he had let in something else too? Something with a keening voice, something that summoned . . .

Perhaps there were reasons he had never listened for the sea before, or for his mother's voice. Perhaps there were reasons, and he had heeded them without ever guessing what they were.

But where did the keening voice summon him to? He closed his eyes and briefly let the streaking pain possess him. He had his answer almost immediately. The voice called him down.

So simple.

He didn't even have to think about it. He only had to go. Down.

How could he not go where the voice called him?

His father was still holding his arm, scratching roughly at the flesh, but the pain was nothing. The nerveways that should have reported it were already fully freighted. Gulping a deep breath, Keiris pulled free. "I can do it," he said. Then, before his father could guess his intention, he leaned to one side and slid from Soshi's back into the water.

Down.

For a moment, as the water closed over him, he doubted. *The hiscapei was calling him, but what was the hiscapei? What form did it take? What was its nature? What did it want with him?* But this was not the time for questions, particularly questions that had no answers. The keening voice was a pain in his head, a driving, piercing agony. It totally possessed him. He kicked as he had mysteriously learned to do and arrowed swiftly from the sun-shot water of the surface toward the darker water below.

Large, slow fish passed him, bumping him with inquisitive

noses. Weeds and grass caught at him. Something rippled through the water, some elongated creature with shimmering spines. Keiris carefully avoided it. The hiscapei was down here somewhere, perhaps hidden in the sand at the sea's bottom, perhaps secreted among boulders and grass, perhaps . . .

But, disconcertingly, time had begun to telescope. Although it seemed he had been in the water for only moments, he had already plunged into the deep cold of shadow. And a moment later he had already taken his first unthinking breath of water.

When he realized what he had done, he was briefly frightened. But the salt water went down easily, filling his lungs as smoothly as if it were air. It didn't burn at all. Bemused, he wondered why he had never guessed before that he could breathe water.

Perhaps it was like swimming: something he had known once and forgotten.

He hung briefly in the water, drawing a second wet breath, a third, wondering what other things he had forgotten, what wonderful, mysterious things. But there was no time for that now. The hiscapei called him. Called . . .

From where?

Suddenly—did it really happen so abruptly or had time telescoped again, folding mysteriously down into itself?— something had changed. He couldn't see.

Briefly he panicked. But only briefly. The water was dark. Why did he expect to see?

He couldn't move, either.

He was slower to recognize that. He kicked, or so it seemed. He beat with hands and feet. But he did not move. He simply hung there, muffled in darkness and silence, as if the water had turned to glass, encapsulating him.

Then he saw the pale shape before him, and exhaustion, the heaviness of water in his lungs, the cold that bore him down—all those were nothing, because there was something in the water before him, something that beckoned with white arms. Something that keened for him.

Eagerly he reached to touch it, but his groping hands passed through empty water.

For a moment he was baffled. For a moment after that he was impatient. It was not as near as it seemed, the pale thing, that calling thing. But he must reach it. Impotently Keiris kicked against the glassy water, struggling uselessly to drive himself forward, to touch fingertips with the wavering shape he saw so dimly. Because he knew from the anguish that raced along his nerveways that the pale wraith must have him.

Must have him for—

Must have him because—

Must have him to—

He didn't know. Frowning, he extended his hand again. Again it met nothing.

Then he recoiled. There was another white shape in the water before him—his father's face. There were other white arms—his father's. They grappled with him, caught him. Before he could react, before he could resist, he felt himself being tugged upward.

Alarm shrieked through his useless limbs. His father was tearing him away from the beckoning wraith. He was tearing him from its very arms, *and it cried for him*. Keiris tried to pull away from his father, he tried to escape, but the water had leached away his strength. His struggle was no more than a series of weak convulsions that sent him reeling quickly into darkness.

Darkness with pain.

Darkness with a crying voice.

Darkness that summoned, reaching white tendril-arms for him.

Then, after a while, the voice was gone and he became marginally aware of other things. He heard his father's voice and Nirini's. He felt their hands upon him. He felt air against his wet limbs and resilient flesh beneath him. An extended spasm of coughing and vomiting shook him, leaving his mouth sour and his throat raw. A long, ragged breath rasped in his chest, the first air he had drawn since he had plunged under the water.

Then there were other things.

Movement.

The passage of time.

The faint warmth of waning sunlight.

The cold of night.

Pain: in his chest, in his throat, behind his eyes.

And finally land, not beneath his own feet but beneath his father's, as Evin carried him ashore.

Evin and Talani placed him upon a springy mattress of dried grasses and covered him with blankets so heavy that he could not throw them off. He tried to roll away. He tried to protest. He could not. In fact, he could not even open his eyes to see who sat beside him through the next hours as he struggled between fevered wakefulness and sleep.

His dreams were troubled and dark.

Then it was dawn, and he shivered awake and stared up into Talani's face. She gazed down at the sand, her small features heavy with grief. Weakly Keiris slipped one hand from beneath the blankets and touched her bare arm.

She started, gazing at him with flaring eyes. For a moment she looked only frightened.

"Talani . . ." he said weakly. He didn't want her to be frightened or grieving. He wanted her to smile, to laugh, to speak happily to him and dispel the cold, the dark he had carried back with him from the bottom of the sea. "Nirini . . . Talani . . ."

She spoke a tentative question in her own language, her eyes momentarily searching his. Then she jumped up and scampered away.

Dizzily Keiris sat and looked after her—and was suddenly awash with a strange, wrenching sadness. He frowned, caught off-guard by the strength of the sensation, by its poignancy. Tears stung his eyes and thickened in his throat. Because Talani had left him? Because she had jumped up and run away? Or was the cloying sense of loss something he had brought back from the deep water, just as he had brought euphoria from the sea pools a few nights before?

It almost seemed so.

Strangely he thought of the stone rermadken he had seen at Black Point. There had been melancholy there, in those carefully carved features. He had taken it for something the artist felt, either for his subject or for the inadequacy of his own work. What if it was something the rermadken had felt instead? What if it was something that reached for them from the depths when the moons met and the hiscapei keened? What if it was a burden they carried back each time they descended to still the hiscapei? What if . . .

But what did he know of that? Of the rermadken, of the hiscapei, of what happened between them in the depths when the moons met? *The dark water, the floating white limbs, the delicate organs that must be parted so carefully if the crying voice was to be stilled. And then the shivering body curled within the nest of cilia, hungry suckers and filaments closing around it.*

He shuddered, terrified of the images that came bubbling unbidden to mind. He did not understand them; he did not want them. They made him sick and afraid. Clumsily he threw off the blankets and pushed himself to his feet. Dizzily he swayed, for a moment not even certain he could support himself. But he must move. He must walk, run, swim. He must erect a screen of activity between himself and the memory of those white arms, because if he did not . . .

What? Would the sadness he felt now drown him? Would the hiscapei call him back to the sea? For what unguessable purpose?

Would he go?

He paused and gazed distractedly over the water, then started at a touch on his shoulder.

"You're awake. How do you feel?"

Keiris turned and immediately flinched from the narrow-eyed keenness of his father's gaze. "Tell me—tell me what's happened," he said. The demand was abrupt, almost brusque.

His father's brows drew tightly together. "Don't you know?"

"I—know. It was—Nirini calls it a hiscapei. In Pehoshi's song it's the deep danger. I heard its voice. But I don't understand. I don't understand why it called me. I don't understand what it wants. I don't understand what it *is*." He had taken images and impressions from Pehoshi's song, but they frightened him, so he was afraid to examine them directly. If his father would interpose words between him and those images, dry words, fleshless words . . .

Keiris shivered, suddenly remembering what he had felt when he emerged from the sea pool, the sense of pinpoint brightnesses scattered throughout his mind. There must be pinpoints of darkness scattered there, too, now, where they had never been before. And he would only discover them by stepping into the place where they cast their shadow.

His father raised his shoulders in a terse shrug. "What is the hiscapei? It's a form of life that roots itself in the deepest furrows of the ocean floor. The densest beds are within the fire zone. Occasionally an isolated individual roots this far south. What did it want? This is budding season. The parent requires prey to feed the new buds. It sensed our presence— and it called."

"It wanted—it wanted me? To feed itself?"

"Just as it's wanted so many of our kind and so many mams. And so many other kinds as well."

"But if I hadn't gone to the sea pools with you . . ."

"Then perhaps you wouldn't have heard it," Evin agreed. "Certainly you wouldn't have heard so keenly. You would have felt little more than Nirini felt. Little more than the mams felt."

Keiris frowned, remembering the way Soshi had shuddered beneath him when he had first become aware of the keening voice, remembering the way Nirini had pressed herself to Kasha's back. "But they did hear," Keiris protested.

"They heard, but they experienced only a faint discomfort, an uneasiness. Because the call was faint, Keiris. Faint and distant."

Keiris touched his lips with the tip of his tongue, aware that his father was not saying everything. Aware that he was waiting for some response before going on. "Then why did I hear it so clearly if it was so faint? If it came from so far away?"

His father shrugged again. "When you came to me, you didn't hear at all. But the potential was there and I took you to the sea pools and awakened it—and, having done that, I can see that it was a far greater potential than either of us guessed. The blood is in you. I knew that from the beginning, of course. Now I know it's stronger in you than I first guessed."

"The blood?"

"Keir, I am a spanner. You know that. Just as the larger mams—the whites, the great grays—hear far more keenly than the smaller mams, so a spanner hears far more keenly than other tribal folk. It's a matter of the blood. Almost all of us in the tribes have some touch of it. The Adenyo carry it, too, no matter how little most of them are aware of it. The fact that you heard as you did, and after your first submersion—"

But panic had come boiling into Keiris' throat. He shook his head, not wanting to hear what his father had to say next. Not wanting to know why his father was a spanner. Not wanting to know what blood it was that had made him that way, what blood had given his father his song and his gift for hearing. Because he carried that blood too. That was what his father was trying to tell him. He carried it, more of it than his father had guessed. And that blood . . .

Then, in the sea, the discovery of a great strangeness.

A strangeness that was almost human in form.

A strangeness that mingled with the people and then parted from them, leaving behind a hybrid folk who carried bits of strangeness in themselves.

Keiris did not want to hear of that now. Strangeness surrounded him already, in the world, in the sea. He was not ready to meet it in himself as well. The prospect charged him with panic.

And how much could it mean, anyway, that he heard so well when he had no voice? He turned and stared out over the water, his body rigid. "I don't know where we are," he said, anxious to speak of anything but a spanner's gifts and their origin. He had not seen what direction they took during the night. He only knew that they stood upon a tiny islet, a black peak sparsely grown with trees, ringed with coarse gray sand. Someone had erected a single hut beyond the tideline. He could see a few rudimentary utensils and supplies stacked within its thatched walls.

"This is Tira dal Tey."

"And the gather—"

"For that we must go on to Misa Hon, another day's travel east of here."

"And the gather begins—"

"Most of the pods of our tribe are there now. If you feel well enough to travel today . . ."

"I feel well enough," Keiris said bleakly. *A strangeness . . .*

. . . almost human in form.

What had his mother said? That she was afraid sometimes that the sea would take her humanity. That it would turn her to something else, some creature from the island tales. Keiris pressed trembling fingers to his temples. He had been afraid once that the land might shift and become water beneath his feet. Now worse had happened. The land had not changed; he had.

Keiris shivered spasmodically, then realized that both his father and Nirini—no, she was Talani upon the land—were watching him silently. He frowned, hesitating. "My sister—has she already reached the gather?" Did his father know?

"Ramiri will reach Misa Hon tonight. As we will if we go now."

"Then we must go." No matter how little he wanted it now—*a strangeness*—he must meet Ramiri. He could not turn back. And what use was delay?

He rode Soshi hard that day. He drove his knees into her flanks. He nudged and urged her, and when that did not satisfy him, he slid into the water and swam instead. His strokes were hard. He punished the water with them, and he punished himself. Then, when he ached too much to swim more, he pulled himself to Soshi's back and rode again.

Mercifully the sun burned swiftly across the sky. Mercifully Nirini did not laugh or try to play, and his father did not speak, although he watched Keiris closely, frowning. Mercifully Soshi did not rebel at the treatment he gave her.

Mercifully each small island they passed lay quiescent in the sea. There was no smoke. There was no lava. There was no tidal wave sweeping out over the sea.

There was bitterness, but that was in him. He had gone to the sea pools to learn of his sister's world. Instead he had sacrificed the sureness, the solidity of his own. The sea-grasses had breathed their mystic breath into him, and he had learned things he did not want to know.

A strangeness almost human in form . . .

There was a hardness to the sun's light that afternoon. It blazed like hot metal at sunset, throwing molten colors upon the water. Keiris, Rudin, and Nirini rode among those sullen colors, and Keiris felt their weight upon every surface of his body.

Then the sun sank and the moons slowly rose, their two orbs joined, silver upon silver, Systris peering from behind the slighter Vukirid. It was very near full drowntide now. At Hyosis the boat master would have ordered the fishing vessels carried up the sea path beyond reach of the crashing water. At Kasoldys the land must be drowning; water must run in palace corridors. In the spits every bone of the serpent's neck was surely submerged.

Yet here the sea appeared no different.

But, glancing around, he saw a difference in Nirini, in Rudin, in the mams. During the last hours of day the sun had cast harsh light upon them. They had seemed driven and strained. Now silver touched them. Soshi and Kasha grinned agreeably as they swam, and Pehoshi moved with giant dignity. Unwillingly Keiris felt the deep drone of the big mam's song in his joints. Mingled with it was his father's song, full of fleeting images and impressions. Worse, moonlight cast soft shadows upon Nirini's face, and the woman laughed from her eyes each time she glanced at Keiris.

Afterward Keiris could not remember which he became aware of first: the torches of Misa Hon or the third silent voice that joined Rudin's and Pehoshi's. Perhaps the two things came at once.

In any case, at some point a hundred blazes appeared on the horizon—and Keiris clutched tight at Soshi's fin as a sweetly piercing voice found its way into his mind. It sang a woman's song, or a girl's. He could not be certain which, but surely it was not a man's. It sang in silver syllables; yet there was something dark, too, as if shadows were near. The song carried images and impressions, but those were faint, fleeting. The emotion it carried was clearer: anticipation and doubt; hesitance; then, deeper, something else he could put no name to.

He glanced up to see his father sliding down Pehoshi's flank into the sea. A moment later Rudin surfaced beside him. Keiris touched dry lips with his tongue. "My sister," he said. No one had to tell him that the voice that had joined his father's and Pehoshi's was Ramiri's.

"Your sister. Do you want to swim with me to meet her?"

Keiris drew a hesitating breath, remembering his sister as he had glimpsed her through Rudin's song a few nights ago: a shadowy silhouette, slight limbs, coiling hair. *Strangeness* . . . His heart began to pound heavily at his ribs, as if he faced a test. Perhaps he was wrong in what he feared; perhaps he had put all the small clues together incorrectly. "I must," he said, not to his father but to himself. He must meet Ramiri, no matter how he wished now that he had never come searching for her. No matter how he wished he had never heard of her birth, of her existence. No matter how he feared to see her face. "A frail child; there were anomalies," his mother had said. "Your sister . . ." his father had twice said, then had stared at the water, saying nothing more.

Perhaps he was wrong.

"Then come," Rudin said.

Keiris knew from the very quietness of the words that Rudin saw his reluctance. He clung for a moment longer to Soshi's back. Then he released a sighing breath and dismounted.

The water was warm tonight. The torches that burned on Misa Hon grew brighter, then were quenched as Keiris followed his father beneath the water's bright surface.

They quickly found Ramiri there, sea snakes guarding her in numbers. Their whip-thin bodies coiled restlessly through the silvered water. Their eyes were red and coldly burning. Ramiri hovered at the center of their twining mass, a slight figure, her hair floating in loose ringlets. Her brow was broad and curving, her eyes wide-spaced and large, like drops of darkness in the paleness of her face. Her nose was shallow, with tiny, perfectly round nostrils. Her lips did not describe an arc but a slightly flattened circle.

She hung in the water there, just beneath the surface, singing no longer. Her gaze moved hesitantly from her father to Keiris. Keiris saw immediately that she was uncertain of him, of his response to her. He saw that she expected him to show surprise—or something stronger. But he was not surprised. She was as he had guessed—as he had guessed so reluctantly that afternoon, once he had begun to understand the things he had learned in the sea pool.

Once he had begun to understand so many unwelcome things.

Why there had been such a powerful gift of hearing waiting to be awakened in him, when he had never guessed before that it existed. Why he had heard the hiscapei so clearly when his father said its voice was distant and faint. Why his father had left Hyosis, disregarding Amelyor's claim to her daughter, and taken Ramiri to grow up in the sea. What blood had been instilled into them all—him, his father, Ramiri—bringing its own watery strangeness.

Now he understood something more: the sense he had had, a few moments before, that he faced a test. He gazed at Ramiri hanging before him in the water, wary of his response, and realized that the test was to greet her without recoiling.

Slowly, deliberately, he released the last of his breath. Silver bubbles flowed upward. Then he kicked himself forward and took the hand his sister hesitantly extended. It was cold to his touch, as cold as the water of the sea—as cold as the water he had thought warm just a few minutes before. He took it, anyway, and held it as sea snakes coiled around them both, their phosphorescent eyes staining the water ruby.

TWELVE

Keiris was glad for the confusion they met on Misa Hon. He was glad for the people who came laughing into the water to greet them. He was glad for the splashing and the hilarity, for the flurrying torches, for the confusion of voices and limbs. Those things made it easier for him to hide what he felt each time he glanced at Ramiri.

Fear of the strangeness she wore like a mantle.

Revulsion at the coiling of snakes upon her shoulders.

Dread of the moment when they must be alone together, when he must try to behave as if he felt the same things for her that he might have felt for any sister.

Affection.

Pride.

Pleasure in her company.

The people of his father's pod converged upon them as they emerged from the water and drew them up the beach to the feasting tables. Men, women, and children, they laughed and talked, half dancing with pleasure. Torches crackled sharply in the breeze, and the smell of the cook fires was tantalizing. When Keiris, Talani, and Evin were seated, children brought baskets of fresh spring water and bathed the salt water from their hair. Then the food came, passed by girls Talani's age. Bright-eyed, teasing, they pressed morsels upon Keiris, and Talani placed her thigh firmly against his and laid a possessive hand upon his knee. Quickly the older people of the pod joined them at the table, talking, laughing, their eyes as bright as the children's.

Everywhere on the beach there were gatherings just like

this one, people gathered around low tables on the sand, feasting and laughing.

But Keiris was little aware of those things. He was little aware of anything but Ramiri sitting at his father's other hand. She did not sit as Evin did, as the other people of the pod did, squarely upon the sand, knees flexed and ankles crossed. Instead she knelt, her head slightly bowed, her hands clasped upon her knees. She had left all but two of her snakes in the water. Those two coiled lightly around her arms and shoulders, ruby eyes peering from the ringlets of her hair. Their speckled hides gleamed by firelight. Their faces were tapered, ending in blunt nostrils, their eyes unwinking.

Keiris was so aware of Ramiri that everything else seemed distant: people, torches, sea. He tried not to bend forward, tried not to glance past his father at her. But he could not help himself. Nor could he help the coldness that touched him when she glanced in his direction at the same moment and he met her eyes, those deep drops of darkness that sat so heavily in her slight face.

A strangeness . . .

A strangeness who had been born at the same hour that he had and to the same parents, in the same chamber of his mother's palace.

His sister, his twin. He drew back, shivering.

And his father hadn't even told him Ramiri was a rermadken. His father had said nothing, although it had seemed once that he might.

It had seemed that he might, but he had stopped himself.

Keiris was so distracted by Ramiri's presence that he was slow to notice several things.

He was slow to notice that the mood of celebration did not touch his father. Evin talked and laughed, he ate and drank, but his eyes remained dark and unsmiling. Occasionally, when he glanced at Ramiri, his face was openly troubled.

By what? Keiris could not guess. But after a while he noticed that it was the same with all the people of his father's pod. They joked with Talani, they laughed with his father, they smiled wordless welcomes at him—but they spoke to Ramiri with careful reserve, their faces telling nothing. Even Talani's face became briefly guarded when she glanced in Ramiri's direction.

Did they all feel as he did? Was no one any more at ease with Ramiri, with her strangeness, than he was?

One thing was clear: The silver of the moons still lay upon them, but it no longer brightened his father, any more than it brightened him.

Still they sat until the food was eaten and the songs sung and all the long, laughing good nights made. Then Evin stood. "We have a small shelter on the hillside. There is room for the four of us." He spoke briefly to Talani. Her gaze flickered brightly to Keiris, and she nodded and jumped up to follow Evin as he led the way through the dissipating group.

The shelter was little more than a roof and three thatched walls set high on the steep, tree-grown hillside. There were wrapped bundles strung from the roof supports but no other furnishings except for the sleeping pads piled in one corner. Keiris helped his father spread those on the floor and stretched out, expecting to lie awake for a while, thinking of all the things that had happened.

He slept immediately.

He slept immediately, but his dreams came like a rising tide. Lost lands, drowned palaces, schools of bright-hued sea creatures, each different from the others . . . He had so much to dream of now. He no longer had only his own experiences, his own memories. He had everything he had taken from Pehoshi's song as well. He had all time to dream of.

It seemed, that night, that he did. It seemed that the night stretched across tens of centuries, that people and mams, so strange he hardly recognized their breed, lived and died while he slept. It seemed that seas dwindled, that skies fumed and changed their color, that worlds ended. And he was at the center of the entire long drama. He was at its heart, living it.

Then it was morning and Ramiri knelt beside him, a diffident hand on his shoulder. "My brother," she said hesitantly, her voice wispy and uncertain. "My brother, will you wake now?"

Keiris sucked a startled breath and came sharply awake. He sat, surprised at the airy insubstantiality of her voice—just as surprised to realize, in his waking confusion, that he had not heard her speak before. She had knelt silently at Evin's side the previous night, saying nothing, only nodding when addressed. "You speak Adenyo," he said.

"Yes, I have your words. I asked Father for them when I was young, and he gave them to me. Will you come with me

for the morning feeding? It is time.'' The snakes coiled
restlessly about her shoulders and neck.

''You're hungry?'' The invitation was hesitant, yet there
was something needful behind it, something that told him she
would be hurt if he refused. Glancing around uneasily, he
saw that Evin had already removed his sleeping pad to the
corner and gone. Talani lay curled on her side, her eyes half
lidded, watching Ramiri without expression.

''We are hungry. Will you come?'' Ramiri repeated. A
flat, tapered head appeared from her hair and peered at Keiris
unwinkingly, as if it waited for his reply.

Keiris met the cold ruby eyes and shuddered involuntarily.
''Do they—do your companions have names?''

Ramiri frowned faintly at the question. ''What would I call
them? They are a help to my voice. But there are so many of
them. How could I give them all names?''

Keiris nodded, searching for some other question to buy
himself a few seconds more. ''And your name, Ramiri—is
that your sea-name or your land-name?''

''I have only the one name,'' she said, looking at him more
closely, as if she found his questions, or his need to ask them,
puzzling. Then she stroked the two snakes, quelling their
restless coiling. ''Will you come?''

Keiris stared down at his mattress. How could he refuse?
''Of course.'' Reluctantly he stood and pulled on his clothes,
glancing at Talani. She lay curled on her side, watching
Ramiri covertly, without expression. She made no offer,
certainly no demand, to join them. Puzzled, Keiris followed
Ramiri from the shelter.

It was early morning; the air was cool and the colors of
dawn were still in the sky, palely tinting it. There were few
people on the steep path. Those who passed, nodded to
Ramiri and quickly averted their eyes. She in turn walked
silently, not speaking again until she and Keiris approached
the water.

The sea was still today, rolling quietly against the sand.
As Ramiri stepped into the water Keiris looked back in
confusion at the tables farther up the beach. There were
people there serving themselves from trays of food. But
Ramiri did not turn in that direction. She continued toward
the water. Keiris hesitated. Was she reluctant to eat with the
others? Or did she like to swim before she ate?

She turned, studying him questioningly, then said with lowered eyes, "Will you come, brother?"

"Of course. I'll come," he said quickly. Perhaps she simply didn't like what the tide folk ate.

Nodding, she walked until the water reached her chin, saying nothing more. Her hair spread behind her and the two snakes slipped away into the quiet waves. Finally she submerged, disappearing quickly under the moving water. Keiris hesitated, then ducked under the water and kicked himself down.

He propelled himself just as quickly back to the surface, a half-suppressed cry in his throat. The water was teeming with sea snakes. They coiled and they glided, their lidless red eyes cold with light.

Ramiri surfaced a moment later, water spilling from her hair. She looked at him in confusion. 'Won't you come?"

Keiris bobbed in the water, quiveringly aware of the swarming of snakes just beneath the surface. "Where—where are we going?"

"To feed. There are brekkie and popon not so far."

He touched his lips with a cold tongue. "I don't know what those are." He had never heard of brekkie and popon—and now that he thought of it, he didn't know who was to eat them. He and Ramiri? Or the snakes?

And had she no idea at all how he felt about the snakes? She seemed not to; she seemed to find his panic confusing.

Ramiri's frown deepened. "I don't know any other names for them. Do you not want to be with me?"

"Of course I want to be with you," he said, embarrassed that she saw his reluctance. Surely even the emphasis he put on the declaration told her something—that it was false.

She hesitated, obviously torn between wanting his company and recognizing that he gave it reluctantly. Then, wordlessly, she dipped beneath the surface again.

Forcing himself, Keiris swam after her, swam after Ramiri and the swarming snakes. He was fastidiously aware of the surface of his skin as he swam, ready to flinch from the lightest touch. After a while he was also aware, uncomfortably, that Ramiri did not surface for breath nearly so often as he did. Challenged, he tried to match her, ducking under the water at the same moment she did, trying not to come up for breath until she came up. But he always surfaced first, gasping, his lungs bursting, while Ramiri did not even seem to notice that there was a contest.

If she sang this morning, he did not hear it. Nor did he recognize that the suspended motes of light that soon appeared in the water were living things until the snakes struck. They seemed to be nothing more than particles of brightness, vividly yellow, fiercely orange, electric blue, a floating enchantment. He hung as quietly as he could in the water, watching the permutation of colors as they first intermingled, then separated into distinct bands again.

Ramiri watched too. But she did not watch with fascination. Instead, he saw, she watched with satisfaction. "They are plenty today, are they not?" she said when she looked up and met his questioning gaze.

And then the snakes struck. They whipped among the slowly changing bands of color and the bright motes scattered in rainbow panic. Only then did Keiris recognize that each mote was an infinitesimal sea creature, brilliantly colored. He kicked himself to the surface, a sour taste rising in his throat, as the snakes swarmed in rapacious hunger.

Shivering, helpless, he floated at the surface, watching the hunt. The brilliant pinpoints scattered through the clear water, snakes darting and striking after them. Ramiri swam swooping circles around the fleeing sea creatures, driving them back toward the feeding snakes.

Keiris hovered near the surface of the water, cold in morning sunlight, until the snakes glided away, sated, and Ramiri bobbed up near him. She glanced around, blinking against the sunlight, then swam toward him. "They are fed."

Hiding his revulsion as well as he could, he asked, "Did you eat too?" Did she feed like the snakes, gorging herself on frightened pinpoints of life?

But weren't the fish the crews brought ashore frightened, too, when the nets fell around them? And hadn't Nandyris told him how brightly their scales glistened when they were first netted and how quickly the luster faded?

Ramiri seemed momentarily troubled by the question. She cocked her head, as if listening for something he had not said aloud. "Do you eat these things?"

"No!"

She seemed briefly disconcerted by the force of his answer. Then she shrugged in self-effacement. "Nor do I. They are much too small, and I don't like live food when I've just

awakened. But I know a quiet sea pool. It is at the far side of
Misa Hon, beyond the gathering place. There are sweet bulbs
in the water. And other things good. Perhaps you would like
to eat there.''

So at least she did not devour living things raw from the
sea. Not in the morning. "Yes," he said. "I'll come."

She disappeared beneath the water without another word,
and they swam back toward Misa Hon, angling so that their
course carried them beyond the beaches where people stirred.
The sun rose in a cloudless sky. Ramiri led Keiris to a quiet
rim of seawater that rose just beyond a narrow beach. The
towering bulk of Misa Hon's dominant peak was nearer here,
an overshadowing presence. Keiris slipped into the pool after
Ramiri cautiously, half expecting grasses to reach for him.
But when he dipped beneath the surface, he saw only a few
pale fish and a scattering of underwater vegetation.

With gestures Ramiri showed him how to harvest the sweet
bulbs that lay beneath the dark sand, only a few inconspicu-
ous fronds marking their place. She showed him how to find
and break free the tiny nutlike nodes that clustered near the
roots of the coarser vegetation. Then, together, they sat on
the black sand and ate, Keiris gingerly at first, Ramiri with
concentration. Twice she slipped back into the water to bring
up fresh bulbs and nodes.

When the meal was done, Ramiri knelt silently on the dark
sand, her two snakes coiled torpidly around her, their speckled skins gleaming. Reluctantly Keiris glanced at the finely
grained flesh of her arm, at the curling delicacy of her
fingers. If he studied those carefully enough, he could almost
forget the prominence of her brow, the shape her mouth took,
the way her eyes sat like drops of darkness in her slight face.

He could almost forget.

When he did not speak, Ramiri said softly, "I never believed that I would know you, brother.''

Keiris frowned at what he heard in her voice, realizing
with sinking heart that she had not brought him here to eat or
to swim with her. She had brought him here because she
wanted to talk with him, perhaps even because she wanted
to forge some bond with him. Hadn't he wanted the same
thing at first, after all, before they had met? Hadn't he
hoped that she would be a sister to him like Nandyris had
been? A companion, someone he could talk to and laugh with.
He drew up his knees and wrapped protective arms around

them, wishing he had not come. Knowing he could not just
get up and leave, however much he wanted. "You—you've
known about me? Always?"

"I've known since I was young that I had a brother who
lived among the Adenyo. Father told me that. And I saw the
palace where you lived once, from the sea."

Keiris shivered involuntarily and didn't know why. "You
saw Hyosis?"

She dipped her head in a diffident nod. "I saw it once
when I played with the other sisters of the kind. Once, when
we were happy because the journey had been completed and
only a few had been lost, we traveled in that direction and
swam in the waters of the coast. I saw the pinkness of your
stone home in the distance, and I wondered about you and my
mother."

He nodded, not knowing what to say.

"Especially I wondered about my mother," she said softly.

So softly. And she watched his face so intently as she said
it. "Yes," he said uneasily. "I used to wonder about my
father."

"And now you have seen him. Now you know him."

"I've seen him," Keiris agreed. Perhaps he even knew
him. But he knew that she did not want to hear about his
meeting with their father. For some reason she would not say
so directly, but she wanted to know about Amelyor. She
wanted him to tell her about Amelyor.

And, he realized helplessly, he did not know what to tell
her. Did she know that Evin had spirited her from the palace
so quickly that Amelyor had never guessed her nature? Did
she know that Amelyor had disavowed her, anyway, until
Nandyris' death? That she had forbidden her staff even to
speak of her? That she had sent Keiris to find her only under
the spur of necessity?

Did she know that Amelyor was so frightened of the inhu-
man in herself that if she ever saw Ramiri, that if she ever
looked into the sea-depth of her eyes, if she ever saw the
snakes that coiled so restlessly around her slight body . . .

One of the snakes glided across her shoulder now and
extended its head toward Keiris, eyes unwinking. He stiffened. "Our mother is kept busy with the horns," he said.
"She has little time for other things."

Ramiri gazed down at the dark sand. "Yes, I have been
told it is that way with the women who blow horns. I listened

for her voice that day, but she did not speak out in the few minutes we lingered there. And I have never seen her, and my father talks about her little. I wounded him that way."

"You wounded him?" He frowned, puzzled at her choice of words.

She glanced down at her hands. "He tore himself from her because of me, because he had to take me to the sea. I could not live as a Nethlor child does. None of the sisters of the kind could live that way. We must have the water, and so my father left my mother and took me to it. And now, whenever he sees me, whenever I am near, the wound of his leaving her bleeds a little. That is why he's so quiet with me, I think, although he talks to other people and laughs. I know that if I question him about my mother, it only makes him more unhappy. So I have asked him nothing for many years now. But I have always wondered so many things: how she looks in the morning when she first gazes up at the sun, how her hair hangs upon her shoulders, how much light her eyes hold. And how does she move, how does she walk? What is her scent?" She moved toward him eagerly, forgetting her diffidence. "I have searched our father's song for these things, but he deliberately keeps them from his mind because it hurts him to think of her. If you would let me hear your song . . ."

Keiris' chest closed tight, and a rapid pulse suddenly beat at his temple. "I have no song," he said, the words harsh, rejecting.

"But surely you do," she said, "although it must be faint, because I have listened and I haven't heard it. Will you make it louder for me? You need only—"

"No!" Inexplicably his heart beat a panicked rhythm in his chest as he jumped to his feet. His fists clenched so tightly, the nails bit his palms. "I have no voice. None at all. My sister did, my sister Nandyris. I do not."

Ramiri sank back on her heels, suddenly very still. She studied him so silently, so intently, that the flesh along his spine began to chill. Then she gently disentangled the more somberly speckled of the two snakes and laid it across her bare knees. "I have not much voice either without my—what did you call them? Companions?"

Keiris glanced down involuntarily and met the serpent's flat gaze. "I have none at all," he said, trying to force his voice to calmness. "Among the Adenyo, men seldom do. That's why men seldom use the horns."

"But you are not truly an Adenyo, brother. You are as much from the tides as from the land, and the blood of the old kind is strong in our family. It expresses itself differently in men than in women, but it is with us both. Here, let me show you. Come to the water with me. It is better there." She rose, returning the snake to her shoulder, stroking it.

"What—what are you going to show me?"

'How small my voice is without my companions, yet how well it carries with their help. That is why this is my first year to swim at the forefront when we travel to the winter waters, because my voice has been so slow to grow. Although that— that, I think, is because I have been much afraid. We learn that when we go to live among the sisters. We learn that our voices are much affected by our fears." She moved toward the water, turning back only when she realized that he did not follow. "Won't you come?" she said plaintively, extending one hand.

Every instinct told him to draw back, not to step into the water with her. But there was a familiar melancholy in her eyes, the same melancholy that had touched him in the carvings he had seen at the black palace. And he had not come here to hurt her. Reluctantly he joined her at the water's edge.

They did not swim far, only beyond the mildly curling breakers. There morning sunlight glinted on the calm waters of the sea, but far in the distance Keiris saw a thin streamer of black smoke rising into the sky. An omen? It felt so, and when Ramiri paused, he gazed at her warily.

"You must close your eyes," she said. "Lie on your back and let the water come all around you. And listen very closely to my voice as it is alone, without my companions."

Uneasily Keiris lay back, hanging rigidly in the water, kicking to stay afloat.

"You must lie still," she urged him. "Very still. Please, let your head fall back. Let your body bend where it wants. The water will hold you."

Reluctantly he let her coach him into a receptive posture. Finally he lay as she wanted him, resting effortlessly on the surface of the water, the sun lightly touching his closed lids.

"Now I am sending my companions away. And you will hear."

He listened but he heard nothing. He lay with eyes tightly shut. He disciplined his breath. He sent every thought from his mind. And heard nothing.

Unless that was her voice, that distant indistinctness, like
an echo caught by the wind. Hanging limply against the
water, he let his breath ebb, and slowly the echo became
clearer, became nearer.

It was the voice he had heard the night before, unmistakably, a silvered voice touched with hesitation and doubt. But
today it did not sing piercingly across the sea. Today he had
to reach to hear it.

Today he had to reach to find his way into his sister's song
and into her memory.

*Their father as seen by a child's eyes, Ramiri's, laughing
into the sun yet shadowed by an unspoken sadness. It was a
sadness Keiris had not noticed, yet Ramiri saw it each time
she looked at their father. She saw it and was darkened by it.*

*The people of their father's pod, warm and laughing, seen
by the same child. She wanted to be just as they were, and so
each day when she awoke, she repeated to herself that she
was a child no different from the others. But saying it did not
make it so. She could not fail to see that. When the people of
the pod glanced her way, their gaiety became forced. In the
water and on the land, they watched her covertly, and she
knew that they thought things of her that separated her from
them.*

*The sea where they all lived—gray-beaks dancing across
the moonlit water, large fish flying with gleaming scales, the
swiftly changing moods of the water and the sky it reflected.
And the enchantment of the islands where they stopped to
refresh themselves. Misa Hon, Vessa Ce, Terita, Useno Te,
the few remaining Adenyos—places of legend, all of them.
Places of event.*

*Then one morning when they had stopped upon Boza Ce, a
woman swathed in living snakes, a woman with eyes like
molten darkness in a face made of fragile bones, appeared
from the tide and bent to lead the fear-stricken child away
with her. Ramiri turned and stretched out one hand, wanting
to cry to her father not to let her go. But there were shadows
upon his face, and she knew she must go where the woman led.
It had been ordained long ago by her blood, the blood she
wanted so badly to deny.*

*The anguish she felt as she let herself be led away was
nothing to the shivering despair she felt later when, deep in
the water, she found herself among the sisters of the old kind.
She looked into their eyes, eyes that had seen the depth and*

mystery of the sea, and cried over and over that she was not like them. No, no. She was like her father. She was like the mother she had not seen. She was like the other children of her father's pod, children whose eyes would never see anything but brightness.

Yet she knew that was not true. She had seen her face reflected often enough in still pools. She knew what kind of face it was. It was a face from the old times, a face from the depths.

Then sea snakes came slithering, cold-eyed, through the water. She recoiled when the first rubbed its seamless flesh against the skin of her arm. She recoiled and knew in the same moment that even if she returned to her father's pod, as he had told her she soon enough would, some part of her could never return. Because now that she had come, she must do as she was bid. She must let the snakes coil around her. And in their embrace she would find another Ramiri, a Ramiri who was not of the tide folk at all, one who was of that whispered breed instead, the sisters of the old kind.

The old kind. That was what the coiling snakes awoke in her. She tried to shut out the rising voices of her sisters. She tried to stifle the unfamiliar voice that rose in her own throat. She had kept it still all these years. But there was something in her that could no longer be denied. The snakes closed around her. They touched her and stroked her and glided across her trembling flesh. And they awoke the old kind, the sad women. Instinctively, as the snakes first caressed her, she knew why the sisters were sad.

Because of so many things. Because their kind was dwindling. Because their gatherings were lonely. Because the hiscapei called in anguish and pain and there were so few sisters to soothe so many voices. The tide folk said that the hiscapei called because they were summoning prey. And, indeed, any of the folk and any of the mams who were drawn too near became prey. But the sisters knew there was more. The sisters knew the hiscapei called with all the anguish of a lonely thing that would touch life, of a hungry thing that would be fed, of a parent that would give to its young what it required to survive. And when they answered its call, they stilled it for a time, until the migrating tide folk could safely pass—and then swam away, giving it back to its anguish.

They gave it back to its anguish if they could tear themselves away. If they could not, if their will weakened and they

*could not bear to abandon the thing to its crying loneliness,
or if their bodies faltered and they could not extricate themselves . . .*

But Keiris could listen no more. There were snakes in the
water. He could not see them, but he could feel the silent
slither of their gathering bodies. Ramiri had sent them away,
but now they were returning; the swarm was gathering around
her again. And if they touched him, if they even brushed
against his skin . . .

What? What would be awakened then? Gasping, suddenly
panicked, he thrashed at the water. Salt water swamped him,
rushing into his nostrils, into his open mouth. Losing buoy-
ancy, he sank, tumbling helplessly through the water. His
staring eyes showed him gliding snakes.

"Brother?" Ramiri abandoned her song and caught at him,
buoying him back to the surface. Her face was poignant with
concern.

He pushed her away, thrusting himself from the water,
coughing and choking. "No!" If the snakes that lashed around
her touched him, if *she* touched him, what would happen to
him then? He thrashed away from her, his legs remembering
how to kick now, his arms remembering how to pull against
the water. Gulping, grunting, he swam with the strength of
panic toward the dark sand.

Ramiri called after him. She swam after him. As he scram-
bled from the sea she rose from the tideline, a dozen snakes
draped around her, flexing their coils nervously. He turned
and stared back, and on her face was not confusion, was not
impatience, was not anger. On her face was hurt.

And a quick, terrible understanding.

Seeing it, Keiris was briefly caught, unable to speak, unable to move. He stood there facing her, seeing that she
understood very well what fear drove him from the water: the
fear that if he remained for even a moment longer, he would
become like her. The fear that if he remained, if he let the
snakes brush his skin and coil on his arms, it would happen to
him, as it had happpned to her. He would become something
he didn't even understand.

Who would he become? What? Certainly he would no
longer be himself.

Please! *I didn't want to hurt you*! he cried silently, heart-
torn, wishing just for the moment that he did have a voice
like hers, like his father's. Wishing he could make her under-

stand. He had not come to injure her, not in body, not in spirit. Last night he had guarded his face against showing her that her strangeness frightened him. Frightened him because of what it hinted about his own blood. Today he had guarded his words.

Now only panic had betrayed him.

Quickly, before she could emerge from the water, he turned and ran along the beach, ran back in the direction from which they had come. Ran, hoping she would not follow.

She did not. Only her silent voice followed him. *I know you did not come to hurt me, Brother. I know. And I did not bring you here to frighten you. I only wanted to know you and to know of my mother.* There were tears in the silent syllables.

He halted then, stricken, a hard fist of terror closing tight on his heart. Slowly he turned and looked back. For a moment he was helpless, stunned.

She had answered him. He had called his anguish to her and she had answered. *The gray-beaks had come to him at the docks of Hyosis. The great white had come to him in the sea temple. And now his sister had answered the very words he had addressed to her.*

If the fist of terror did not loosen its grip, his heart would burst.

Terror? No, it was not terror that choked him, that strangled him, that sent him stumbling and gasping up the beach again. It was certainty, a crushing certainty. The strangeness was in him. It permeated him. It infiltrated him. It possessed him. He could not deny it now.

He had called to Ramiri and she had answered him.

THIRTEEN

THERE WAS ONE thing to do. Keiris knew that with aching certainty as he ran up the beach and climbed the hillside path. There was one thing.

He must wall the betraying voice into the darkest corner of his mind. He must barricade it there until it died of slow suffocation. And he must return to Neth. Now.

He must return to his mother's palace in silence and live there that way for the rest of his days. He must return and never go to sea again, body or mind.

He resolved that as he ran along the beach, as he staggered and stumbled up the hillside to his father's shelter and threw himself down on the floor. His breath was harsh. His chest burned. But at least he knew what he must do.

He was crouched there, thinking of the how of it—how to find Soshi, how to plot a course back to Neth—when Talani slipped silently into the shelter, studied him for a moment, then knelt beside him. She touched his arm lightly, murmuring a few words in her own language. She saw his mood, he realized distractedly, and she offered him sympathy.

His father came next. Keiris recognized his step on the path, then on the lightly thatched floor of the shelter. Evin entered and stood with no word, his face shadowed and pale. "So you've decided you must return to Hyosis without your sister," he said finally. The words were distant, carefully dispassionate.

Keiris looked up at him with surprise. "How do you know that?"

"It was the only decision you could make. And I see by

your face that you have made a decision. You have decided that the people of Hyosis are no more ready for Ramiri than you are. And you are not ready at all. Are you?''

"I'm not," Keiris admitted dully. "And certainly they are not." No matter how courteously his mother, her aides, the people of the palace might receive Ramiri if he invited her to visit Hyosis, the strain and the disbelief would be there, and Ramiri would feel them. Certainly he could never take her to the academy for scholars like Harridys to scowl over and to scorn. The Nethlor, the simple people, might accept her. The Adenyo never could, because she was living testimony to the fact that the tide folk and the rermadken were alive still—not just in the sea but in the Adenyo themselves.

Ramiri had been born to an Adenyo mother, after all; born in a palace like any Adenyo child.

The Adenyo were no more ready for that than Keiris was.

"So your journey has come to nothing, at least in that. There is no one to take the dais when Amelyor steps down but yourself."

Keiris' head snapped up sharply. "Myself?"

"Who else do you have to offer?"

A pulse hammered at Keiris' temple, making him suddenly dizzy. "*No*. I have no one to offer." And he was sorry for that. The people of Hyosis deserved to fish the sea in safety. But to think that *he* would take the dais . . .

His father knelt. "You've learned to hear, haven't you? The gift came quickly and strongly. I think that if you reach past your fears, you'll find that you have a voice, too, the voice of a spanner. And you know the sea better than any other person living on Neth."

Keiris stared at his father, reluctantly admitting that what he said was true. There was no one on Neth who had gone where he had gone, who had seen what he had seen. There was no one who knew what he knew.

And he had a voice. Perhaps not a spanner's voice but voice enough.

He had a voice and he had condemned it to die, unused. He touched the shell horn at his neck with trembling fingers. "I have no voice, and I want to go now, back to Neth," he said. "I want to go today."

Slowly his father stood again, looking down at him with a frown that saw far too much. "No. The journey back to Neth is a long one, and the hiscapei are in season. You can't travel alone, and I have no one to send with you."

For the first time Keiris felt the sting of anger. Or was it only fear finding a safer focus? "Then take me back yourself. You're the one who brought me here. I wouldn't have come if you had told me when we first met—if you had told me about Ramiri."

His father raised one brow. "Would you not?"

"I wouldn't have come."

"And if you hadn't come, what word would you have to take back to Hyosis?"

Keiris drew a painful breath. "The same word I have now." That his search had been unsuccessful. That when Amelyor reached full cessation, the crews must go to sea unprotected. They must offer their lives to feed their families or they must disband, even though their hearts died in doing it. Keiris shook his head, feeling the sudden bitterness of tears in his throat.

His father studied him with weighing eyes. "I can't take you back to Neth, Keiris, and I can't send you back, not now. If you want, you can come to the summer feeding grounds with us. You can make the migration. Or you can wait here for me. When I return in the fall, I will travel back to Black Point with you."

"Ramiri—" Keiris said involuntarily. Was it even a choice if Ramiri would travel with them on the journey north? If he must see her each day, if he must constantly guard against hurting her again, as he had today.

Evin turned, frowning at the hillside growth beyond the shelter. "She will make the migration with the sisters of her kind."

"She won't travel with you?"

Evin continued to stare at the hillside. A muscle in his jaw jumped. "The sisters swim ahead of us through the fire zone so that—" He broke off, his face no longer just pale but gray with some unspoken strain.

Keiris was puzzled by the sudden tightening of his lips, by his color. It almost seemed the color of fear. But he wasn't so distracted that he forgot his own misgivings. "I'll wait for you here," he said. If the rermadken traveled with the others, he would not make the journey.

Evin turned back with a pale flash of anger. "There are some things you haven't learned, aren't there?"

"Are you any better?" Keiris demanded, stung. "Is any-one else? I saw how people looked at Ramiri last night. I saw how you looked at her. Everyone was laughing and talking, but they hardly spoke to Ramiri. And she knows how you feel. She knows you would still be with Amelyor if it weren't for her, if she hadn't been—the way she is. She sees that on your face every time you look at her. She—" He stopped, surprised that he had become so passionately his sister's advocate. Embarrassed, too, that he had spoken so impulsively—and said so much.

His father was looking at him hard, fists closed tight. "You speak of things you don't understand. Your sister—"

"She knows she hurt you by being as she is. She knows—"

"No. She doesn't hurt me by being one of the sisters, any more than you hurt me by being an Adenyo from Neth. Not in the way you mean. She's as beautiful to me as Amelyor was, as you are. She is my flesh and I have nothing but love for her, nothing but pride, nothing but concern. What hurts me, what makes me afraid, and surely she knows it if she has thought about it at all . . ."

Keiris held his breath, waiting for him to go on.

But he did not. Evin frowned intently, his jaw drawn tight. "Surely you know it too," he said in a low voice.

"But I don't," Keiris said, confused.

Evin studied him, several things touching his face in suc-cession: anger, pain, regret. "No, perhaps you don't. Perhaps you aren't ready to know," he said. "Perhaps you need never know." He turned and gazed again at the hillside beyond the shelter. When he turned back, he had purged all expression from his face. "Don't think less of yourself," he said crypti-cally. For a moment he took Keiris' hands, pressing them tight. Then he turned and left the shelter.

Keiris stared after him blankly, clutching the shell horn. Perhaps he would never know? Perhaps he need never know?

Know what? And why think less of himself for not know-ing it, whatever it was? His father had gone so abruptly, almost as if he were afraid that if he stayed, he would say something he would regret. But what? Keiris rubbed taut muscles at the base of his neck.

He was marginally aware that Talani had roused herself and run after Evin. He retreated to a corner of the shelter and hunched there, running his father's words through his mind again, reviewing his own responses. He was not satisfied with the things he had said, with the way he had said them.

He was not satisfied with the way he felt, either. He hadn't come so far to feel like a child. He had not walked the neckbones of Neth, he had not plunged into the ocean, he had not followed his father so far, only to feel ignorant and lacking and small-minded.

Slowly he became aware of the quiet of the hillside. There were no people on the paths now. They had gathered on the beach, but the sounds of their celebration did not reach this far. Nor did the sound of the breakers.

It was quiet today, and it would be quiet on Misa Hon for many months to come while he waited for his father to return.

It would be quiet except for the surf against the sand. Except for the breeze in the trees. Except, perhaps, for the occasional grinding motion of the earth.

It would be quiet except for the questions he asked himself every day. And the memories and the regrets. *Ramiri's moon-silver voice the first time he had heard it . . . Her uncertainty, her diffidence when they met . . . And today, her hurt understanding when she stood in the tidewater looking after him . . .*

Suddenly uncomfortable, Keiris jumped up and fled the shelter. He hesitated outside, glancing up the path and down, then picked his way up the rugged hillside. The path was narrow and overgrown. Trees and vines grew profusely, brilliant with blossoms.

The contrast with the darkness of his mood was stark. He had come so far to find Ramiri. And he had not been seeking her just because his mother had sent him. He had come hoping she would fill the place Nandyris had left vacant. He had hoped she would be a companion, a friend, someone to share meals and stories with. And she had wanted the same things of him; she had shown him that.

How could it have hurt to spend a few hours with her? How could it have hurt to ask her to join him on the beach, to sit together where the swarming snakes could not reach them and tell her the things she wanted to know? She wanted to hear his song. Couldn't he have offered words instead? Wouldn't she have taken them for better than nothing?

And really, what harm could it do to sing for her? The voice was there. Could it hurt to use it once—just once?

Could it hurt as long as he did not go into the water when the snakes were near?

What harm could it do to go back to the beach now?

He started at a sound in the vines, then turned as Talani stepped near. She paused, studying him with uncharacteristic hesitance, uncertain of his welcome. Her expression reminded him so painfully of Ramiri's that he held out his hands.

She caught them eagerly, squeezing them, her eyes glinting. "Keiris, I stay with you," she said. She offered the words as a gift, triumphantly.

Keiris laughed despite himself. "Did my father tell you to say that?"

She tilted her head, smiling. "With you," she echoed.

"Evin? Did my father teach you those words?"

"Evin," she agreed.

"Are there others? Do you have others?"

Her smile remained in place, faltering just a little. "Keiris, I stay with you," she said again.

So she had only those four words. Yet how many gifts had she offered him in their short acquaintance? Food, guidance, instruction, companionship . . . "Stay," he said. If only she would be quiet. If only she would not begin to chatter, to tease, to play.

She seemed to understand. She sat quietly for a while, sometimes looking intently into his face, sometimes lying back and gazing up at the sky through the trees. Finally, when he continued to sit somberly, doing nothing, she rose and wandered away.

What harm?

He weighed the question, lying back against the hard ground, eyes closed, one hand curled around Nandyris' shell horn.

What harm?

Deliberately he released a long breath, relaxing tensed muscles, gently releasing all extraneous thoughts.

The rustling of trees and vines, the occasional sounds of the hillside—he released those, too, until he drifted without planning into a twilight state somewhere between sleeping and waking.

The song began so quietly that at first he didn't recognize it as his own. It began with memories and impressions so unfamiliar, he thought they must belong to someone else. Then he recognized them as the memories of infancy, hazy and warm, full of easily satisfied hungers and long, cradled sleeps. Quickly the first days of life slipped past, and his awareness filled with daunting heights and with the fascination of ordinary things that had not yet become ordinary.

Amelyor, Nandyris, Lylis, Pendirys and Pinador . . . After a while he learned what his hands could do, and he reached out for the people who bent over him. Eventually he picked himself up with great effort to follow those he liked best.

He picked himself up, and the years went rapidly after that. He walked, he played, he learned. He ran with Nandyris beside the water. He hid with her in storm-safes on sunny afternoons and ran with her on the plaza when it stormed. He held his breath as she dared one danger and then another. And then one morning, all of childhood had passed, all of early youth was gone, and Nandyris went away and didn't return.

The song ran past more rapidly then. His mother called him to her chambers, and reluctantly he braved the neckbones of Neth for her. He braved the sea. He braved the unknown, and there was Ramiri. And he saw, in the half dream of his song, that she was not as alien as he had thought. She was of the same flesh that he was. She felt the same things he felt: love, pain, fear, hope.

And so the decision was made, not in thought but in song. He would give her what she wanted. He would not wall away his voice to die until Ramiri knew all the things she wanted to know.

How could he do anything else for his sister? Hardly thinking of what he did, he rose from the vines and started down the hillside. He made his way, not toward the beach where his father's people celebrated but toward the quiet beach where he had last seen Ramiri. Talani followed him, strangely quiet, sometimes touching his arm inquiringly, more often simply keeping pace.

She stayed with him.

She stayed, increasingly troubled, but he hardly noticed that. He was thinking of Ramiri, of the things he wanted to share with her.

The beach where he had left her was still when they reached it. The tide had retreated, leaving an expanse of glistening black sand. There were no shells or strands of weed. Nor was there any sign of Ramiri.

But was that so surprising? She had gone. He would have to call her back. Undiscouraged, he sat and hugged his drawn-up legs, pressing his forehead to his knees. He reached out.

He heard his own voice clearly this time, as clearly as if he spoke aloud. It was distinct and distinctive, his own and only his own. And he didn't use it just to call for Ramiri. He used it to send her singing snatches of memory too.

Their mother walking across her chamber floor, her white gown shining against her dark skin, her feet bare on the fur rug.

Their mother at the dais, too caught up in her duties even to notice who walked along the seaside path.

Nandyris running through sparsely flowering spring orchards; she was Ramiri's sister, too, after all.

The cliffs that overlooked the fishing docks, the wind-twisted trees that grew there.

The thin-walled bowls that Kristis set the table with, so delicate that light glowed through them.

The sunrise window of the palace meeting chamber.

He sent her all those things and so many more. He caught them in his mind and sent them, bright and glowing, to Ramiri. He sent her the sounds of the palace, the timbre of Amelyor's voice when she called to her aides, the cries of the shore birds that fished in the surf. He sent his own feelings as well: his love for Kristis and Tracador and Norrid, the awe he felt for Amelyor, his grief when the gray-beaks brought him Nandyris' shell horn.

He sent Ramiri all those things, but she did not come. Nor did he hear any answering voice to tell him that she heard. After a while he raised his head and gazed across the water. Surely if she heard, she understood. And surely if she understood, she could forgive him for the morning.

Perhaps she could not. And perhaps it was not even a matter of forgiving. Perhaps she was simply reluctant to join him and be hurt again.

Slowly he realized that Talani still sat beside him. He glanced at her distractedly, then looked quickly back. Tears coursed down her face, leaving wet tracks. She did not brush them away. But when she realized that he looked at her, she bit her lip and clasped his arm tightly, almost beseechingly. Then she jumped up and ran away, ran as swiftly down the beach as he had run that morning.

He stood, staring after her, not understanding. "Talani— what is it?"

She did not pause or turn back. She ran, stumbling a little, her bare legs flashing.

"Talani!" But it was no use. She did not stop, and she did not answer.

Keiris looked back over the sea, briefly torn. But there was no sign of Ramiri. Confused, anxious, he ran after Talani.

He heard the sounds of celebration long before he reached the feasting tables. The songs were loud and rowdy, accompanied by exuberant cries and the call of shell horns. As he drew near he saw that the tide folk danced as they sang. Long lines of people stamped their way up and down the sandy beach, confronting other long lines. The lines pushed and shoved at each other. When a line was broken, its two parts danced away in opposite directions, still clinging together and laughing. People from lines that had been completely broken darted among them, throwing themselves against the clasped arms of those who still held their lines.

Keiris hesitated, then moved slowly along the beach until he found his father.

Evin sat silently among a small number of his own people under a thatched canopy. The celebration seemed not to touch him. Nor did it touch the people who sat with him. Talani crouched beside him, her head bowed. She looked up with a half-stifled sob as Keiris approached.

"Please," Keiris said when his father glanced up, "what did I do wrong?"

Evin seemed momentarily surprised by the question, as if he had not noticed Talani crying beside him. Rousing himself, he touched her shoulder and stroked her hair, questioning her with a distracted frown. She shook her head, offering apologetic words.

"What is it?" And why was his father so distracted, so pale?

"She says it is not worth speaking of, not now, not when . . ." He frowned, his gaze wandering abstractedly across the beach.

Keiris followed his gaze and saw nothing. Troubled, he knelt near his father. "Please, if she won't tell me what's wrong, what can I do? She said she would stay with me. We went to the beach together, the beach on the far side of the island. Then she cried and ran away."

Evin frowned faintly and questioned Talani again in their own tongue. She only shook her head at first. Finally she began to speak, a long, tearful recitation. She wiped at her eyes with the back of her hand, her mouth quivering.

When she had finished, Evin touched her hair gently. "She says you went to the far beach and sang, and she was nowhere in your song. She was nowhere at all, although she vowed to stay here with you through the entire summer to see that you were well. She vowed that, even though you've never let her pick the third blossom. She is the only one of her friends who has been spurned this way, you see. She is the only one who feels unwanted. And when she tried to make a song of her own to ask if you didn't care about her at all, she couldn't. Her voice is faint, very faint; the old blood expresses itself very little in her. She couldn't make you hear."

Keiris felt his heart plummet. "I—I wasn't listening. I was—I was trying to call Ramiri back. I was trying to tell her I was sorry for something that happened this morning. I wasn't listening for Talani at all."

His father shrugged. "Even if you had been listening, you probably wouldn't have heard. But tomorrow, in the afternoon, the sisters will come with the snakes. Talani will dance with them and handle the snakes. Then, if you want to reassure her, you will listen to her song."

"The snakes?" Keiris said uncomprehendingly.

"We use them as the sisters do, to amplify our voices. Tomorrow people who are mute for the rest of the year will sing with the rest of us for a while, for a few hours. We create a bonding before we undertake the migration that way. The singing makes the gather a gather."

Keiris nodded, half understanding. But his thoughts were too much with Ramiri to dwell long on Talani's problem. "Ramiri—she isn't here? Now? With you?"

"She's with the sisters, in the sea. They have their own gather today. Then tomorrow they come to join our gather."

So that was why Ramiri had not come when he called. She probably had not even heard. "The others, the other sisters—are they just as Ramiri is?"

"They're much like her."

"And they come from parents like you and my mother? They come from the people who have the most rermadken blood?" A hard question; in asking it he admitted that the old strain was in his blood too.

Evin shook his head. "Not always. There are factors that seem to sleep for generations without expressing themselves. Then they all awaken together in a single individual, and that

individual comes to us as if she had descended directly from
the old kind. She has the appearance, she has the capacities—
and ultimately she must assume the responsibilities. As Ramiri
soon must do."

Keiris frowned uneasily. Capacities. Responsibilities. He
knew that Ramiri could remain underwater far longer than he
could. But what other capacities did she have? And what
responsibilities? He glanced away from his father, glanced
toward the point where sky met sea, and felt a stirring of
unease. *The rermadken were sad because of so many things:
because their kind was dwindling, because their gatherings
were lonely, because the hiscapei called in anguish and pain
and there were so few sisters to soothe so many voices.* Was
that what his father meant? That the rermadken swam at the
forefront of the migration so that they could still the hiscapei?

But how did they still them? Frowningly, reluctantly, he
called up a snatch from Pehoshi's song. *The dark water, the
floating white limbs, the delicate organs that must be parted
so carefully if the crying voice was to be stilled. And then the
shivering body curled within the nest of cilia . . .*

Was Ramiri's to be one of those shivering bodies? Must
she give herself to the hiscapei, pretending to be prey, and
then extricate herself somehow, when the tide folk had passed
safely?

Was that one of a rermadken's responsibilities? And if it
was . . .

He shuddered, his own fears suddenly small. He met his
father's eyes and realized how self-concerned he must have
seemed earlier. Realized, too, why his father was tense, why
his father was silent, why his father sat at the center of
celebration and did not smile or laugh. Realized, even, why
his father was quiet in Ramiri's company. Because he had only
to look into the dark drops of her eyes to read the future there,
the terrifying future.

Tomorrow night the migration would begin. And Ramiri
was one of those who must offer herself so the tide folk and
their mams could pass.

The impulse came then, and he spoke immediately, before
it could evaporate. "I'm going with you. On the migration."
He could do nothing to relieve what his father must be feeling
this afternoon. He could do nothing to protect Ramiri. But at
least he could go with them instead of sitting alone on a
deserted island.

A quick bleakness touched Evin's eyes. "Do you want to do that, Keir? Talani will stay here with you. She'll see that the time passes."

"I want to come," Keiris said. What else could he do?

"You need not even come to the beach tomorrow afternoon when the sisters bring the snakes. Talani will show you a place where you can wait on the hillside. Although I do ask one thing of you: that you let her come to you and sing when she is ready. That you give her your full attention for that short time. She's done a lot for you."

Keiris met the bleakness in his father's eyes, confused. His father didn't want him to come to the beach? He didn't want him to see Ramiri again? When earlier . . . "I'll listen. And tomorrow night I'll come," he said. And then, because Talani was watching him with questioning eyes, he said, "Please, will you ask Talani if she will show me again where the bathing place is? And then if she will join the dancing with me?" He had reparations to make.

Evin frowned, then nodded and spoke briefly to Talani.

Talani stood, her head still bowed, looking at Keiris from under her lashes. When he extended his hand, she was slow to take it. But she had not led him far from the beach before uncertainty dropped away and she began to skip and chatter as they climbed the hillside.

The bathing place was in a secluded hollow where vines created shadowing curtains. The water was cold. They splashed each other, and Keiris shivered so violently that they both laughed. And an hour later, when they both wore a single flower tucked behind one ear and Talani lingered pensively over a third blossom, some vagrant impulse made Keiris nod. Talani laughed triumphantly as she plucked the flower.

When they went back down the path, they both wore long strings of blossoms. The scent of them was dizzying. Touching soft petals, Keiris listened to the singing and laughing from below and decided impulsively that tomorrow was soon enough to wonder if he would regret his decision to go with his father, to wonder if he could meet the challenge of the migration, to wonder why he had let Talani string flowers for him when he must leave the tide folk at the end of summer. Tonight there were games and dancing and tables laden with food. Tonight he would be as young as Talani and as little troubled.

FOURTEEN

No ONE WAS as untroubled as Keiris wanted to be. He learned that as afternoon became first evening, then night. In the afternoon the people laughed and played. But the dusk, when it came, rolled in like a shadow from the sea, foggy and chill. Then the tide folk began to eat too hungrily, to drink too deeply. Their laughter became labored, their games bruising. Earlier, children had passed fruit juice in large pitchers. Keiris could not identify what the pitchers contained now except that it was stinging and bitter and it made him choke. Yet each time he emptied his cup, someone filled it and he drank again. He didn't know why he drank except that he felt the same chill everyone felt.

Later he was not certain when he began to stumble and to speak thickly in Adenyo to people who could not understand a word he said. It didn't seem so remarkable at the time since people were moving unsteadily all around him. Many of them spoke just as thickly as he did, pounding him heavily on the back, embracing him—and filling his cup again.

Nor was he certain when he finally fell asleep—or where. He knew only that his thoughts grew increasingly disconnected until finally he had a moment's confused impression that he was falling. Then, sometime much later, he awoke in his father's shelter, dizzy and nauseated, his entire body aching.

Stiffly he sat, trying to orient himself.

It was daylight and he was alone. Except for the pad he lay upon, all the bedding was piled in the corner. The blossoms Talani had strung for him the afternoon before were at his neck, wilted and crushed. With unsteady fingers he slipped them over his head and discarded them. Dizzily he stood.

He made his unsteady way out of the shelter, weaker than he had thought. He met no one as he picked his way downhill. His ears buzzed and ached, and a sour taste rose in his throat. Twice he stumbled and fell. Finally he vomited into the undergrowth. When he had done that, he felt better.

He felt better until he reached the bottom of the trail and emerged upon the beach. There he halted, sucking a long, painful breath, trying to control the fresh surge of nausea.

The tide folk sat on the beach in silent ranks. Some were gathered in family groups, others in larger groups. Occasionally entire pods sat together in broad semicircles, a hundred or more people shoulder-to-shoulder and knee-to-knee. There were no bright clothes today. There were no strands of blossoms. There was no laughing, no singing, no celebration. There was no food or drink.

There were only the silent people—and at the tideline, long, carved posts pounded into the sand. Keiris touched his lips with a tongue suddenly dry. Snakes coiled upon the posts in writhing masses, and the sea delivered more with each breaker. They glided in on the whitecapped water, whip-thin bodies lashing nervously, and wrapped themselves upon the carved posts. Occasionally a flattened head appeared from one of the coiling masses and red eyes briefly glowed.

Drawing a long breath, Keiris glanced distractedly at the sun and realized it was midday.

It was midday and the sun's light was bright and hard. Shuddering, trying not to look at the writhing posts, Keiris glanced down the beach. The people who sat on the sand were still, concentrated. Frowning, uneasy, he picked his way toward his father's canopy.

Perhaps a dozen people sat with his father today. Their faces were sallow. Evin sat as the others sat, with legs crossed and head half bowed. Yet he was apart from them. A muscle trembled in his temple; another jumped in his jaw.

"Talani . . ." Keiris said, kneeling tentatively, peering around. She was not among the people under the canopy.

"She is with her own pod today." Evin touched Keiris' knee but did not look at him. He seemed not to look at anything, in fact, although his eyes were narrowed and his pupils were drawn to pinpoints.

"Should I—"

"No, you should sit with me now, if you won't go away and wait for her to come to you afterward."

"I won't." He did not fully understand what was to happen today, but he was decided upon one thing. If he was to join the migration, then he would join everything that preceded it.

"Then sit here with the rest of us and listen. You will hear them very soon."

Keiris shivered with a moment's penetrating cold. "I'll hear—" No matter how resolved he was, apprehension still carried its sting.

His father glanced at him for the first time, distantly. "You'll hear the rermadken coming from their own gather, singing the oldest songs of the sea. We all take our sea-names then, when the eldest sisters cross the tideline. We wear them through the afternoon and evening, until the tide comes at its highest and we begin the migration. This is the only time we take our sea-names when we're upon land." Remote, frowning, he gazed toward the water. "When you were born, I chose a sea-name for you. I never had the chance to bestow it."

Keiris stirred uneasily, disturbed by his father's tone, by his frowning abstraction. "Would you give it to me now?"

"If you want it."

"I want it." More, he wanted his father to think for a few minutes of something besides Ramiri.

"Then tell me how you like it: Lirion, a name from one of our oldest stories."

Keiris frowned, turning the unfamiliar syllables over in his mind. They meant nothing to him. "Will you tell me the story?"

Briefly his father seemed to come back from the distance. He addressed an intent glance at Keiris. "If you want. It was this. Lirion was born to the Soli-niki pod of the Kirltika tribe. He became a man in the days of the first parting of the rermadken and our people. The sisters had mingled with us for nine generations at that time, but when the eldest of them urged a parting, all those in whom the old blood predominated followed her away. No one knows, to this time, why she urged the parting. So Lirion lived in a time of loss and change, when the people were troubled and unsettled. He was more troubled than most because someone he had loved had followed the sisters away. Her name was Damira, and his heart cried for her for seasons afterward. But on this night he went into the water and looked up, and to his surprise he recognized Damira's light in a small, bright star winking overhead. He recognized her light when he thought he had lost her forever. He was so overjoyed that he followed the star as the heavens changed. He followed the star, singing after it, calling to it, telling it all the secrets of his heart. Eventually, when he tired, when he thought he could swim no more, a great white heard his need and came to carry him on his search—his moonsteed. Lirion and Rikahashi are out there still—swimming and searching as the heavens turn. Sometimes, on very bright nights, our people see them. Sometimes, on dark nights, we hear Lirion calling to Damira's star to brighten for him. And sometimes, when the clouds are deep, when no stars shine through at all, we hear him crying.''

Keiris felt a chill move down his spine. ''It isn't a happy story.''

''No. Keiris is your glad name, Lirion your sad one. How can a child grow, after all, if he has two happy names? There must be balance.'' Evin's voice faded, and briefly his attention turned inward again. When he spoke again, it was softly. ''Keiris, it isn't too late for you to go back up the hillside.''

Something in his tone made Keiris chill. ''What do you mean?''

''I mean that if you join the gather, you'll be as I am. Torn between two ways of life. Oh, you'll return to Hyosis. I have no doubt of it. But we'll be in your blood, too, and in your heart and in your mind, from this day forward. You'll never leave us, not entirely. You'll never leave the tribes, any more than I've ever completely left Amelyor and Hyosis.''

The second chill was sharper, colder. ''You can return to Hyosis. You can come back with me.''

''I can go with you when my calling is here? When I'm the only one with voice enough, with stamina enough, to hold the pod together in heavy seas?''

''Nestrin—''

''His voice is waning. He can span for me briefly, when we're running through quiet seas. Otherwise, no.''

''And there's no one else?''

''There are two children, my brother's son and daughter. They're with their mother's tribe now. In five years, in six, they'll be ready for the span. Not before. Otherwise there are only people for quiet seas, like Nestrin. The gifts are stronger in us than in the Adenyo, but they must serve over greater distances, too, and in far heavier seas. I don't just join the members of my own pod together, you see. I talk ahead with pods running to the north, and I convey information back to pods running to the south. Sometimes, when the rermadken are hard-pressed, we join our voices and try to drown out the call of the hiscapei. Although . . .''

Keiris glanced at him tensely, waiting for him to go on.

''Although that serves us very little when the hiscapei are in full season, especially if they've rooted in numbers in channels where we didn't expect to encounter them. It's always harder when they surprise us that way, when we're not prepared.''

Keiris shifted uneasily. ''Why do you migrate when they're in season? Aren't there times when they're quiet?''

His father shrugged. ''They're quiet in the winter, during their dormant period. And during the very hottest days of summer. But the dates of the migration aren't ours to set. We follow the mams. In the summer they must feed in the north, where the waters are far richer than here. They can harvest enough there in just a few months to carry them for many months in less abundant waters. Then, near the end of summer, the calves are born and we all travel south to the warmer waters for winter. That migration is easier because the hiscapei have completed their reproductive cycle by that time. And, of course, by then the maiden rermadken, those serving their first year at the forefront, are more experienced. They're better able to free themselves from the hiscapei after the tribes have passed safely.'' He paused. ''But you know at least some of this, don't you, Keiris?''

Keiris nodded reluctantly, drawing on images from Pehoshi's song. *Fall, when the sun's rays grew weak and the water darkened. Fall, when the growing time ended and the young drifted away on the current to root and to begin calling weakly for their own prey. Fall, when the parent-voices waned toward their winter dormancy.*

His father clasped his arm, interrupting the flow of images. ''Keiris, if you want to wait on the hillside, go now. Immediately.''

The quick pressure of his fingers, the urgency of his voice

startled Keiris. He glanced up and saw that all along the beach, people had begun to shift and stir, looking toward the sea. The snakes writhed on their posts with fresh agitation.

There was a disturbance in the sea. That was Keiris' first impression, that the rushing pattern of the breakers had been disrupted, making the water tumble upon the beach in broken rhythm. Then he saw that there were forms bobbing in the water—women pulling themselves out of the foaming sea. Women walking breast-deep, waist-deep, thigh-deep. Slight women, fragile women, overburdened with wet, coiling hair and eyes full of darkness.

"Now, Keiris. Go now if you intend to go."

Go because the rermadken had come. Keiris caught his lower lip in his teeth. "No," he said, although at that moment he wanted nothing more than to flee the beach, the silently waiting tide folk, the emerging women. "No."

His father's fingers tightened on his arm. "Then stay with us, Lirion."

Lirion, because the first rermadken had emerged from the water and now stood above the tideline. Lirion, because the second had followed her, and the third. Keiris caught his breath, his heart jarring at his ribs.

They were tiny, just as Ramiri was, with delicately made limbs and fragile faces. Some wore their curling hair so long, it covered them to their knees. Others showed the bareness of their flesh. Their sisterhood was clear in the heavy darkness of their eyes, in the curve of their lips, in the depth of their brows. Keiris could not see the human in them. Not today, as they emerged together from the water. It was hidden, submerged—perhaps, today, lost entirely. His glance flicked uneasily from one to another. He did not see Ramiri, and he didn't know if he was relieved or disappointed.

The first women to cross the tideline had hair streaked with silver and features softened by fine lines. Their approach brought a new stillness to the tide folk and a new agitation to the sea snakes. The creatures whipped and lashed on their posts, extending tapered heads, bobbing and swaying and tasting the air with flickering black tongues. For a moment Keiris thought he heard a high whine in the air, and he pressed his fingers to his ears. But the whine persisted.

It only died when the rermadken approached the posts and extended their arms to the serpents. The snakes were upon them immediately, wrapping themselves around necks, torsos, and limbs, a restless, coiling burden.

Keiris heard the song of the rermadken then. He heard it with everyone. It was as if a single silver voice quivered alive, coiling around the waiting people just as the snakes coiled around the rermadken. It was light, it was elastic, it was binding. It caught the awareness and commanded it totally. One moment Keiris sat upon the beach in the midday sunlight, surrounded by the people of his father's pod. The next moment he swam alone in an ancient sea.

He should have gone. He should have waited on the hillside.

He was in the sea of a hundred centuries before, swimming alone among lantern-eyed fish and creatures armored in iridescent plates. He was alone, and the songs of the rermadken rang through him, delicate silver threads that thrilled and anguished at once. Songs of love and pleasure and joy. Songs of terror too. Songs of wrenching losses and chasms where sunlight never reached. Songs as strange, in their way, as the songs Pehoshi had sung him. Songs far more frightening.

Songs of aeons. Songs of forever.

Songs of waxings and wanings, of minglings and separations. Songs of strangeness, inborn and compelling.

He never should have stayed to hear these songs. They spoke things to him he didn't want to hear. They spoke to his blood, that small sea contained by his flesh. They spoke and tides rose and beat against his mind, alien tides that threatened to erode the final certainties of his life.

He never should have stayed.

But he remained through all the sea-songs. He remained, the silver thread binding him, commanding him.

He remained, only shivering back to awareness of his surroundings when the rermadken returned the sea snakes to their posts and knelt in the foam at the water's edge. They hunched there with heads bowed and their clasped hands thrust forward, as if in supplication. For a moment Keiris heard the whining again, high-pitched, almost inaudible. Then it faded. There was only the sound of the sea against the sand.

Somehow it was dusk. And it was cold. Keiris stared blankly around at people who seemed imprisoned by the cold gray twilight. His father touched his arm. "Are you all right?"

"Yes." Although in truth he was too stunned to be certain. He wondered if he looked like the others around him, drained and gray. "What—what happens next?"

"The passing of the snakes."

Keiris' lips turned cold, his tongue dry. "The—passing?"

"The rermadken will carry them among us and let us handle them. You remember what I told you, don't you?"

Keiris shuddered violently. He remembered. The passing of the snakes made the gather a gather. Because with the passing of the snakes, those whose voices could not be heard otherwise would sing for a while. They would sing with the other people of the tribe. And when finally the gather was made, he could never leave. He might return to Neth, he might trudge its bony length to Hyosis, but a part of him would remain with the tide folk. The sea would be in him.

He stared at the snakes where they coiled on the carved posts. "Do you—do you touch them?"

"All of us touch them. They like our warmth. Those who need most to have their voices raised dance with them. They dance along with the rermadken."

So the snakes would be passed, and he would be expected to touch them as everyone did.

Keiris felt the inner trembling first. It was like the cold that caught him at the same moment: reasonless, gripping, total. He drew a quivering breath and stared down at his hands. They were still, still and pale. Like carved stone. That solid. That immobile. But inside he was shuddering so violently, his blood seemed to crash at his eardrums.

His blood seemed to beat against his skin, just as the sea beat the shore. His blood that was only incarnadine seawater, his blood that carried secrets and mysteries in it, rushing them to the separate cells of his body without his consent—until recently without even his knowledge.

How many more secrets would it carry if he stayed for the passing of the snakes? How many more mysteries? How much more like seawater would his blood become?

This was the blood that fed every organ of his body. How could he live again as an Adenyo once the full strength of the sea was awakened in his blood?

There was one answer: He could not.

He was on his feet before he knew it. He was on his feet staring at the writhing serpents, at the flickering torches, at the rermadken prostrated at the tideline. He was aware of his father looking up at him, of the other people of the pod gazing at him in surprise.

"No longer," he said to them all. He could stay no longer. He should not have stayed as long as this.

He turned and fled the shelter. Fled the tide folk. Fled the beach.

Fled himself, as well as he could.

He ran. He ran up the hillside in the dark, picking his way from imperfect memory, stumbling, losing himself, finding his way again. He did not guess his destination until he heard the rush of water.

The bathing place. The rushing stream, the cold fall, the pool itself, secluded in its shadowed dell. He threw himself down, gasping for breath. His heartbeat was a muffled concussion. Laying one hand on his chest, he could feel each separate beat against his palm.

His heart was trapped there, trying to escape.

He was trapped, trying to escape the ancient sea that had risen in him with the rermadkens' song. He hugged himself, teeth chattering, and felt a sudden, desperate hunger for home. His feet ached for the soil of Neth. They ached for the rocky hillside beyond the palace, for the coarse sand of the seaside path, for the jagged cliff's edge where he and Nandyris had played. They ached, too, for polished palace floors, for the fur rug in his mother's chambers, for the fiber carpets he put down in his own chambers in winter. And his body ached for the embrace of people he loved: Kristis, Tracador, Norrid, Tardis. He was hungry for faces he knew, food he knew, places he knew.

He was so hungry, it was a pain. He hugged himself tighter and wondered what he must do. Go with the tide folk as he had said he would? Everything in him rebelled against that. Wait here, then? Wait for fall when his father could guide him back to Neth?

He wanted to do neither. He wanted his home now. He wanted the safety of Neth, the security of the palace, the protection of his own chambers. How could he be anything but himself within the walls of his own chambers? How could he be anyone but the person he had always known himself to be?

But he could not go home now. The sea was wide and he did not know the way.

He sat with his forehead pressed to his knees, hugging himself, until he no longer trembled. Then, exhausted, he raised his head and glanced around. The moons had just crested the horizon. Their silvered edges blazed through the trees. They touched the surface of the pool with light. He gazed down into the water, briefly losing himself in its insubstantial brightness.

He found no answers there. All he found, some timeless period later, was Talani's face. It quivered alive on the surface of the water. For moments Keiris did not react. Then, slowly, he raised his head.

Talani—no, she was Nirini tonight—stood watching him solemnly. She wore snakes upon her shoulders, two of them, their tongues flickering restlessly. "Lirion," she said softly, stepping forward, kneeling beside him.

Involuntarily he recoiled. "My name—my name is Keiris," he said stiffly.

"Lirion, I am Nirini of the pod of Kadiri the spanner. Kadiri is cousin to Rudin, your father, and to me he is distant kin. My mother is Medra, born to the pod of Parsedri, and my father is Nicolo of the pod we swim with now. This is who I am. I have not been able to tell you before."

Keiris looked at her in surprise. Then he realized that she had not suddenly learned to speak Adenyo. This was her silent voice, the voice so small that he had never heard it before. She spoke through the snakes.

I have never been able to tell you who I am, so you think I am only a child. You think I have no mind, only laughter. You think I have no soul, only a spirit that runs like water, with much noise and little effect. But those things are not true at all. I have a mind and I have a soul. If I had the words of your language, I could show you them.

Tonight I can show you them even though I do not have your language.

Tonight I can show you the woman I am if you will let me. Will you listen to me tonight, Lirion?

Keiris drew a long, unsteady breath. He had promised his father that he would do just that. And only the night before he had worn flowers strung by Nirini's hand, pledging himself to her for the summer. And that other night, beside the sea pool . . .

Remembering, he felt the raw clutch of panic. That other night he had briefly seen the woman she was. He did not want to see again tonight. Because, he realized, he wanted one thing to remain constant in the confusion of the night, at least one thing. And that was Nirini. He wanted her to remain a child, laughing and lighthearted. He wanted her to remain as she said, a spirit that ran like water, with much noise and little effect.

When she had first tried to pluck flowers for him, he had rejected her because she was a child, not a woman. Now he wanted a child. Now—desperately—he wanted only a simple, laughing child. Because nothing else was simple tonight. Nothing else at all.

He pressed trembling fingertips to his temples, carefully finding words to lull her. *I'll listen later. Now—now I want to play in the pool.*

A frown touched her face. She drew back. *Lirion . . .*

Put the—put the snakes away for a few minutes and play with me. Will you?

There is not much time.

Then we will play quickly. Are you permitted—are you permitted to keep the snakes with you? When the migration begins?

They will stay with me for a while. For a day or two. Once they become hungry, they will leave.

Then put them—put them here on the ground. Make a nest in the leaves for them. And play with me. Play with me because I don't want to hear your song. I don't want to learn that you are a woman, complex and full, with your own mysteries and heartbreaks. I only want a child who won't trouble me with anything. Because I am troubled enough by myself.

She made a hollow in the leaves for the snakes but reluctantly. They coiled tightly around each other, rigid and nervous, as if the ground were a foreign place. Their eyes winked out of the shadows as Keiris led Nirini to the pool.

They splashed silver water upon each other, and it was as cold as it had been the afternoon before. But Keiris did not cry out as he had then, and neither of them laughed. Nirini followed him in the motions of play, but there was no spontaneity, no gaiety. She glanced too often at the moons, gauging their progress across the sky. She looked too often for the winking red eyes of the snakes. Keiris shivered in the cold water. Miserably Nirini shivered against him.

Then they were huddled beside the pool, clothes pulled over their damp bodies, Nirini crying quietly with disappointment. Keiris stroked her hair, but that only made her look up hopefully. That only made her utter a few words in her own tongue and reach tentatively for the snakes that had glided near.

No, he told her silently. *Tonight I can't listen to your song. Tonight . . . tonight . . .*

Then you don't care for me as I care for you. She had disregarded his plea. The snakes were coiled on her arms, winking at him.

I care for you, he said helplessly. *I care for you. But tonight . . .* He sighed, then pressed his temples, briefly projecting to her the full confusion of his mood.

She drew back, her face twisting. For a moment she did not touch him, did not attempt to speak again. She sat with eyes averted and lips pressed tight. Then she clasped his arm. *Please, Lirion, at least let me speak to you for a moment. You've shown me how you feel. You've shown me that you are torn and hurting. I want to say—if you stay here, I will stay with you. If you go north with your father's pod, we will go together. And when you return to Neth, I will return with you.*

It was his turn to draw back. He looked at her in surprise. *You could never live there.*

I can live anywhere you are.

But we are—I thought we pledged ourselves only for the summer.

We did, but I will pick other flowers for you. I will pick flowers for you for as many times as we both can see the blossoms and smell them. And I will do everything else for you that you want done. I will do everything, Lirion.

He bowed his head helplessly, feeling the cold stirrings of guilt. She had been right a few moments before when she had said he did not care for her as she cared for him. He felt affection and a gentle desire and once, beside the sea pool, he had felt awe. But he could never offer what she had just offered: to follow where he led, to live as he lived.

He could not offer her that kind of love, and suddenly he felt constrained that she offered it. He did not want her to make sacrifices for him, to give up her family, her friends, the life she knew. He did not want to be responsible for her happiness or unhappiness. And his reasons were entirely self-ish. Tonight the terms and patterns of his own life were confusing enough. If he must pause and consider the terms and patterns of her life as well . . .

You will feel differently some other time, he said, pulling back from her. *I don't know your ways well, but my father told me one thing. He told me that your people care much less for permanence than mine do.*

That is why I'm offering it! she cried back. *Because you require it. It is the way among your people; Rudin explained it to me. You want a woman who will be yours for all her life. I am a woman, and I'll make myself yours through every season. And I have just told you my genealogy. I have just told you the names of my parents and their pods. Isn't it what you want? You are confused and unhappy, and I don't want you to be so. So I have offered you—I have offered you—Haven't I offered you what you want?*

He shook his head, more helplessly than before. *I want—* But he could not tell her what he wanted without hurting her. Because all he wanted tonight was to be alone.

And did she even want to spend her life with him? Or was she only making a gesture she would regret later, an impulsive gesture? How well did she know her own feelings?

The snakes winked at him, mocking. He closed his eyes briefly. *Nirini,* he said finally, *I want to think. I want to think of what you have said. Please go down to the beach and wait for me. Wait with my father. I'll—I'll come soon.*

No! I won't leave you now. I—

But it's what I want. It's what I need. I'll come soon.

She argued more, but finally she went, casting behind a lingering, troubled glance.

She went, and he was alone on the hillside. Alone with the risen moons. Alone with the silvered water. Alone with a confusion that he could not resolve.

He sat for a while and then, without thinking, he picked his way down the hillside again. He did not go in the direction of the beach where his father's people were gathered. He went instead toward the other beach where he had gone with Ramiri the morning before. Perhaps he would find clarity there.

He found only dark sand and light-struck water and overhead a sky vivid with stars. He stood on the narrow beach looking up at the stars, wondering numbly how many there were, wondering if his mother stood on the seaward plaza looking at the same stars. Wondering if Kristis saw them from her quarters this night. Wondering if Tardis sailed under them.

He stood wondering when and how he would ever reach his home again.

He stood wishing for Hyosis.

FIFTEEN

HE STOOD WISHING and the moons sailed overhead. He stood wishing and the water rose. He stood wishing and drowntide came, full drowntide, the hour when the sea stood at its highest.

He stood wishing and wondering and empty and afraid, with no idea what to do next. Trudge around the island and rejoin his father's people? Go with them to the northern waters? Or remain here, alone, until they returned in the fall?

He only wanted to return to Hyosis.

The hunger that swept over him then was sharper, more poignant, than the hunger he had felt earlier on the hillside. He closed his eyes and Hyosis shimmered alive around him: palace walls; long, gleaming corridors; windows opening upon sunrise and sunset. The familiar smells of the palace were in the air. Listening, Keiris heard the voices of people he knew: Kristis, Tracador, Tardis, his mother. He heard the sea, too—not the crashing drowntide sea but a gentler, more distant sea.

The illusion was so real, he even heard the deep call of the sounding horn from the seaward plaza.

He heard the call three times before he realized it did not come from Hyosis, that it was not his mother's sounding horn at all. The sound was deeper than that, nearer. It was not so much a wail as a boom.

Reluctantly he opened his eyes.

At first he did not understand what he saw. A gleaming whiteness. A resplendence. A majesty, moon-silvered vapor rising from it like a geyser.

189

A great white. It loomed in the water just beyond the breakers. It sounded again, and vapors rose from its blowhole and dissipated into the air.

"Pehoshi." Surprised, Keiris uttered the white's name aloud. And here was Soshi, too, darting in the surf, sleek body waggling.

Soshi was summoning him. He recognized that immediately. In the same moment he sinkingly realized that he need think no longer of what he was to do next. It was time for the migration to begin, and his father had sent Soshi and Pehoshi for him. How could he refuse to go?

There was no way. His father expected his company. But still he hesitated for moments before wading into the water.

He had already reached Soshi, had already seated himself on her back, when he heard Nirini's voice over the sound of the surf.

"Lirion! Lirion!" And then some plea in her own language.

Startled, he glanced back and saw her running across the narrow beach and into the water. The sea snakes were coiled around her arms and neck, lashing in agitation. Her dark hair fluttered. He slid off Soshi's back, his voice sharply impatient. "Nirini, I told you—"

But she did not understand Adenyo. *I told you to go back to my father and wait.*

And I told you I would not leave you. So I went into the trees and waited and then I followed you here. Lirion . . .

Keiris frowned at the barely bridled hysteria he heard in her voice. *Come then,* he said. Did she think he would leave her behind?

Strangely she hesitated, water washing at her thighs, and turned to look back at the bulk of Misa Hon. *Lirion . . .*

Keiris was momentarily puzzled. Her expression, the tone of her thoughts, suggested apprehension, even fear. But what was there to fear? The sea? It was her home. The mams? Why would she fear Soshi and Pehoshi? *Come,* he repeated. *You ride Soshi. I'll swim out to meet Pehoshi.*

She darted a startled glance at him and, forgetting to use her silent voice, addressed him in her own tongue. The words were questioning, breathless.

He raised an impatient hand. *And the snakes . . .* If they were to ride the big white even a short distance together, he would not have the snakes. *Send the snakes away.*

Nirini's face contracted in a grimace of distress. She drew

a long, sobbing breath. *But you didn't listen to me sing. You—*

I won't have the snakes, he insisted. *Later I'll listen to you. Later you can get other snakes.* Surely there were still hundreds coiled on the posts on the beach. And he *would* listen when they rejoined the tide folk. He would keep his promise.

Still Nirini hesitated, glancing back at the bulk of the island again. She seemed torn, unable to move. Inexplicably tears glinted in her eyes. Finally, with visible effort, she plunged forward, stooping and disgorging the snakes into the sea. She swam toward Keiris with uneven strokes.

When she came nearer, he saw that her face was bloodless, her small features pinched, her eyes frightened. Her hands, when she clasped his, were cold and trembling.

Simply because he had made her send the snakes away? Because he had told her he would not listen to her song until later? But she had been pale and frightened before that.

"Here. Let me help you up." She had never needed help before, but tonight she did. And she was staring at Pehoshi with something like dread.

The great white hung in the darkness like the lingering afterimage of a dream. By sunlight Pehoshi's flesh had been marred by scuffs and scars, but tonight moonlight healed every irregularity. Tonight the white was a creature of legend and light. Awed, Keiris forgot Nirini's fright as he swam beside Soshi toward the big white.

Then he was helping Nirini to the white's back, bolstering and supporting her, puzzled and concerned again by the violent trembling he felt in her. But he was distracted too. His father had never invited him to ride the white. The flesh was so much smoother, so much more yielding than he had expected. He grappled awkwardly, trying to make his way up the creature's back without gouging it.

Then he sat as he had seen his father sit, high above the water.

The creature began to swim, the motion smooth, gliding. Keiris gazed out over the water and wondered if his father had felt this same wonder, this same enchantment, the first time he rode the big white. Clasping the smooth flesh between his knees, pressing his palms against it, it almost seemed he could feel the steady rush of the white's blood, the deep sigh of its respiration. Gradually his own heartbeat slowed to meet the white's, and Keiris felt the change as a deep, slow relaxation. But when he glanced back at Nirini, her eyes were frightened and staring. He frowned, confused. *Please, why are you afraid?*

Of course, she could not answer. The snakes were gone; they had disappeared in the water. Nirini could only meet Keiris' questioning gaze, then dip her head, fresh tears gleaming in her eyes.

Puzzled, Keiris tried to shrug off her mood as the white glided easily through the silvered water. Soon he saw torches on the beach. Soon he saw the silhouettes of the tide folk against tall bonfires and caught distant snatches of silent melody. He pressed the white's flesh harder with knees and palms, trying to shut out the wispy, intermingling songs. The white responded by sounding, its solid flesh jarring. Vapor rose in a shrouding plume.

Distracted, Keiris was slow to realize that Pehoshi was gliding no nearer the shore. Soon the torches and bonfires that had been ahead only a few minutes before were falling behind. Keiris looked back, frowning—and realized with a stopping heart that Pehoshi was not carrying them to join his father on the beach. Nor was Pehoshi carrying them northward, in the direction of the migration. The stars were wrong. Pehoshi was carrying them away from Misa Hon, southward and westward.

Confused, Keiris turned to look back at Nirini. She met his questioning gaze, and silver tears welled in her eyes and slid down her cheeks.

Keiris drew a long, steadying breath, trying to repress the sharp rise of fear. The white flesh under him was real. It yielded to his pressing hands. It had substance and texture. Yet what was happening seemed as far beyond understanding, as far beyond control as a dream. Pehoshi had come for him. And now Pehoshi was carrying him silently away.

Pehoshi was carrying him beyond sight of land. Torches and bonfires were winking into obscurity behind them. Ahead was nothing but the sea.

The empty sea.

And Nirini could explain nothing. He had made her send the snakes away.

For minutes he could not think at all. Pehoshi? Could Pehoshi tell him why they were going out to sea? Keiris stroked the white flesh, wondering. He had heard Pehoshi's song. He had taken memories from it, images and impressions and even long tales told in a symbolic idiom far different from his own. Could he ask Pehoshi a specific question? And understand the answer if it came?

What choice had he but to try? He could not even see the bonfires now. The fear he had suppressed was rising sharply.

Bowing his head, he pressed the palms of both hands to the mam's resilient flesh. Silently he pleaded, *Where are you taking us, Pehoshi? Didn't my father send you to bring us back to him? Where are we going?*

Pehoshi seemed to tremble under him. Briefly, for the barest portion of a second, Keiris thought he heard a deep voice, but he could not comprehend what it said.

He pressed harder at the white flesh, marginally aware that Nirini had slipped back from him toward the white's tail. *Pehoshi, do you understand me? Where are you taking us? My father*—he concentrated, creating an image of his father—*where did my father tell you to take us? Pehoshi, where?*

There was no answer from the creature who carried them.

Instead his answer came from the water below. "Brother, this is not Pehoshi."

Startled, Keiris turned and stared down. "What—"

Ramiri swam in the silvered water, her snakes darting beside her. "This is not Pehoshi," she repeated. Her voice was neither so wispy nor so hesitant as Keiris remembered. Still, it came faintly.

Keiris couldn't tell which disconcerted him most: Ramiri's sudden appearance or what she said. He gazed down at her, confused. She seemed small in the water. Her face was a pale oval, her eyes heavy and dark, like small, captured seas. The familiar melancholy was in them. "Not . . ." Keiris frowned, remembering his first impression that moonlight had buffed the scuffs and scars from Pehoshi's flanks. And he had noticed other differences, too, he realized, small differences. He had noticed them and disregarded them.

But if this was not Pehoshi, whose white was it? Why had it come? And where was it taking them? He hesitated, then slid down the white's back into the water, leaving Nirini perched alone. He held himself stiffly as Ramiri's snakes swam near, black tongues flickering. "Ramiri, if this isn't Pehoshi, who sent him?"

Ramiri's lashes fluttered with surprise. "No one sends a moonsteed. A moonsteed simply comes."

Keiris darted a blank glance at the looming white, for a moment not understanding what she said. A moonsteed . . . simply comes? Did she mean . . . ? "It came? It came to me?" he demanded, shaken. This was a moonsteed? And it had come to him as Pehoshi had come once to his father. As Rikahashi had come to an earlier Lirion? "Why? And its name?"

She cocked her head, surprised again by his ignorance. "Who knows why a moonsteed comes, Brother? Most spanners have them, and most other folk do not."

"But I'm not a spanner."

She acknowledged his protest with a slight frown before going on. "And it has a name but not one it can tell you. You must give it another, to be used between the two of you."

"Any name I choose?"

"Any name it will answer to. If you give it a name it does not like, it will not respond."

"If I called it—if I called it—" But nothing came to mind. And, gazing into the creature's eye, he was struck by a new thought. He licked his lips, disturbed. "Before I ever thought of coming here, there was a white," he said. "I called it before I knew I had a voice. I called it without intending to." He remembered clearly the pallor of white flesh in the water temple. He remembered his own awe and fright. And he remembered Tardis' anger.

"Then it was this one," Ramiri said.

Had it followed him all that way? All these days? "But it never approached me again until tonight," he mused. It had never approached until tonight, when he had stood on the beach wishing desperately for Hyosis. Until tonight, when he had stood calling up images of home, memories of people and places he longed for. Tonight, when he had stood wondering if he would ever see his mother again, if he would ever sleep in his own bed again, if he would ever eat another meal from Tracador's kitchen.

He shivered, understanding then why the white had come. Understanding, too, why it had carried him past the shores of Misa Hon and taken him southward and westward.

"It's taking me home," he said softly. "To Hyosis."

Ramiri's dark eyes flickered. "Do you want to go there?"

"Yes."

"Then that is where it is taking you. Once a moonsteed

fully gives itself, it carries its master wherever he most needs to go.''

And Nirini . . . Suddenly Keiris understood the other thing that had puzzled him: Nirini's fear, her tears. She had guessed what he had not: that the white had come to carry him back to Neth. And, true to her promise, she had come with him. She had come although it meant leaving everyone and everything familiar behind. She had come trembling and crying.

And he did not want that. There was no reason for it. Whatever attachment she felt for him could never outweigh her need for her family, for her pod, for all the ways and customs of her life. Bobbing in the water, holding himself aloof from Ramiri's snakes, Keiris saw that clearly.

"Ramiri, tell her—tell Nirini—that she is not to come any farther with me. Soshi is here. Soshi can carry her back." Even if the migration had begun, surely Soshi could catch up with the others. They had not left the torches and bonfire of Misa Hon behind so very long ago.

"You want me to tell her that you do not want her?" The query was hesitant. Ramiri glanced uneasily up at Nirini.

"No. I want you to tell her—" Keiris groped briefly, and then his thoughts came clear, completely clear. "Tell her that I am sorry to leave her. She is the first mate I've taken, and she will always be first in my heart. But she would be unhappy living among the Adenyo, and I would feel her unhappiness even more than she would. Because if I let her come with me, I would be responsible for it. And I want to be responsible for her happiness instead. I want to be responsible for sending her back to her own people." The sense of resolution he felt was marred by one question: Why couldn't he have put his feelings in order earlier, when he could have expressed them directly to Nirini?

Ramiri hung for a moment in the water, her eyes deep with shadow. She said doubtfully, "I will tell her these things." Stretching out her arms, she beckoned her snakes. When they had coiled around her, she climbed to the white's back and slipped one comforting arm around Nirini.

Nirini's first reaction, as Ramiri spoke, was to protest. But even from where he paddled in the water Keiris could see that there was another, deeper response: relief. Although she shook her head, although she objected aloud, the pinched look slowly left Nirini's mouth. Color came back to her cheeks.

But when Ramiri moved to slide back into the water, Nirini

detained her. She spoke with animation, touching the snakes
that coiled around Ramiri's slight shoulders.

"She will go back because you ask it. Your asking, in the
way you have asked, supersedes the promise she made to
you," Ramiri explained when Nirini had spoken. "But you
made a promise to her that you must keep. You promised to
hear her song."

Keiris stiffened. "There isn't time. The migration—"

"There is enough time for what she wants."

And he *had* promised. "Will you let her use your snakes?"
he asked reluctantly.

"I will permit it." Gravely Ramiri sent the snakes gliding
from her shoulders to Nirini's. She stroked them reassuringly
as they anchored themselves there. She spoke just as reassuringly to Nirini. Then she slipped back into the water.

Keiris gazed up. Nirini sat waiting for him, sad and pleased
at once. Reluctantly he pulled himself from the water and
joined her on the white's back, keeping a careful distance
from the restlessly swaying snakes.

She began to speak immediately, stroking the snakes with
one hand, her voice light and clear. *Do you remember the day
we met, Lirion? I was a child then, just as you thought. I
wanted the things a child wants: to laugh, to play. But when I
met you, I learned that a woman slept in me. And I learned
what a woman feels, what a woman wants, how a woman
laughs, and how she tries to entice. All those things were
waiting to be awakened in me. You wakened them, but you
were afraid of them. So you tried not to see.*

I didn't see, Keiris said uneasily. Her eyes were luminous,
her face bright, disturbingly so.

Perhaps you did not, she conceded. *But you see now, don't
you? I was a child and I was happy. But a woman awoke in
me when you came. My mother told me once that people are
like that. There are things sleeping in them, and life is simply
a long awakening of those things. Do you believe that?*

I—I don't know. But surely he did know. Otherwise why
did her words make him so profoundly uneasy?

*I believe it now. And I'm telling you because I want you
to understand why I must sing you a woman's song. I can still
laugh and play like a child, but this is the voice that moves in
me tonight. This is the song.*

Keiris drew back then, involuntarily, but he could not
escape Nirini's lightly caroling voice and all the things it

held: the joys, the pleasures, the triumphs, the occasional small defeats. Touching the coiled snakes, stroking them, she offered Keiris everything she had captured from life: memories, images, sensations. She offered him texture and dimension and detail, an entire tapestry woven of her own soul. She offered light and color and movement and an overriding brightness of spirit.

She offered him the sea as well, in all its moods and seasons, sunny and bright or sullen and storming. She offered him her people, too, and he saw that they had moods and seasons as well. He saw that sometimes their simplicity became complexity, that sometimes their peace became strife, that sometimes they were as sullen and storming as the sea.

But only sometimes. Only very occasionally.

He saw, not wanting to, how good it was to be a person of the sea tribes. He saw how good it was, most of the time, to be Talani upon the land, Nirini in the sea.

He saw how wise he had been to insist that she remain behind.

He even saw, for the first time, that it would be difficult to leave her.

At first he thought that was the reason for the sadness he felt then—that tonight he would part from Nirini. He thought that was the cause for the tiny pain that erupted in his chest as she sang. He thought that was the cause for the slowly growing anguish he felt.

He thought that until Nirini's voice shivered and was abruptly still. The bright images of her song vanished. She gazed at him with stricken eyes, her face losing all its brightness, all its color. Keiris stared back at her, trying to understand her sudden silence, her pallor. Trying to understand why the white shuddered under them, its flesh quivering violently.

The pain grew. It intensified. It keened.

It summoned.

Then he understood.

Down.

He must go down.

The hiscapei called him.

White arms, empty and cold . . .

He shook himself, trying to cast out the pain, the summons. This time, at least, he knew what called him. He knew what it wanted of him. The hiscapei wanted prey—and he had not come so far for that.

He had not, but the keening had already begun to numb him. He edged away from Nirini, casting off her clinging hands, and stared down into the dark water. All he saw was Ramiri looking up at him, her eyes no longer melancholy but stricken.

It was the creature's anguish that compelled him. How could he hear the hiscapei keen and cry and do nothing? All it wanted was to be comforted. All it wanted was to have its pain assuaged. And he could do that. He could do that so easily.

All he had to do was go down.

Down.

He was in the water. He was kicking, he was tumbling, he was plunging. Never mind that darkness blinded him. Never mind that the weight of the water pressed heavily upon him. Never mind that he hadn't even taken time to fill his lungs before sliding down the white's flanks. The hiscapei's anguish was shrill. It was unbearable.

He didn't even have to think what direction to take in the black water. The keening shrill drew him surely. And he hardly noticed when he took his first gulping breath of salt water. By then he was totally possessed by the hiscapei's anguish.

A flash of white, and for an instant Keiris thought he had found the hiscapei. But it was Nirini instead. She was a paleness that hung before him, eyes wide and senseless, and then tumbled away in a poorly coordinated flurry of limbs.

And that was wrong. Even through the growing thickness of his thoughts Keiris realized that. Nirini was like a fish in the water, swift, graceful, unafraid. She did not flounder and tumble, her eyes full of fear.

For a moment he was torn. The hiscapei's voice had reached an excruciating pitch. It burned along his nerveways. It called. But Nirini was in trouble. Nirini . . .

Concern for Nirini briefly overrode the hiscapei's need. With increasingly uncooperative limbs Keiris tried to struggle in the direction she had taken. He tried to follow the dimming paleness of her limbs. Once, reaching out, he thought he touched her hand. It was cold and limp. But before he could grasp it, it pulled away.

And then, before he could grope again for her, the hiscapei's voice was suddenly stilled.

Pain vanished. Anguish died. Keiris hung suspended in the

.dark water, suddenly aware of the burn of salt water in his
throat and nose, suddenly aware of the suffocating heaviness
of it in his lungs. He stared around him and did not see
Nirini. Stifling the reflexive urge to gulp water into his lungs
again, he kicked once, weakly, and let the water buoy him.

Coughing and choking, he reached the surface. He gasped
and gagged, fighting for air. Then Nirini was in his arms,
cold and shuddering. They clung together for long moments
before struggling to the back of the waiting white. Keiris
crouched on the creature's wide back, shivering violently,
vaguely aware that Nirini was softly crying.

When finally Keiris was able to look around coherently,
the water was empty. There was no sign of what had happened. There was . . .

The water was empty. But why was that so disturbing?
Why shouldn't the water be empty?

Because when Nirini had begun her song, Ramiri had been
swimming near.

She was not near now. She was nowhere to be seen.

She was nowhere to be seen, and the hiscapei was silent.
Suddenly Keiris was not cold but numb again. He stared at
Nirini. "My sister . . ." His lips formed the words stiffly.

Nirini did not answer. She touched her bedraggled hair and
drew a soft, wordless breath. She stared down into the empty
water. Then she looked up and met his glance again and bit
her lip, her eyes widening with a horror that matched his.

Horror because there was no summons from the hiscapei
now, no summons at all. The anguished keening was still.
There was only silence, a terrible, empty silence. And Keiris
knew with growing terror that there could be but one reason
for that. Far below, the hiscapei had closed its wavering
white arms on prey.

"Ramiri!" he cried to the empty water. His breath caught
in his throat and stuck there. He could not draw another. Yet
he managed to cry again. "Ramiri!" The syllables of her
name were raw with pain.

The only answer was silence.

SIXTEEN

KEIRIS CALLED BUT the only answer was silence—silence and the angry sob of his own breath. He pressed one knuckle hard to his teeth, punishing himself. He had been so preoccupied with his own concerns that he hadn't even wondered when Ramiri suddenly appeared in this empty quarter of the sea. Now, too late, he realized that she must have learned, somehow, that he was traveling through dangerous straits and had come to escort him, just as her sisters escorted the tide folk on their migration. She had come to protect him from the keening voices of the sea.

Keiris jarred one clenched fist against the white's resilient back, angry at his thoughtlessness—and his helplessness. What was he to do? Search the surface of the water again? He had done that. Call Ramiri's name? He had done that too. Could he do nothing else but urge the white to a safe distance and wait to see if Ramiri extricated herself?

But what had his father said? That in her maiden season a rermadken was more vulnerable to the hiscapei's spell than later, when she was more experienced.

And this was Ramiri's maiden season. "My father . . ." But Evin was on Misa Hon—or at sea, leading his pod in the migration. Keiris bit his lip. One hand, he realized dimly, was clenched on Nandyris' shell horn. The other pounded in frustration at the white's back. How long could Ramiri remain underwater? He didn't know.

'Lirion . . .''

Keiris shrugged Nirini's hand off his shoulder, clinging to the white's back for a moment longer. Then, impulsively, he pulled the shell horn over his head and spilled it into Nirini's hands. *Wait here. Wait for me,* he instructed, and slid down the white's flank into the sea. He could not simply sit here, waiting. And he could not urge the white away. Ramiri had only done what a rermadken did. But Keiris remembered his father's pallor, his silence these past days, too clearly. And Ramiri would not be in the hiscapei's arms if Keiris had done as he promised and remained on the beach for the gather.

The water was cold, moonlight a satin-brightness on its surface. Bracing himself, Keiris plunged beneath the surface and kicked himself downward.

He quickly lost himself in the featureless water. After the first moments he could not tell if his kicking feet were driving him deeper or if he was swimming in useless circles. Finally, when his lungs cried for breath, he let himself float free. Breaking through the silver-skimmed surface, he gulped for breath, oriented himself, then turned and dived again. Nirini cried after him, but the words meant nothing.

He plunged toward the bottom four times before he finally caught a glimpse of paleness there. And at last, on his sixth dive, he hovered in the water looking at the white thing that held his sister.

He had not been prepared to find the hiscapei beautiful. But he did. Taller than a man, it stood loosely rooted in the ocean bottom, wavering and pale, with long, slender arms that eddied in the current. Faintly luminescent cilia and filaments tasted the water around it. A tightly wrapped bud grew from its base, its immature arms curled into a truncated cone. For a moment, looking at the creature and its half-formed offspring, Keiris felt the things Ramiri had described to him in her song: He felt the hiscapei's loneliness and its need. This was not a creature that could swim free, seeking what it required. Instead it stood rooted and alone in this deserted quarter of the sea, calling out in its hunger, crying for some creature to feed it and its growing bud. And if nothing came . . .

If nothing came, its roots would shrivel. Its bud would wither. Its lacy arms would curl in upon themselves in help-less death.

Did he want that? Did he want this wavering paleness to die with no one to temper its anguish, no one to nourish its bud? Did he want . . .

Keiris shuddered involuntarily, catching a bare glimpse of

a fragile form curled deep within the nest of drifting leaves before bursting lungs drove him back to the surface.

Breaking through the water, he fought for breath, shaken. The hiscapei was not calling now, yet it had exercised some kind of influence even in its silence. He had hovered there with lungs aching, more concerned for the hiscapei than for his sister, curled in its embrace.

How much longer could she crouch there without drowning? And how tightly did the white arms and the pink filaments hold her? How much strength would it require to pull free?

Did Ramiri want to pull free? Keiris understood better now what he had learned from her song when they swam together. The sisters of the old kind stilled the hiscapei until the tide folk passed safely. Then they swam away, giving it back to its anguish—giving it back if they could tear themselves free. But if their will weakened, if they could not bear to abandon the hiscapei to its crying loneliness . . .

He had lingered, himself, pitying the hiscapei, and the creature was not even crying now.

Keiris hung there in the water, kicking to keep afloat, and was struck by an unwelcome new thought: If he pulled Ramiri from the hiscapei's arms, surely the creature would begin to cry again. Could he steel himself to disregard the keening call? Could Ramiri steel herself, fresh from its arms?

And if the hiscapei cried again, how could he keep Nirini from being drawn back into the water? She did not hear as keenly as he did, but the hiscapei was almost directly below. He looked up to where she sat on the white's back, shivering and frightened. She had retrieved Ramiri's sea snakes. They coiled nervously on her shoulders, their eyes vividly red. Soshi lay low in the water at the white's side, as if sheltering behind its protecting bulk.

Aware of moments passing, precious moments, Keiris pulled himself clumsily up the white's back. He clasped Nirini's cold fingers. *You must go*, he instructed her. *You must go with Soshi back to Misa Hon*. He could not think of her and Ramiri too.

She looked up at him blankly. *I must go? What about you? I can't leave Ramiri here. But you—*

Her small features drew into a sharp frown. *Do you think I will go and leave you here?*

You must. There's nothing you can do. You— But she was

shaking her head, protesting. Keiris pressed her hands tight, his patience abruptly exhausted. *Nirini, I'm asking you to go! I can't look after you and myself too!* He regretted his brusqueness almost immediately. But there was no time to waste in argument.

Nirini drew back from him, her eyes filling with a hard, cold light. *If you can say that to me, then you heard nothing I told you tonight. You want to send me away like a child. You want to send me away—*

Nirini, I'm sending you for my father, Keiris interposed desperately. Why hadn't he thought of that in the first place? *You must find him and tell him that I need help. That Ramiri needs help. He'll send someone. Or he'll come. He— Didn't he tell me that sometimes the spanners join their voices to drown out the hiscapei?* Surely she would go if he gave her some mission. And perhaps there *was* time. Perhaps if his father could come quickly enough . . .

She pulled her hands free of his and clasped his arm. *They do. And the other rermadken sing and call, too, when one of the sisters is caught and can't free herself. But I can't bring your father that quickly. Even if you called him yourself, this moment, he couldn't come in time.* She faltered, frowning up at him uncertainly before she rushed on. *You're the only spanner near enough. And, Keiris . . .*

The only spanner . . . Blood ran from his face. He wrenched his arms from her grasping fingers. *I'm no spanner.*

You have a spanner's voice. Everyone who has heard it recognizes that. It isn't trained but it's strong. It's as strong as Evin's.

He shook his head angrily. Of all the things he wanted to hear—that she would go, that she would bring his father, that together they could extricate Ramiri from the hiscapei—this was not one. He had a voice, and he had slipped into the careless habit of using it. But to tell him it was a voice that could span the waters as his father's voice did . . .

He did not want a spanner's voice. All he wanted was to return to the safety of land, to sun-washed palace walls, to his own chambers, to familiar voices and sounds.

The white stirred restlessly, and Keiris realized abruptly that the creature understood his thoughts and was orienting itself tentatively to the south and the west.

Stricken by his unconscious betrayal, Keiris took Nirini's arms. *You say you aren't a child. Then behave like a woman and do what needs to be done: go—so I can try to free my sister. Nirini, go!* There's nothing you can do here and nothing I can do while you are here.

She did not yield easily, but finally she slid down the white's flank and rode away on Soshi's back, darting a single tearful glance back. Keiris looked after her and knew he probably would never meet loyalty like hers again. He wished he felt less constrained by it.

Then he plunged into the water again.

This time he was prepared for the distracting emotion he felt as he approached the hiscapei. He tried to concentrate instead on the increasing heaviness of his limbs, on the discomfort of his straining lungs. The water was dark, but he could see the hiscapei clearly as he swam near.

He could see Ramiri less clearly. She was curled tightly at the center of the white mass, unmoving, her eyes closed. For a chilling moment he was afraid he was already too late. But when he touched her shoulder, he felt the shiver of life in her. And from the wispy sigh that touched his thoughts he knew she recognized who had come.

Ramiri, come with me. Please come with me. His lungs were bursting again, but he groped to find her hand, to press it as he formed the silent plea.

Go . . . Be safe . . . Her voice was faint.

I'll be safe. I let the hiscapei call me down once, but it won't happen again. I wasn't ready. Now I am. Come with me.

Go, Brother. I was born for this. You left the gather, and I went to find you on the shore and saw you ride away on your moonsteed. And I followed because I was born to keep you safe. I'm of the old blood and you're of the new, and that is the way of it.

No!

Yes. This is the way. The way . . .

Then my way is to see you safe! Ramiri—

And then he had to kick his way to the surface again. He rested for a moment against the white's massive side, sick and aching. If he could reach the bottom more quickly, before the air in his lungs was exhausted . . .

He shuddered as red eyes gleamed up at him from the dark water. Nirini had discharged Ramiri's snakes as she rode away. They glided near, eyes phosphorescent, and instinctively Keiris shrank back against the white.

The white, who could dive with a speed and strength Keiris could never match. The white, who could carry him quickly down, if he could only cling tightly enough. The white, who could get him to Ramiri while he still had breath to sustain him.

He looked up at the big creature, completely forgetting the gliding snakes. Suddenly it seemed important to find a name for the white. How could he speak with it if it had no name? For a moment he groped blankly, remembering the first time the white had appeared, remembering its giant paleness in the sun chamber of the water temple. Remembering his stunned fear. If he had known then how the creature honored him . . .

There was an archaic word Sorrys had taught him, a word no one used now. Instinctively Keiris guessed it had been set aside when the Adenyo first turned their faces from the sea. Because when one said *chehalli,* one said *sea-blessed.*

"Chehalli," he said aloud. Then, climbing to the creature's back, he pressed his palms against its white flesh. *Will you be my sea-blessing, Chehalli?*

Did he only imagine it or did the white answer him with a deep, assenting voice? How long would it take him, he wondered, to fully know the creature? Years, perhaps, but he didn't have years now. Quickly Keiris placed his face against the white's back. The flesh was surprisingly smooth. *There is a place I want to go, Chehalli. It is below, at the bottom of the water. There is a hiscapei there. I must go to the hiscapei.* As well as he could, he put his need into images, trying to give the white some sense of the direction he had taken through the dark water to find the hiscapei.

The white shuddered and shifted slightly in the water, but it did not submerge.

Keiris felt a quick twinge of misgiving. Was the name wrong? Did the white fail to understand what he wanted?

Or did it understand only too well? Keiris frowned. He knew he must go to the hiscapei, but he feared it too. Did the white sense his ambivalence?

He shifted uneasily on the broad back. How could he convince the white of his need when that need was tinged so heavily with fear?

If he asked the white to take him to his sister instead . . .

Pressing his face to Chehalli's back, he called up Ramiri's face: fragile bones, eyes like dark drops, curling hair. *My*

*sister, Chehalli—take me to my sister. She needs me. I must
go to my sister.*

Briefly the great, white shivered. Then, so swiftly, so
smoothly that Keiris had barely a second to respond, it submerged. One moment Keiris was sitting on the white's broad
back. The next, water´was rushing past him, tumbling him
back toward Chehalli's powerful tail. Blindly he seized for a
handhold and found himself clinging to the white's dorsal fin.
He hugged the fin with all four limbs, his eyes squeezed tight
against the rushing water.

Then they were at the bottom of the sea. They had descended so swiftly, Keiris required precious seconds to orient himself. There were two pale shapes in the dark water
now: Chehalli and the hiscapei, Ramiri curled motionless
within its enshrouding arms. Was she still alive? Could she
be? Heart pounding, Keiris kicked free of Chehalli's back
and swam to part the wavering white leaves. He touched his
sister's shoulder.

Her response was so weak, alarm closed a cold hand on his
heart. *Ramiri, come with me. Come now.* She could not stay
here much longer and live.

Brother, are you here again?

*I'm here. I've brought my moonsteed. He'll carry us both
away. He'll carry us quickly. And we won't listen when the
hiscapei tries to call us back. We'll close our minds. We can
do it. You know we can do it. Come, please!*

Yes, I'll come. . . .

But she did not move to extricate herself. She remained
curled blindly in the nest of cilia. Keiris reached after her,
catching her by one arm, trying to ignore the suckered filaments that wavered near to taste his bare skin. If he could tug
her free . . .

But if he did that, the hiscapei would be empty and alone.
There would be nothing to nourish its leaves, nothing to feed
its bud. And the bud must be fed if it was to grow, if it was to
break free and ride the ocean currents to its own anchorage, if
it was one day to form a bud of its own.

He could not leave the hiscapei here alone, hungry and
needy. He could not—

Keiris exhaled sharply, alarmed. The filaments that had
curled around his arm were pulling gently at him, even
though the hiscapei already had prey. And he felt the beginning of an oppressive sadness. It was so barren here. The

currents that swept across the ocean floor were so cold. Even
in the brightest hours of day no light fell here. It was dark,
always dark.

Lonely.

Dark.

Barren.

The bud . . .

He drew salt water into his lungs without realizing it. It
wasn't until he felt pale leaves closing gently around his torso
that fear outstripped everything else. Terror-driven, he kicked
himself sharply backward, ripping his arms free of the suckered filaments. Then Chehalli was nudging him with broad
flukes, urging him back toward the surface.

Keiris broke through the water sputtering and coughing and
knew, with a certainty that was bone-deep, that he did not
dare go down again. Not if he wanted to live.

He knew, too, with the same certainty, that he could never
return to Hyosis if he swam away and left Ramiri to the
hiscapei.

He did not even chill when Ramiri's snakes glided near,
dark tongues flickering. He was cold, he was gripped with
bone-terror, his arm stung where the hiscapei had tasted it.
But he was angry too.

The hiscapei needed his sister.

He needed her too.

The hiscapei was lonely at the bottom of a dark sea.

He felt the dark, too, and he was as lonely as any creature—
lonely and lost and far from home. He had a people, he had a
place, and he was hungry for them, as hungry as the hiscapei
for prey. Yet they were beyond reach. They would remain
forever beyond reach if he could not free Ramiri. How could
he buy passage home at the price of his sister's life?

Chehalli stirred at his side, sounding loudly. The snakes
circled restlessly. The stars were distant, as distant as help. If
only he could summon Ramiri from here. If only he could cry
his need to her as keenly as the hiscapei had cried. If only he
could compel her with *his* anguish . . .

He hesitated, bobbing gently in the water. He had a voice,
a spanner's voice. Nirini said it, his father said it, and so it
must be true, however little he wanted it. If he called to
Ramiri with all his need and all his eloquence . . .

The snakes glided nearer. Their eyes were coldly burning.
If he called as loudly as he could . . .

He pressed shaking fingers to his forehead, briefly discouraged. If he called and failed, he would have thrown away another handful of precious moments. Ramiri could not survive much longer under the water.

The snakes raised inquisitive heads. Their eyes seemed to be the only things alive in the sea.

The snakes . . .

He recognized then, thunderstruck, what his choice was: to call with his untrained spanner's voice and perhaps fail. Or to augment his voice. To make it as powerful as he could make it. To call with Ramiri's snakes coiled around him. To call with all the power of the sea that slumbered—unwelcome—in his blood.

For a moment he could not move. His lungs emptied and would not fill again. He tried to kick, to paddle, and could not. Weakly, raggedly, he drifted against Chehalli's side, as if the big white could somehow hide him.

But there was no shelter in Chehalli's shadow. There was no shelter anywhere. Because Keiris saw clearly what he must do. He saw the only thing he *could* do. And remembering what had happened that afternoon when he listened to the rermadken's song, he guessed its consequences.

He wanted to pause then. He wanted to take time to think, to weigh, to consider his decision from every perspective. But there *was* no time. And, as far as he could see, there was no alternative, none he could live with.

He closed his eyes and drew one long breath, wondering what would have happened by the time he let it out again. Wondering how he would have changed. How the world would have changed. Then, tense, trembling, he stretched out his arms to Ramiri's snakes.

They came boldly. They came sinuously. They came and closed their coils around him. They were unexpectedly muscular, their skin cold and tough. Keiris felt their touch like the stroke of panic. He could not move. He could not breathe. He could only quiver helplessly, his body rigid. He might have been a post pounded into the sand. He had as much mobility, as much will, as the snakes settled themselves on his shoulders.

The cold brilliance of their eyes filled his. From somewhere he heard a whining sound. He winced as it grew louder, more penetrating.

Briefly he was aware of little but the thinly screaming

whine and the sensations that accompanied it. His fingers, his toes—first tingled, then numbed. Heat darted down all the pathways of his nervous system. He felt a sharply metallic taste on his tongue. Then, swiftly, a massive internal turbulence gripped him, as if his blood had suddenly changed course in his veins. Perhaps it really had. How else explain the way his every perspective shifted, the way every thought and perception suddenly altered?

Images flashed in his mind of a palace sitting beside the sea. Its pink stones gleamed in the sun. Yet, looking at it, he felt a sense of oppression, as if the palace were a place of confinement, a place where stale air was trapped in closed corridors and people moved like bloodless shadows, mysterious and ineffectual in their ways. How could the Nethlor live there, closed off from the sea, what sunlight they enjoyed strained into attenuated shafts by the narrow windows?

As he watched, a heavy-limbed form appeared on the landward plaza. Kristis—he knew her immediately. But he had never noticed before how painfully gravity pulled at her, nor how unhealthy her complexion. If she could walk into the sea and let the water buoy her while the sun browned her face and warmed her stiffened joints . . .

But she would never do that. No Nethlor woman swam in the sea. When the Nethlor went to sea, they went balanced fearfully in wooden shells. They went guided by a woman as afraid of the sea and its creatures as themselves. They cast themselves into the water's greatness, made a trembling raid upon its plenty, and then retreated to the narrow ridge of rock that was their prison.

Because that was what Neth was, not a home but a prison. Worse, it was a prison whose doors stood open. But how could its inmates venture free when they were deaf to the voices of the sea—and mute as well? Did they even guess at their confinement, at their diminution?

And his mother? Nandyris? Keiris shook his head. There was no time for this painful exercise. There was no time to subject all his memories to this hurtful reexamination. Choking back the tide of images, he climbed quickly to Chehalli's back. Every muscle rigid, he raised one hand and stroked the snakes.

With all the force of the pain he felt, he called to Ramiri and told her how much he needed her. He told her in a voice that rang in every direction. He told her how badly he needed a sister in this lonely and frightening world: someone to share stories and meals with, someone to talk with of intimate things, someone to provide stability as the universe shifted and changed. He told her how he had loved Nandyris and how he mourned her loss, even now. He told her what the loss of a second sister would cost him.

With all the force of the loss he felt, he called to Ramiri. He held back nothing of his anguish. He held back nothing of his need. Because he needed Ramiri far more than the hiscapei did. The hiscapei could call some other prey. He had no other twin. They had been born together. If she died tonight, they would die together, in spirit if not in body. Because if she died, his life would be barren from this night on. Her death would be a sacrifice that bought nothing.

But if she pulled free of the filaments that held her, if she pushed aside the hiscapei's white arms, if she came to him, he would sing to her for as long as she wanted. He would sing to her of their mother, of the way her hair gleamed in the sun, of the timbre of her voice, of the white of her gown against her dark limbs. He would sing to her of the palace, too; of the Nethlor who were his family; of their kindness and strength. He would sing to her of all the bright moments of his life. He would sing to her of Nandyris, his sister and hers too.

If she did not come to him, he would be rootless and lonely and despairing for every remaining day of his life.

He called and cried. He keened in a voice to rival the hiscapei's. He was not ashamed to do it.

But Ramiri did not appear.

He pleaded. He let his voice fill with tears. He let the snakes coil around his neck and wind themselves over his face. Their tongues flickered against his cheekbones. Their cold flesh touched him everywhere.

The water remained empty.

Finally, bitterly, he knew he had failed. He bowed his head and let his voice die. He did not even remove the snakes from his shoulders. There was no need. The old blood no longer lay dormant; it was fully awakened now. It ran freely in his veins, coloring his perceptions and his memories. It would never be silent again.

Already, through his grief, he saw things in the sea he had not seen before. He was aware of currents and rhythms, of colors and hues that had been invisible to him before. He had always cherished stability. Now the movement of the water seemed full of promise—and the horizon called him. If he honed his senses keenly enough, he knew he could find his way from one quarter of the sea to another simply by appraising minute changes in water temperature and salinity.

He wanted to do that, because he was full of restlessness now. It was the season for migration. The north waters called. Distant mountain peaks, flashing shoals of fish, vivid skies, and brisk air—these were the things of summer. Even through his despair he had an appetite for them. He had an appetite for the journey, too, for its dangers as well as its beauties. He wanted to test himself in the fire zone. He wanted to race against sleek young mams. He wanted to pick his way up sheer rock faces and throw himself down into the cold water.

He had an appetite for those things, and he was ashamed.

He was ashamed until he realized that he felt the first pain of the hiscapei's call again. He raised his head and looked out over the water, his senses sharpening.

Stunned, caught between a sudden, dangerous hope and despair, he saw an ill-defined paleness rising from the water nearby. It drifted lazily up through the separate layers of water and slowly became a human form: arms, legs, torso—a half-drowned face, Ramiri's.

For one long instant his breath clutched in his chest. He released it in a hoarse cry and slid into the water. The hiscapei's plaint was rising, becoming more keenly anguished. He hardly heard. Ramiri had heard his plea. She had freed herself.

If only it hadn't been too late. She hung totally limp in his arms as he pulled her to Chehalli's back. Her limbs were lax and unresponding. Her chest did not seem to rise and fall. Her skin was blistered where she had ripped free of filaments and cilia. He pressed one ear to her breast and heard nothing.

But she was alive. He felt the life in her, a faint presence, struggling back toward consciousness. Quickly he did what instinct told him. He urged Chehalli to swim back toward the safety of Misa Hon. He turned Ramiri on her stomach and pressed on her back to force the water from her lungs. And he cried his gratitude loudly, drowning the hiscapei's rising plaint.

It seemed a long time before Ramiri opened her eyes. They were as dark, as huge as he remembered, but they were no longer strange. They were only his sister's eyes. Her gaze was stunned, groping. He met it with relief. "I was afraid you wouldn't come back," he said.

"The deep danger had me," she said faintly. "I wanted to free myself, but I couldn't. Not until—not until I heard you call me back. Do you hear the danger crying? Do you hear it calling again?"

"I hear it," he said. "But it's faint. It can't touch us now." In fact, in the time it had required to bring her to her senses, they had left the hiscapei far behind. Its voice was no more than a thread of pain.

"No more danger," she echoed. She closed her eyes, weakly, and lay quietly in his arms for a while. When she looked up again, she seemed stronger. "You said that you needed me, brother."

"I need you," he affirmed, his voice husky. Everything he had said while the snakes coiled around him was true. They had been born together; the world would be empty for him without her. "I need you. You're my sister."

She sighed. "And I think that you made me promises." Her familiar diffidence had returned. When she spoke, her eyelashes dropped, as if she were afraid to confide too directly what she wanted.

"I made you promises," he agreed.

"You promised me what I asked for the day we swam together. Was it yesterday?"

"It was yesterday."

"You promised to tell me . . . things of our mother. All kinds of things. And things of your home and your people. I know I will never go there. I would not be happy on the land. I think people who live there must become very tired, walking on the rocks all day. I can't guess what they do when they want to float. But I would like to know of your life. I would like to know of you."

"I want you to know," he agreed. That was true too. She was not Nandyris. She was diffident, not bold; hesitant, not laughing. But those were only superficial differences. Beneath lay the same courage, the same promise.

So they rode together on Chehalli's back, and Keiris sang Ramiri songs of the beautiful land he had come from, of the shining palace where they both had been born, of the mother who had borne them. He sang songs of their laughing sister, Nandyris; of the Nethlor, strong and kind; of sunrises and sunsets framed in broad windows; of meals arranged on delicate platters.

He sang of these things as he had seen them before he had touched the sea snakes and felt his blood boil up with turbulence and change. He sang of them as he had seen them before he had recognized how narrow life was upon the land, before he had realized how sterile the soil was, how ungiving, how empty of things that brought wonder and joy. He sang of them as he had seen them before he had recognized that his beloved Nethlor were deaf and mute and that the land imposed some of its own narrowness upon them, shuttering their eyes to the full wonder and plenty of the sea that lay just beyond their shores, making them afraid of the very element that supported their survival. Lessening them.

He sang, and of all the people who came swimming to meet them as they approached the shores of Misa Hon, only his father understood why he cried.

EPILOGUE

THE MORNING WAS bleak. Keiris stood on the balcony of the hut he and Talani had shared since the tribe had returned from the northern waters and saw no color anywhere: in the sky, in the sea, on the land. Part of that was the hour of the day, of course: The sun had not yet risen. Part of it was the season. It was late autumn; winter storms were coming soon. And part of it was his mood.

He was leaving the tide folk. He had announced his decision at the singing five nights ago, and last night there had been feasting and dancing in his honor. The leave-taking ceremonies had lasted until both moons had set. Now his father had taken the path to the beach to call Pehoshi and Chehalli for the journey. His footsteps had awakened Keiris just minutes ago.

And the morning was bleak. Reluctantly Keiris stepped back into the hut. Talani lay with her eyes closed, one hand resting on the swell of her abdomen. Keiris hesitated for a long time, looking down at her. Could he blame her for feigning sleep, for refusing to speak to him one last time before he left? What was there left to say after everything that had already been said? After the tears, the hurt silences, the whispered declarations? *You know I don't want to go,* he offered silently.

But was that true? Or was he only trying to absolve himself? Because it wasn't entirely duty that called him away. He had met the test of the migration. He had enjoyed the pleasures of a northern summer. He had tasted the things he had wanted to taste and done the things he had wanted to do.

But these last weeks his memories of the palace had begun to shimmer again. He thought of his mother, waiting for news. He thought of Kristis and Tracador, worried by now at his long absence. And he thought of the winter sea, he thought of the Nethlor fishing crews, and he recognized again how brave they were to set into the storming waters in fragile wooden shells. And all to feed their families, because the land could not support them.

Yes, there was much of duty in his decision. They needed him, those people, far more than anyone here needed him. Amelyor's voice would wane soon. When it did, the Nethlor of Hyosis would need someone to stand in the dais and relay news of the sea. And who could do it better than him?

No one. Perhaps, when he returned, he could even show the Nethlor that there were friends in the sea, human and mam, waiting to be discovered. Certainly he would try. Because how were they to learn those things if he didn't teach them? It was their need that had led him to search out his father and the tide folk in the first place.

But, beyond those things, he was hungry again for the palace, for his mother, for his friends. He was hungry for the familiar sights and sounds and smells of home.

But admit those things to Talani? How could he?

So he only said, again, *I must go now*. He projected a little of his pain to her, a little of his regret, a little of his sorrow at leaving her and the child. And then he stepped out of the hut, quickly. If he lingered, if he said more, it would help nothing.

Still he hesitated on the balcony, catching his lower lip in his teeth. Then, quickly again, before he could waver, he descended and ran down the trail. People were already waking in the huts, speaking to each other in low voices, stepping to their balconies to stretch, but he made himself blind to the familiar sights of morning, deaf to its sounds. If he stopped now, if he stopped before he reached the beach . . .

Ramiri was waiting there for him at the edge of the water. He saw her as soon as he emerged from the trees. Saw her and reached out to her and immediately felt the comfort of her response. He paused, remembering how they had groped for words the first day they swam together. Now they hardly had to speak. The closeness that had developed over the summer was that strong, that sure.

She held out her arms and he held her, pressing her so hard that it must have hurt. She didn't protest. Nor did she tell him she was as saddened by his going as he was. They had conspired not to speak of that, not silently, not aloud. "You've promised to come to the waters of Hyosis next fall, after the tribes return from the north," he reminded her, keeping his tone light.

"I'll come," she promised. "Oh, I'll come. Perhaps—perhaps I'll even come ashore for a few hours and see some of your favorite places."

'I'll show you them. I'll have Kristis pack a lunch for us both, and afterward we can swim together." But he probably would not tell even Kristis whom he went to meet. Would the Nethlor be ready so soon to hear of the rermadken?

Ramiri shuddered delicately at that. "I'll find my own meal, brother."

He laughed. If she could ignore the tears that had gathered at the corners of her eyes, he could ignore his own. "So you won't be brave enough to eat from my kitchen even once?" Ramiri suffered a rermadken's fastidious revulsion at the prospect of eating anything that had not been harvested or caught within the hour.

"Did you eat everything I offered you this summer?"

Of course, he had not. Some things were inedible even freshly caught.

Keiris—are you ready? His father's voice. Turning, Keiris looked toward the horizon and saw Pehoshi and Chehalli, white against the gray of early morning. His father sat on the older white's back. He waved, beckoning.

A moment. But it would take more than a moment to say everything he wanted to say to Ramiri. He saw that and she saw it, so they didn't try. Instead they embraced again and he said impulsively, "Be a sister to Talani, will you?"

"In every way."

Then it was time to go. Time to leave behind allegiances and responsibilities to resume other allegiances and responsibilities. Keiris felt the thickness of tears in his throat. He waved to Ramiri, then quickly plunged into the water and swam to where his father and the two whites waited.

It didn't help that Pehoshi sounded as they glided toward the open sea or that Chehalli echoed the lonely sound. It didn't help that the sun chose that moment to crest the horizon, creating a hurting shimmer on the sea's surface. It didn't help that when Keiris looked back, Talani had joined

Ramiri on the beach. They stood with hands clasped. Reluctantly, half heartedly, Talani raised her free hand in farewell.

It didn't help that she stood with arm raised until the shoreline faded entirely from sight.

"I'm leaving a child behind," Keiris said when they could see nothing but sea. The surface of the water was bright now with dawn, the air clear. Yet all Keiris felt was emptiness. He knew the child Talani carried would be well cared for, well loved. The people of her pod and his father's would see to that. But to leave it, to simply go away and leave it without even seeing its face . . .

Rudin stroked Pehoshi's white flesh thoughtfully. "I left one, too, Keir, and it was hard. But eventually he came to me, and now we've had three seasons together. You'll have seasons with your son, and you and I will have others together as well."

"Perhaps," Keiris said, although he could not imagine when or how. And he shrank from thinking of the future now, with the pain of departure so keen. How could he be at once empty and full of pain?

He did not ride happily that day. Chehalli dived to feed, but Keiris waited at the surface instead of clinging to the white's back for the excitement of the hunt. Later his father foraged for them both, but Keiris could not eat. And when his father tried to talk with him, he answered in reluctant monosyllables, refusing to meet Rudin's eyes. Finally his father tried no longer.

What if he reached Hyosis and found it as narrow, as sunless as it had seemed the night he handled the snakes? What if he could never find pleasure or even comfort in the old ways of his life again? Time and again he closed his eyes and deliberately emptied his mind of unwelcome questions. Time and again they returned.

He slept poorly that night, cushioned on Chehalli's back. He dreamed of the child, dreamed it was born without features, with only a smooth, unformed face, and he awoke with a start, barely stifling a cry. When he caught his breath, he glanced over and saw that his father watched him from Pehoshi's back, silently, concerned.

Just as silently Keiris turned his face away and settled back into the posture of sleep. After a while he actually slept again but uneasily.

He began the second day unhappily too. The brightness of

sky and water, the leaping of fish, Chehalli's surging strength beneath him . . . None of those things touched him. As he rode, he had brief, waking dreams of a barren land, of a palace that was little more than a warren of pink stone, of a people incapable of seeing beyond the limits of their own lives. His dreams were little more than visions; brief, self-contained despairs that forced themselves into his consciousness, then vanished, leaving only an aching heaviness.

His father watched him and carefully said nothing. But finally, shortly after midday, Rudin urged Pehoshi to Chehalli's side and said, "Perhaps you don't see it now, Keiris, but you have more than most people."

"Or less," Keiris suggested, sorry that the response seemed sullen.

His father stroked Pehoshi's white flank, shrugging. "There have been many times when I felt that way, many times when it seemed I could not reach for what I wanted without giving up something else I wanted just as badly. Finally I learned to ask myself this: Am I to be happy because I know both land and sea? Or unhappy because I can't have them both at once? It's a choice, one I've made a hundred times. Or more.

"There will be a time when you can come back to the tribes, you know. Just as there will be a time, eventually, when I can return to Neth. My brother's son will be ready for the span in five years, perhaps six. It seems long now, but there will be times before then when I can come for short visits, just as Ramiri intends to come. And when I have surrendered the span, I can spend entire seasons with you. Whole years if I want. If I still have my voice, and I think I will, I can take the dais so you can return to the pod for a while."

Keiris drew a shaky breath, seeing possibilities he had not seen before, brightening with them. If his father took the dais, he could swim with Nirini again. He could hold his child while it was still young. And Amelyor . . . ? He looked up at his father. "My mother . . . ?"

Rudin glanced away toward the horizon, frowning slightly. "Would she be pleased to see me if I returned to Hyosis?"

Did he doubt it? "You know she would. That was the last thing she said before she sent me away. That if you didn't want to relinquish Ramiri, you could come back to Hyosis with her."

"Amelyor said that?"

"Yes. And other things." But perhaps he should let Amelyor tell him those things for herself.

"So if I returned to Hyosis with you—not now, not today, but one day . . ."

"She would be pleased."

His father glanced away again, his eyes narrowing thoughtfully. When he spoke again, it was in measured tones, as if he had thought long of what he wanted to say next. "When you reach the palace, ask her just how pleased she would be, Keiris. Ask her if she would be pleased enough to walk into the sea with me next spring and join the migration."

Keiris stared at his father in surprise. He wanted Amelyor to join the migration, to swim with the pod? The suggestion took his breath. Could his mother set aside her fears as he had set aside his? He tried but could not imagine her on Pehoshi's back. Nor could he imagine her submerging herself in the sea pools. Or feasting with the tribes on Misa Hon.

But he could imagine her walking into the sea with his father. He could imagine her taking the first step.

He had taken the first step. He had dared the drowntide, and it had carried him all the way to the northern waters.

"I'll ask her," he said. "If you'll come near enough the shore, perhaps you can hear her answer yourself."

"In the spring I'll do that," his father promised. "I'll come and I'll listen. But now we must separate. Another hour will carry you ashore at Hyosis."

"So soon?" Keiris felt a sharp pang of regret. If he had known the journey was to be so brief, he might have been more responsive to his father the night and the day before.

But his mood had been dark then. Now it had lightened. He had left Talani, he had left the child, he had left Ramiri, he had left the pod. But he had left none of them forever. His father had reassured him of that.

"So soon," his father said. "I don't want to swim too near. I don't want to hear Amelyor's voice until I can answer it."

And so they parted, sliding into the water to embrace, then waving as their two whites carried them away in opposite directions. Keiris looked back until he could see his father no longer. Then he called out once, *In the spring*. He let the bittersweet of his mood ring in his voice.

In the spring, came the response, echoing the same feeling.

For a time after that Keiris rode with his head bowed. Even

Chehalli seemed saddened. But Chehalli was one of the coastal mams of Neth, so this was a journey home for the big white. *We'll speak often,* Keiris promised, rubbing the smooth, white flesh. *I'll call to you every day. You'll tell me where the crews can find the best catch and whether there are storms or predators. On nights when its warm, I'll come to the water so we can swim together. And if my sister or my father come this way, you'll tell me. when they approach.*

He felt the deep rumble of Chehalli's assent. Then he saw the first smudge of the coastline in the distance. Catching his breath, he gripped the white's flesh with his knees.

Swiftly the smudge darkened and took on full definition—so swiftly, in fact, that Keiris was not ready for the first full blaze of pink stones against blue sky. The sight took his breath. Tears stung his eyes, tears of gratitude and relief.

It was beautiful, just as he remembered. The land was dark and rugged, the palace stones warm with sunlight. He had forgotten how pink they were, how brilliant. The sheds, the docks—he saw them with the eyes of a landsman again. They were solid and reassuring. Safe harbor, proof against any storm. And the Nethlor would be the same solid folk who met hard conditions with courage and endeavor. He would have no trouble finding the same beauty in them he had seen before. Relieved and overjoyed at once, Keiris urged Chehalli toward the shore.

But when he left Chehalli's back a few minutes later, when he slid down into the water and waded to the tideline, he looked back and the sea beckoned too. It built tall waves for him to ride. It tantalized him with its depth and its power and its thousand mysteries. Its voices called.

Keiris hesitated, torn between two worlds, knowing he would always be torn. But torn between two bright and challenging worlds. Torn between two beloved families of people. Torn between good and good.

It was not a bad fate. No, not at all.

Still, it was a long time before he turned and walked up the seaward path toward the palace.